Joshua Turner is a debut author with a passion for blending genres, from fantasy and crime thrillers to horror and romance. His first book, *Fallen and Found,* showcases his love for creating complex characters filled with mystery and emotion. Josh finds inspiration in immersive worlds both on the page and the screen. When he's not writing, you'll find him exploring new books, enjoying games, and crafting the next chapter in his storytelling journey. *Fallen and Found* is his first step into the world of fiction.

Joshua Turner

FALLEN AND FOUND

AUSTIN MACAULEY PUBLISHERS
LONDON * CAMBRIDGE * NEW YORK * SHARJAH

Copyright © Joshua Turner 2025

The right of Joshua Turner to be identified as author of this work has been asserted by the author in accordance with sections 77 and 78 of the Copyright, Designs and Patents Act 1988.

All rights reserved. No part of this publication may be reproduced, stored in a retrieval system, or transmitted in any form or by any means, electronic, mechanical, photocopying, recording, or otherwise, without the prior permission of the publishers.

Any person who commits any unauthorised act in relation to this publication may be liable to criminal prosecution and civil claims for damages.

This is a work of fiction. Names, characters, businesses, places, events, locales, and incidents are either the products of the author's imagination or used in a fictitious manner. Any resemblance to actual persons, living or dead, or actual events is purely coincidental.

A CIP catalogue record for this title is available from the British Library.

ISBN 9781035888993 (Paperback)
ISBN 9781035889006 (ePub e-book)

www.austinmacauley.com

First Published 2025
Austin Macauley Publishers Ltd®
1 Canada Square
Canary Wharf
London
E14 5AA

I would like to thank Austin Macauley Publishers for believing in this book and helping bring it to life.
Also, to my family and friends for your encouragement and support for this book and for me.

Table of Contents

Prologue	**11**
Chapter 1: A Sudden Loss	**13**
Chapter 2: The New Detective	**18**
Chapter 3: Secrets in the Lab	**21**
Chapter 4: Uncovering the Past	**28**
Chapter 5: A Lead Emerges	**32**
Chapter 6: The Connection	**37**
Chapter 7: Confrontation at the Estate	**41**
Chapter 8: Breaking and Entering	**46**
Chapter 9: A Desperate Night	**50**
Chapter 10: Aftermath	**54**
Chapter 11: A New Mission	**59**
Chapter 12: The Hunt Begins	**62**
Chapter 13: A Shadowy Figure	**66**
Chapter 14: Unlikely Allies	**70**
Chapter 15: The Betrayal	**75**
Chapter 16: The Pursuit	**78**
Chapter 17: A Dangerous Game	**81**
Chapter 18: Traps and Deceptions	**87**
Chapter 19: The Price of Power	**91**

Chapter 20: Revelations	95
Chapter 21: The Net Tightens	98
Chapter 22: The Lion's Den	104
Chapter 23: The Cost of Truth	111
Chapter 24: Alliances Tested	116
Chapter 25: The Final Piece	122
Chapter 26: Confronting the Enemy	125
Chapter 27: A Twist in the Tale	129
Chapter 28: The Betrayal Unmasked	131
Chapter 29: Closing In	135
Chapter 30: The Final Confrontation	139
Chapter 31: A Last Stand	142
Chapter 32: The Truth Revealed	145
Chapter 33: The Aftermath	148
Chapter 34: A New Beginning	151
Chapter 35: Hidden Agendas	154
Chapter 36: Unfinished Business	156
Chapter 37: The Reckoning	159
Chapter 38: Secrets Unravelled	163
Chapter 39: The Shadow of Doubt	167
Chapter 40: In the Crosshairs	170
Chapter 41: The Enemy Within	173
Chapter 42: A Fragile Alliance	177
Chapter 43: The Price of Victory	180
Chapter 44: The Final Countdown	186
Chapter 45: A Dangerous Gambit	187
Chapter 46: The Fall	190

Chapter 47: The Lost Path	193
Chapter 48: A Glimmer of Hope	197
Chapter 49: The Choice	202
Chapter 50: The Last Battle	205
Chapter 51: The Endgame	208
Chapter 52: The Sacrifice	212
Chapter 53: The Aftermath	215
Chapter 54: A New Dawn	219
Chapter 55: The Phoenix Rises	222
Chapter 56: A New Era	226
Chapter 57: Redemption	230
Chapter 58: A Future Forged	233

Prologue

The rain fell steadily on the streets of London, each drop tapping a rhythmic pattern on the pavement as the city remained shrouded in a sombre veil. Beneath the cover of darkness, a lone figure moved with purpose through the narrow alleyways, the trench coat flapping against their legs with each hurried step. The dim glow of streetlamps cast elongated shadows, obscuring the identity of the stranger.

Dr Robert Harper clutched his briefcase tightly, his heart pounding in sync with the rhythm of the rain. His normally composed demeanour was now fractured, his mind racing with the revelations he had uncovered. In the secluded sanctuary of his lab, Robert had stumbled upon a discovery that could derail his revolutionary discovery in the field of artificial intelligence—an innovation that promised to heal broken minds, to restore memories lost to the ravages of time.

But such power was a double-edged sword. The same breakthrough that could cure also held the potential to control, to manipulate. Robert had always been guided by a strict ethical compass and a commitment to using technology for the betterment of humanity. Yet, he knew that not everyone shared his vision. In the wrong hands, his research could lead to unimaginable consequences.

A flash of movement caught his eye, and Robert quickened his pace, glancing over his shoulder. The alleyway behind him was empty, but the sense of being watched persisted. He turned a corner, and his destination came into view—a nondescript building with a single light flickering above the entrance. The house of a colleague that he trusted, hoping to shake the tail following and escape to safety.

As he moved down the alley, a chill ran down his spine. The streets were eerily silent now, the rain a steady drumbeat in the background. Robert's thoughts turned to his daughter, Emily, and his long-lost twin brother, Shay. He had kept so much from them, believing it was for their safety. But now, he wondered if he had made the right choices.

Without warning, a sharp pain pierced his side, and Robert stumbled; his vision blurring. He looked down to see blood spreading across his shirt, the briefcase now a distant memory. He fell to the ground, his strength ebbing away, he reached for his phone, struggling to unlock it and he managed to dial a number. Shay, a renowned detective and Robert's twin brother called out, "Hello…Robbie…ROBERT?" Robert managed to mumble something, but it was too late, he had lost too much blood and in his final moments, his mind was filled with images of his family—their faces, their voices, their love.

The rain continued to fall, washing away the evidence of the night's events, but the secrets Robert had uncovered would not remain buried for long. The echoes of his memory would reverberate through time, setting in motion a chain of events that would challenge the very fabric of technological and medical boundaries.

Chapter 1
A Sudden Loss

The kettle whistled softly, filling the small kitchen with the comforting sound of boiling water. Emily Harper stared at it, her mind lost in a fog of nerves and anticipation. Morning light filtered through the half-drawn curtains, casting a soft glow on the cluttered dining table. Today was her first day as a detective, and despite the years of training and hard work that had led her here, she couldn't shake the anxiety gnawing at her insides.

She sighed, pushing a lock of blonde hair behind her ear. It had been a restless night, her thoughts oscillating between excitement and dread. What if she wasn't ready? What if she made a mistake? The expectations weighed heavily on her, and it didn't help that her father, Dr Robert Harper, was so proud of her new role. He had been the one person she could always turn to for advice, his steady presence a constant in her life. She had spoken to him just last night, his voice filled with the usual mix of warmth and concern.

As the kettle's whistle grew louder, Emily snapped out of her thoughts and reached to turn off the stove. She poured the boiling water over the tea bag, watching the dark liquid swirl as it steeped. The simple task grounded her, momentarily easing her anxiety.

A sharp knock at the door jolted her from her thoughts. She glanced at the clock—6:30 am. Who could be knocking at this hour? With a sense of foreboding, she rose and walked to the door, her heart pounding in her chest.

When she opened the door, two police officers stood on the porch, their expressions grim. Recognition flickered as she saw the familiar faces of Donny, a senior officer she'd seen around the station, and a younger officer she didn't recognise.

"Emily Harper?" Donny asked, his voice gentle but serious.

"Yes, that's me," she replied, her voice barely above a whisper. A knot of dread tightened in her stomach.

Donny removed his hat, a gesture that deepened the sinking feeling in Emily's chest. "I'm sorry to inform you that your father, Dr Robert Harper, was found dead early this morning. It appears to be murder."

The world seemed to tilt on its axis. Emily's vision blurred as the weight of Donny's words crashed over her. "Murder?" She managed to say, her voice shaky. "How…how did this happen?"

Donny exchanged a glance with his colleague before answering, "We don't have all the details yet. When you're ready, we'll need you to come down to the station to give a statement."

Emily nodded numbly, barely processing the words. The officers expressed their condolences before leaving her standing in the doorway, feeling as if the ground had been pulled out from under her. She closed the door and leaned against it, her legs trembling.

She had only spoken to her father last night. He had sounded worried, almost frantic, but she had brushed it off as stress from work. Guilt gnawed at her as she replayed their conversation in her mind. What had he been trying to tell her?

The tea sat forgotten on the counter as Emily sank into a chair, her thoughts spinning. She felt lost, alone, and utterly unprepared for the wave of grief that was about to wash over her.

***

The day of the funeral was a blur of faces, condolences, and shared grief. The small chapel was filled with friends, colleagues, and family, all gathered to pay their respects to a man who had touched so many lives. Emily stood at the front; her eyes fixed on the simple wooden coffin that held her father's body. She felt a mix of sorrow and anger, a burning desire to find out who had taken him from her.

After the service, as the mourners began to disperse, Emily found herself standing alone by the grave. The rain had started to fall, a soft drizzle that seemed to echo her inner turmoil. She was about to leave when she noticed a figure approaching—a tall man with a weathered face and piercing blue eyes.

"Emily Harper?" He asked, his voice gentle yet firm.

She nodded "Excuse me?" She said softly, a wave of emotion flowing over her.

The man responded, "I am Shay Walsh; I knew your father. I am a…"

She cut him off, "You're the private detective, I have heard stories about you in the department."

Shay gave a small nod, his expression a mixture of sadness and determination. "Your father was a good man, Emily. One of the best. I'm deeply sorry for your loss."

"Thank you," she replied, her voice thick with emotion. "I don't know what to do. The police don't seem to have any leads, and I…I need to know why this happened. And they won't let me on the case as I have only been a detective for a couple of weeks."

Shay's eyes softened with empathy. "Your father and I were close. He shared a lot with me about his work and his concerns. If there's anyone who can help you uncover the truth, it's me." They walked to a nearby bench, seeking shelter from the rain under the branches of a large oak tree. As they sat, Shay pulled out a leather-bound notebook and handed it to her.

"This was your father's," he explained. "He entrusted it to me a few weeks before his death. It's filled with his notes and thoughts about his research. I believe it's the key to understanding what happened to him." Emily took the notebook, feeling a surge of hope mixed with apprehension. She opened it to the first page, her father's familiar handwriting bringing a fresh wave of grief.

"Thank you, Shay. I don't know where to start, but I know I can't do this alone."

Shay placed a reassuring hand on her shoulder. "You're not alone, Emily. We'll figure this out together. Your father was onto something big, something that threatened powerful people. We need to uncover the truth and make sure his legacy is honoured."

Emily and Shay sat in the quiet of the cemetery for a few moments longer, each lost in their thoughts. The rain had slowed to a light drizzle, the droplets creating a soft rhythm against the leaves above. Finally, Emily stood, clutching her father's notebook to her chest.

"We should go somewhere we can talk more freely," she said, glancing around at the remaining mourners. "There's a café not far from here. It was one of my father's favourites."

Shay nodded, standing and offering a supportive arm as they made their way to the exit. They walked in silence, the gravity of their mission hanging heavily between them.

***

The café was quaint and quiet, with a comforting warmth that contrasted sharply with the dreary weather outside. Emily and Shay took a seat in a corner booth, away from prying eyes and ears. A waitress approached, and they both ordered coffee, grateful for something to anchor them at the moment.

Emily placed the notebook on the table, her fingers tracing the worn cover. "This notebook…it's like having a part of him with me. I just wish I had understood more of what he was working on before it was too late."

Shay leaned forward, his gaze steady. "Your father was a visionary, Emily. He saw the potential to change the world, but he also saw the dangers. His work was always about finding the balance, about ensuring technology served humanity, not the other way around." Emily nodded, flipping open the notebook to the first page. The neat script was a comfort, a connection to the man she had lost. "He mentioned something about a breakthrough. Do you know what he was working on?"

Shay sighed, rubbing his temples. "I cannot remember, my memory isn't what it used to be. I just know he was working on something technological…" he trailed off.

"Shay? Are you ok?" Emily looked at him inquisitively, this great detective that she had heard so many stories of, looked lost, almost dumbfounded.

"Sorry, I remember him saying that he was working with Blackwood Technologies," Shay said, snapping back to reality.

Emily's eyes widened. "Blackwood Technologies…that's a huge company. What would they want with my father's research?"

Shay's expression darkened. "That's what we need to find out. Your father's research made him a target. And we need to uncover who was after him—and why."

Their conversation was interrupted by the arrival of their coffee. Emily wrapped her hands around the warm cup, taking a moment to steady herself. "Where do we start?"

Shay took a sip of his coffee, his mind clearly working through the possibilities. "We start by going through this notebook. It's likely your father left clues that can point us in the right direction. Then, we'll need to access his lab and see what else we can find."

Emily nodded, determination hardening her features. "I'll make arrangements to access the lab. I know someone who can help."

They spent the next hour discussing their plan, going over the details and potential obstacles. Emily's grief was still raw, but with Shay's guidance and her father's notebook, she felt a renewed sense of purpose. Whatever secrets her father had uncovered, she was determined to bring them to light—and to ensure that his death would not be in vain.

Chapter 2
The New Detective

The morning sunlight streamed through the tall windows of the precinct, casting long shadows across the bustling station. The familiar sounds of ringing phones, clacking keyboards, and low conversations filled the air as officers moved with purpose, engrossed in their respective tasks. For Emily Harper, the day felt like a surreal blur. Less than 24 hours ago, she had learnt that her father had been murdered. Today, she was about to face the reality of it all.

Taking a deep breath, Emily adjusted her coat and made her way to Chief Inspector Caldwell's office, her heart pounding in her chest. The gravity of her father's death weighed heavily on her, but she knew she had to keep her composure. This was her first day as a detective, and she had to prove that she could handle the responsibility—even if her world had been shattered overnight.

She knocked on the door, her knuckles rapping sharply against the wood.

"Come in," came Caldwell's gruff voice from inside.

Emily pushed the door open and stepped into the office, meeting Caldwell's piercing gaze. He was a stern man, his grey hair and furrowed brow giving him an air of authority that few dared to challenge. He motioned for her to sit.

"Harper," he said, leaning back in his chair. "I'm sorry for your loss. Robert was a good man."

"Thank you, sir," Emily replied, her voice steady, though her emotions churned beneath the surface. "I need to speak with you about my father's case."

Caldwell's eyebrows rose slightly, a hint of curiosity in his eyes. "I assumed you would. What's on your mind?"

Emily took a deep breath, gathering her thoughts. "Sir, I believe there's more to my father's murder than a simple robbery gone wrong. I've found some of his notes that suggest his work with Blackwood Technologies was involved. I need to take over the case to ensure a thorough investigation."

Caldwell studied her for a moment, his expression unreadable. "You're too close to this, Emily. You know that. Personal biases can interfere with an investigation, especially one of this magnitude."

"I understand, sir," Emily replied, leaning forward, her eyes locked on his. "But my father's work was ground-breaking. It could explain why he was killed. I'm not asking for special treatment—I just want to make sure the truth comes out."

Caldwell rubbed his chin thoughtfully. "And you have evidence to support this theory?"

Emily nodded, determination hardening her voice. "I do, sir. But I need access to all the case files and resources to pursue it properly. I can't do that unless I'm officially on the case."

Before Caldwell could respond, the door to his office swung open, and Shay Walsh walked in, his presence commanding immediate attention. He was a tall man, with silver hair that contrasted sharply with his sharp blue eyes, which seemed to miss nothing. His tailored suit and confident stride spoke of years of experience and tactical expertise.

"Chief Caldwell, I believe I can help with that," Shay announced, his voice calm and confident.

Caldwell's eyes narrowed as he looked at Shay. "Walsh, what are you doing here?"

Shay stepped forward, holding up a file. "I've been looking into Dr Harper's case independently. Given my history with Robert and my expertise, I think it's clear that Emily and I should handle this together. Besides, you know my track record. I've solved several high-profile cases for the department."

Caldwell's scepticism softened slightly as he considered the proposal. "I'm aware of your record, Walsh. But this is highly irregular. Emily is an officer of the law, and you're a private detective. How do you propose we handle this?"

Shay smiled the kind of smile that hinted he'd thought this through. "Simple. I take over the investigation as a private detective, and Emily assists me in an unofficial capacity. She has the insight and personal stake necessary to see this through, and I have the resources and experience to ensure it's done right."

Caldwell leaned back in his chair, weighing the options. "This is highly unconventional. But given the circumstances and your history…I'm willing to consider it. However, Emily, you'll be working under Shay's supervision. Any official reports or findings will come through him."

Emily felt a surge of hope. "Thank you, sir. I promise we'll get to the bottom of this."

Caldwell nodded, his expression still serious but more accepting. "Don't make me regret this, Harper. This case is sensitive and has far-reaching implications. Do your job, and do it well."

Shay extended a hand to Emily, a look of determination in his eyes. "We've got a lot of work ahead of us. Let's get started."

As they left Caldwell's office, Emily felt a mixture of relief and anticipation. She was on the case, and with Shay's support, they had a real chance at uncovering the truth behind her father's murder. The weight of her father's death still hung heavy, but now there was a spark of purpose—a mission to find out who was responsible and why.

Back at her desk, Emily gathered her things, feeling the weight of the task ahead, but also a renewed sense of determination. Shay sat down across from her, laying out a plan.

"We'll need to be methodical about this," Shay said, his voice steady. "First, we need to go through all the evidence we have and follow up on any leads. Arabella Blackwood and Blackwood Tech are our primary suspects, but we need to be discreet. They have resources and influence."

Emily nodded. "Agreed. We should start by interviewing people who worked closely with my father. They might have seen or heard something that can help us."

Shay smiled. "Exactly. And we'll also need to secure any files and documents related to your father's research. The more we know about what he was working on, the better we can understand who would want to kill him."

Emily looked down at her father's notebook, her fingers tracing the worn cover. "This notebook is our starting point," she said softly. "It's the last piece of him I have left, and I'm not going to let his death be in vain."

Shay nodded, his expression serious. "We'll find out the truth, Emily. Whatever it takes."

As they prepared to dive into the investigation, Emily felt a sense of resolve harden within her. The road ahead would be long and difficult, but she knew that with Shay by her side, they would uncover the truth—and bring her father's killer to justice.

Chapter 3
Secrets in the Lab

The evening sky was painted in hues of deep purple and orange as Emily Harper approached the police station's forensic lab. Her heart pounded with a mix of anxiety and determination. She had spent the entire day working alongside Shay, sifting through her father's notes and trying to make sense of the clues he had left behind. But one thing was clear—whatever secrets her father had uncovered, they were well-hidden, and the key to understanding them lay in his lab.

As she pushed open the heavy glass door of the forensic department, the familiar scent of chemicals and sterile equipment greeted her. The lab was a maze of workstations, each cluttered with the tools of the trade—microscopes, computers, and files piled high. Emily's eyes scanned the room until they landed on Jamie Parker, her best friend and the department's top forensic technician.

Jamie was hunched over a microscope, her long brown hair pulled back in a loose ponytail, the goggles perched on her head giving her a quirky, yet professional appearance. She looked up as Emily approached, a warm smile spreading across her face.

"Emily, how are you holding up?" Jamie asked, her green eyes full of concern.

Emily managed a small smile, grateful for her friend's support. "I'm...I'm managing," she replied, her voice tinged with exhaustion. "But I need your help, Jamie. I need to get into my father's lab, and I need someone I can trust."

Jamie's expression shifted from concern to determination. "Of course. Whatever you need, I'm here for you."

Emily took a deep breath, her hands tightening around the notebook she held. "There's something in his lab, Jamie. Something that could explain why he was killed. We need to find it."

Jamie nodded, already moving to gather her tools. "We'll go after hours. Security will be minimal, and we'll have the place to ourselves. Are you ready for this?"

"More than ever," Emily replied, her voice steady with resolve.

***

As the city lights flickered on, casting a soft glow over the streets, Emily and Jamie arrived at the research facility where Dr Robert Harper had spent countless hours working on his ground-breaking projects. The building was a sleek, modern structure of glass and steel, its reflective surfaces shimmering in the night. It stood as a testament to the cutting-edge research that had taken place within its walls, yet tonight, it seemed ominous, shrouded in the mystery of Robert Harper's death.

Jamie used her credentials to bypass the initial security measures, and they slipped inside undetected. The corridors were silent, the hum of computers and the faint glow of monitors the only signs of life. As they made their way to Dr Harper's private lab, Emily couldn't help but feel a pang of nostalgia. This was where her father had dedicated himself to his work, where he had poured his heart and soul into his research. It was strange to be here without him.

"This is it," Emily whispered as they reached a secured door at the end of a long hallway. She handed Jamie a key card, her fingers trembling slightly. "His most important files should be in here."

Jamie nodded, inserting the key card into the reader. The door clicked open, revealing a room filled with advanced equipment, shelves lined with notebooks, and a large central workstation. Emily stepped inside, her eyes scanning the familiar setup. It felt surreal to be here, knowing her father would never work in this space again.

"Where do we start?" Jamie asked, her voice a soft whisper in the quiet lab.

Emily led her to a secured cabinet at the back of the room. "My father always kept his most critical files locked away. If there's anything here that can help us, it'll be in this cabinet."

Jamie knelt beside the cabinet and began working on the lock. Her fingers moved deftly, and after a few tense moments, there was a soft click. "Got it," Jamie said, standing up and stepping back as Emily opened the cabinet door.

Inside, they found a collection of documents, data drives, and a small, black notebook. Emily's heart raced as she pulled out the notebook, recognising her father's handwriting on the cover.

"This is it," she murmured, flipping through the pages. The notebook was filled with diagrams, equations, and notes—pieces of a puzzle that Emily was determined to solve. As she skimmed the entries, she noticed frequent references to 'Neural Integration' and 'Project Echelon,' terms that were unfamiliar to her.

"Look at this," Jamie said, holding up a series of encrypted data drives. "These could contain the missing pieces of your father's research. We'll need to decrypt them, but I have the tools to do it."

Emily nodded, her eyes scanning the files for anything that stood out. "He was on the verge of something big, Jamie. I can feel it. We need to find out exactly what he discovered—and who wanted him silenced."

Just as they began gathering the files and drives, the sound of footsteps echoed through the hallway, growing louder with each passing second. Emily's heart skipped a beat as she and Jamie exchanged worried glances.

"We need to hide," Jamie whispered urgently. "Now."

They quickly ducked behind a row of cabinets, holding their breath as the footsteps drew nearer. The lab door creaked open, and a beam of light swept across the room.

"Who's there?" A voice called out, filled with authority and suspicion.

Emily's heart pounded in her chest as she recognised the voice—it was one of Blackwood Tech's security officers. They stayed perfectly still, hoping the darkness and the maze of equipment would keep them hidden.

After what felt like an eternity, the officer muttered something under his breath and closed the door, his footsteps fading away. Emily and Jamie waited a few more minutes, ensuring the coast was clear before emerging from their hiding spot.

"We need to get out of here," Emily said, her voice trembling with adrenaline. "Now."

Jamie nodded, and they quickly gathered the remaining files and data drives, stuffing them into their bags before making their way to the exit. The tension in the air was palpable as they slipped out of the building and hurried to Emily's car.

Once inside, they drove in silence, the weight of what they had just discovered hanging heavily between them. As they reached Emily's flat, the adrenaline began to fade, replaced by a deep exhaustion.

***

Back at Emily's flat, they set up their equipment and began the painstaking process of decrypting the data drives. The room was filled with the soft hum of computers and the rapid clicking of keys as they worked late into the night. The atmosphere was tense, the only sounds being their focused breathing and the occasional rustle of papers.

Finally, as dawn began to break, Jamie let out a triumphant cry. "Got it! Emily, look at this."

Emily rushed over, her eyes scanning the decrypted files. They contained detailed notes on her father's breakthrough—how he had developed an AI algorithm capable of repairing damaged neural pathways, potentially curing diseases like Alzheimer's. But there was more—references to a shadowy figure within Blackwood Tech who had been pressuring Robert to hand over his research.

"This is it," Emily said, her voice filled with a mix of awe and determination. "This is what they killed him for."

Jamie placed a hand on Emily's shoulder, their eyes meeting with a mix of solidarity and unspoken emotions. "We're on the right track. But this is just the beginning. We need to find more evidence and bring this to light."

The morning sun cast a pale light through the curtains of Emily's flat, illuminating the cluttered workspace. The decrypted files lay spread out across the table, a testament to their progress and a harbinger of the battles yet to come.

Emily rubbed her tired eyes and glanced at Jamie, who was reviewing the data with intense focus. Despite the exhaustion, there was a fire in Jamie's eyes that caught Emily's attention. She couldn't help but be captivated by Jamie's beauty, especially in moments like these. The soft glow of the computer screen highlighted Jamie's features, casting a gentle light over her smooth skin and accentuating the sharpness of her jawline.

Jamie's long brown hair cascaded over her shoulders, a few loose strands falling into her face as she leaned forward, utterly absorbed in the information before her. Emily watched as Jamie absentmindedly tucked a stray lock behind her ear, her fingers delicate and sure.

There was something mesmerising about the way Jamie worked—her green eyes darting across the screen with a mixture of determination and passion. The intensity of her gaze, the way her eyebrows furrowed slightly in concentration and the slight curve of her lips as she uncovered each piece of data—all of it made Emily's heart skip a beat.

Jamie's beauty was not just in her appearance, but in the fierce intelligence and unwavering dedication she displayed. Emily found herself in awe of Jamie's ability to push through fatigue, driven by an inner fire that seemed inexhaustible. At that moment, Emily felt a swell of admiration and affection, grateful to have someone so remarkable by her side.

"We need to be strategic about this," Jamie said, breaking the silence. "We can't just storm into Blackwood Tech and accuse Arabella. We need solid proof and allies who can help us take her down."

Emily nodded. "Agreed. We need to inform Shay. His connections and experience are going to be invaluable. And we need to keep this out of official channels for now. We can't trust that there aren't moles within the police force."

Jamie leaned back, her expression thoughtful. "We also need to think about our safety. Blackwood Tech won't hesitate to use their resources against us if they find out what we're doing."

Emily's phone buzzed and she glanced at the screen to see a message from Shay. He wanted to meet to discuss their findings. She showed the message to Jamie, who nodded in agreement.

"Let's meet him at the park," Emily suggested. "It's public enough to be safe, but we can still talk without being overheard."

***

The park was a tranquil oasis amidst the bustling city, its green expanse offering a brief respite from the intensity of their mission. Emily and Jamie arrived first, finding a secluded bench shaded by a large oak tree. The air was cool and fresh, carrying the scent of blooming flowers and damp earth. It was a stark contrast to the tension they felt inside.

Shay arrived shortly after, his eyes sharp despite the weariness etched on his face. He greeted them with a nod, taking a seat on the bench with a weary smile.

"Morning," Shay said, his voice steady. "What have you found?"

Emily and Jamie quickly brought him up to speed, showing him the decrypted files and explaining their plan. Shay listened intently, his expression growing more serious with each revelation.

"This is bigger than I thought," Shay said, his voice grave. "If your father's research can do what he claimed, it could revolutionise medicine. But in the wrong hands…"

"Exactly," Emily said, her determination hardening. "We need to expose Blackwood Tech's unethical practices and ensure my father's research is used for good. But we can't do it alone. We need allies."

Shay nodded. "I have a few contacts that might be able to help. Old friends in the intelligence community who owe me a favour or two. We'll need to tread carefully, though. Arabella is well-connected and won't hesitate to retaliate."

"First, we need to secure these files," Jamie said. "I'll set up a secure backup and encrypt everything again. We can't afford to lose this data."

Shay stood, his eyes scanning the park for any signs of danger. "I'll reach out to my contacts and see what I can dig up. We'll need all the support we can get."

***

Back at the police station, Emily and Jamie worked tirelessly to secure the files and review their plan. They knew the road ahead would be perilous, but they were ready to face whatever came their way. As they sat side by side, reviewing the encrypted data, the unspoken tension between them simmered just beneath the surface.

Jamie glanced at Emily, her expression softening. "We make a good team, you know. I'm glad we're doing this together."

Emily met her gaze, a small smile tugging at her lips. "Me too. I couldn't do this without you, Jamie."

For a moment, the weight of their mission lifted, and they were just two friends sharing a quiet moment amidst the chaos. The bond between them, strengthened by their shared resolve and the lingering romantic tension, was a source of comfort and strength.

As the day turned to night, Emily's thoughts returned to her father. She traced her fingers over the photograph on her desk, silently renewing her vow. "We'll find the truth, Dad. We'll make sure your work changes the world for the better."

Chapter 4
Uncovering the Past

Shay Walsh sat in his dimly lit office, surrounded by the detritus of a once-brilliant career. The walls were lined with accolades and framed newspaper clippings heralding his successes as a world-class detective. Yet, amidst the clutter of trophies and certificates, the present reality loomed large—a growing stack of notebooks filled with the fragmented memories he clung to as his mind continued its slow, cruel betrayal.

He rubbed his temples, trying to push away the fog that had settled over his thoughts. The conversation with Emily and Jamie at the park had rekindled something within him—a spark of purpose—but it also stirred up a whirlwind of confusion. Robert Harper had been a significant figure in his life, yet the connection felt distant and incomplete.

Shay flipped through one of his notebooks, searching for any mention of Robert. His fingers paused over an entry dated five years ago: "Met with Robert Harper today. Discussed advancements in AI and its potential implications. Brilliant man, deeply committed to his work."

He read the entry over and over, trying to latch onto the memory. He knew Robert had been more than just an acquaintance, but the details eluded him. With a heavy sigh, Shay closed the notebook and leaned back in his chair, staring at the ceiling. Why was it so hard to remember?

A knock at the door pulled him from his reverie. He called out for the visitor to enter, and a young woman stepped inside, carrying a folder.

"Mr Walsh, I have the background check you requested," she said, placing the folder on his desk.

"Thanks, Claire," Shay replied, his voice tinged with fatigue. "Leave it here. I'll look it over later."

Claire hesitated; her eyes filled with concern. "Are you okay? You've been working non-stop since the Harper case came up."

Shay managed a weak smile. "Just trying to stay busy. This case...it's important."

Claire nodded, her worry evident. "If you need anything, let me know."

After she left, Shay opened the folder, but the words blurred together, failing to hold his attention. He pushed it aside and stood, pacing the room to clear his mind. He needed answers, and he knew the only way to get them was to dive deeper into the past—his past and Robert's.

Shay Walsh sat at his cluttered desk, a cup of coffee growing cold beside him. His hands trembled slightly as he flipped through his meticulously kept notes—the lifeline he relied on to navigate his deteriorating memory. Hours had passed since he'd first started sifting through everything he had on Robert Harper, hoping to trigger a more concrete memory. The faint light from a nearby lamp cast shadows across the room, making it feel even more isolated and distant from the world outside.

Among the photographs, one caught his eye—a faded picture of two young boys, identical in appearance, smiling at the camera. He turned the photo over and read the handwritten note on the back: 'Shay and Robert, age 6.' The name of the orphanage, scrawled beneath, sent a shiver down his spine. The building seemed familiar to him, like a place he had once known intimately but had since lost to the fog of time.

Shay's heart pounded as he stared at the photo, the realisation dawning on him. Robert wasn't just a colleague or an acquaintance—he was his twin brother. The knowledge hit him like a wave, overwhelming and disorienting. Memories, fragmented and hazy, began to surface. He remembered the orphanage, the way they had clung to each other for comfort, the promises they had made to protect one another before they were separated. How could he have forgotten something so fundamental?

He clutched the photo in his hands, his knuckles whitening with the pressure. Alzheimer's had started to take so much from him, but this felt like a deeper betrayal—a loss of self, of history, of the bond that had once defined his life. The fog that had clouded his mind seemed thicker than ever, and he realised with a pang of fear that if he didn't hold on to this memory now, it could slip away forever.

Shay knew he needed to talk to Emily, to piece together the fragments of his past. But how could he face her, knowing he had failed to remember something so important? He felt a mix of shame and desperation as he reached for his phone.

***

The next morning, Emily was surprised to see Shay waiting for her outside her flat. His face was pale, and his eyes held a mixture of confusion and determination. The early-morning sunlight did little to soften the lines of worry etched into his features.

"Shay, what's wrong?" She asked, her concern evident in her voice.

Without a word, Shay handed her the photograph, his hands trembling. Emily took the photo, her eyes widening as she saw the two identical boys staring back at her. She turned the photo over and read the note, her breath catching in her throat.

"Shay…I didn't know," she whispered, her voice barely audible. "You're Robert's brother? His twin?"

Shay nodded, his voice thick with emotion. "I don't know how I could have forgotten, Emily. I don't know how long it's been buried in the depths of my mind, but I remember now. We were separated as kids and sent to different families. He must have known, but…I didn't. Not until now."

Emily felt a surge of emotions—shock, sadness, and a deep sense of connection to Shay. "He never mentioned you, at least not to me. Maybe he wanted to protect us both, or maybe he thought you'd remember on your own."

Shay's gaze dropped to the ground, his voice barely above a whisper. "I've lost so much to this disease, Emily. But this…this is more than I can bear. I need to understand what happened. I need to know why he never told you."

Emily placed a comforting hand on Shay's arm, her voice steady with resolve. "We'll figure this out together, Shay. You're not alone in this."

Before they could delve further into their thoughts, Emily's phone buzzed, interrupting the moment. It was Jamie, her voice urgent. "Emily, I found something. Meet me at the lab as soon as you can. It's important."

Emily exchanged a determined look with Shay. "Let's go," she said. "We're one step closer to the truth."

***

At the lab, Jamie was waiting for them, her laptop open to a series of decrypted documents. The room was filled with the low hum of machinery and the soft glow of screens, giving it an almost otherworldly feel. Jamie looked up as they entered, her expression a mix of excitement and concern.

"I decrypted more of your father's files," Jamie began, barely able to contain the urgency in her voice. "There are mentions of a secret project—something he was working on outside of Blackwood Tech. It's all connected to his breakthrough in AI and neural repair."

Shay leaned over the laptop, his eyes scanning the documents with a renewed focus. The fog in his mind seemed to lift, if only for a moment, as he immersed himself in the details. "This could be it. The key to everything."

Emily nodded, feeling a surge of hope. "We need to dig deeper, find out exactly what this project was, and how it ties into my father's murder. And we need to do it fast before Blackwood Tech catches wind of what we're doing."

As they pored over the newly uncovered files, a sense of clarity began to form. The pieces of the puzzle were slowly falling into place, and with each discovery, Emily felt they were one step closer to uncovering the truth. But with that clarity came the realisation of just how dangerous their mission had become. The stakes were higher than ever, and there was no turning back.

"We're in this together," Shay said quietly, his voice filled with both resolve and a lingering sense of loss. "For Robert and for the truth."

Emily met his gaze, her own determination mirrored in his eyes. "For Robert," she agreed, a fierce protectiveness burning within her.

As they left the lab, the weight of their mission hung heavy in the air, but so too did a sense of purpose. They had uncovered more than they ever expected, and now, they were on the brink of revealing secrets that could change everything. The truth was within reach, but so was the danger—and they knew that the next steps they took would be critical in deciding their fate.

Chapter 5
A Lead Emerges

The first rays of morning light filtered through the tall windows of the police precinct, casting long shadows across the station floor. Emily Harper walked in, her steps steady but her mind racing. The familiar buzz of activity surrounded her—ringing phones, clacking keyboards, the low hum of conversations—but today, the atmosphere felt different. The knowledge of what she and Shay had uncovered weighed heavily on her, a mix of dread and determination swirling in her chest.

As she made her way to her desk, Emily couldn't shake the sense of urgency gnawing at her. The decrypted files, the memories Shay had unearthed, the danger that loomed over them—it all pointed to something far bigger than she had anticipated. But she was ready. Whatever it took, she would uncover the truth behind her father's murder.

"Morning, DI Harper," a familiar voice called out.

Emily looked up to see Detective Sergeant Mark Turner approaching, a stack of files in his hands. He was a seasoned detective, with greying hair and a calm demeanour that belied the intensity of his work. Emily had always admired his steady presence, especially on days like this.

"Morning, Mark," Emily replied, offering a small smile. "What's on the agenda for today?"

Mark handed her a few of the files, his expression thoughtful. "Routine cases, mostly, but there's something you should look into. We've got a new lead on that tech firm break-in from last week. The one at Blackwood Technologies."

Emily's heart skipped a beat. "Blackwood Technologies? What kind of lead?"

Mark lowered his voice, glancing around to make sure they weren't overheard. "Forensics found traces of a unique polymer on-site—something that's not easy to come by. I cross-referenced it with known suppliers, and it turns out it's linked to a small network of labs that specialise in cutting-edge AI tech. And here's the kicker—the polymer matches materials used in your father's lab."

Emily's mind raced as she processed the information. The break-in at Blackwood Tech, her father's research, the encrypted files—it was all connected. But how? And why?

"This could be the break we've been waiting for," Emily said, her voice tinged with urgency. "We need to follow up on this. Did you find any other connections?"

Mark nodded, handing her a separate report. "I also ran the fingerprints we found at the scene. We got a hit—a former Blackwood Tech employee named Marcus Reed. He was let go about six months ago, under circumstances that were, let's say, less than transparent."

"Marcus Reed…" Emily murmured, the name ringing a distant bell. She flipped through her father's notebook, searching for any mention of him. "Yes, here it is. My father mentioned Reed a few times, but not in detail. Just that they had a professional relationship that became strained."

Mark frowned. "Strained how?"

Emily looked up, her eyes meeting Mark's. "It seems Reed was ambitious, maybe too ambitious. My father wrote that Reed didn't always agree with the ethical constraints he insisted on. Whatever my father was working on, Reed might have wanted it for himself."

Mark's expression darkened. "If that's the case, he could be a key player in all of this. We need to find him and see what he knows."

Emily nodded, her resolve hardening. "Agreed. Let's bring Shay into this. We'll need all the help we can get."

***

Later that afternoon, Emily and Mark met Shay in a small conference room at the precinct. The walls were lined with case boards and evidence files, the space charged with the energy of countless investigations. Shay was already there, reviewing the reports with a focused intensity that made Emily momentarily forget about his struggles with memory loss.

"Good to see you, Shay," Emily said, closing the door behind her.

Shay looked up, a small smile playing on his lips. "You too, Emily. Mark filled me in on the new lead. Marcus Reed is definitely someone we need to talk to."

Mark pulled up a chair and sat down, his expression serious. "I've been looking into Reed's background. He was part of the team working on your father's project, but he was let go after a disagreement with the higher-ups at Blackwood Tech. The details are murky, but it's clear he didn't leave on good terms."

Shay nodded thoughtfully. "If Reed was involved in the break-in, he might have been trying to get his hands on something he believed he was owed—or perhaps something he felt was his to begin with. We need to find out what he knows about your father's research."

Emily leaned forward, her fingers tracing the edges of her father's notebook. "We need to approach this carefully. If Reed is involved in something illegal, he could be dangerous. But he might also be our best shot at finding out who else is involved."

Shay's eyes sharpened, a flicker of the old detective fire lighting them up. "I've been digging through my old contacts, trying to see if I can find any information on Reed's whereabouts. I've got a few leads that might pan out."

Mark glanced between them, his expression thoughtful. "We need to get a team together and move quickly. If Reed is our link to Blackwood Tech and your father's work, we can't afford to lose him."

Emily nodded, her determination resolute. "Let's do it. The sooner we find him, the sooner we can get to the truth."

***

The sun was setting as Emily, Mark, and Shay pulled up outside the address they had traced to Marcus Reed. The building was a rundown apartment complex on the outskirts of the city, its façade cracked and weathered. The setting sun cast long shadows across the parking lot, giving the place an eerie, abandoned feel.

"This is it," Mark said, glancing up at the building. "Reed's last known address."

Emily felt a shiver run down her spine as she scanned the surroundings. The place felt wrong as if it had been forgotten by time and everyone in it. She exchanged a glance with Shay, who gave her a reassuring nod.

"Let's be careful," Shay said quietly. "We don't know what we're walking into."

They made their way to the third floor, where Reed's apartment was located. The hallway was dimly lit, the flickering lights adding to the sense of unease. Emily could feel her pulse quicken as they reached the door marked with Reed's number.

Mark knocked on the door, the sound echoing down the hallway. For a moment, there was silence. Then, after what felt like an eternity, the door creaked open.

Marcus Reed stood in the doorway, his eyes darting between the three of them. He looked dishevelled, a shadow of the man Emily had seen in the old photos—his hair unkempt, his clothes rumpled. But it was his eyes that caught her attention. There was something frantic in them, a wildness that spoke of fear or desperation.

"Marcus Reed?" Mark asked, his voice steady.

Reed hesitated, then nodded. "Yeah…what do you want?"

"We're investigating the break-in at Blackwood Tech," Emily said, stepping forward. "And we know you were involved. We also know you worked with my father, Dr Robert Harper."

At the mention of her father's name, Reed's expression shifted—first to surprise, then to something darker. "I don't know what you're talking about," he said, but his voice lacked conviction.

Emily pressed on, her tone firm. "We're not here to arrest you, Marcus. We just want to know what happened. My father trusted you once, and I need to understand why he was killed. Please, if you know anything, now's the time to speak up."

For a moment, Reed seemed to consider his options. His eyes flicked to the hallway behind them as if weighing the possibility of escape. Then, with a resigned sigh, he stepped back and motioned for them to enter.

"Fine. But you're not going to like what you hear," Reed said, his voice tinged with bitterness.

The apartment was as rundown as the building itself—cluttered with papers, electronic parts, and the unmistakable signs of a man who had been living in isolation. The smell of stale coffee and unwashed dishes hung in the air, adding to the oppressive atmosphere.

They took seats around a small, rickety table piled high with blueprints and diagrams. Reed sat across from them, his hands fidgeting nervously.

"I know why you're here," Reed began, his voice low. "And you're right. I did break into Blackwood Tech. But it's not what you think."

Emily leaned forward, her eyes fixed on Reed's. "Then tell us what happened."

Reed ran a hand through his hair, his gaze distant. "After I was fired, I discovered that Blackwood Tech was planning to use your father's research for something…unethical. They wanted to weaponise it, turn it into something that could be used for control, not healing."

Emily's heart pounded as she listened. "So you broke in to stop them?"

Reed nodded, his expression pained. "I was trying to find the data and destroy it before they could use it. But I couldn't find everything I needed. They must have moved it to a more secure location. Your father was right to be cautious, but it also made it impossible for me to do what I needed to do."

Shay leaned in, his voice calm but insistent. "Do you know who's behind this? Who's leading the effort to weaponise the research?"

Reed hesitated, then nodded slowly. "Edward Mason. He's one of the top executives at Blackwood Tech. Ruthless, power-hungry…he's the one who's been pushing to use the neural chip for purposes your father would never have agreed to."

Emily's jaw tightened; her mind racing. "We need to stop him, Marcus. But we can't do it alone. We need your help."

Reed looked at her, a flicker of something—hope, maybe—crossing his features. "I'll help you. But you have to promise me one thing."

"What's that?" Emily asked.

"Promise me you'll stop them. Promise me you won't let Mason get away with this," Reed said, his voice filled with a desperation that was impossible to ignore.

Emily placed a hand on Reed's arm, her voice firm and resolute. "We promise, Marcus. We'll make sure my father's work is used for good."

As they left Reed's apartment, Emily felt a renewed sense of purpose. They had a name, a lead, and an ally. The pieces were starting to come together, but the danger was only growing. Edward Mason was their next target, and she knew that the fight for justice was just beginning.

Chapter 6
The Connection

The low hum of the city buzzed around Emily Harper as she sat in the backseat of Shay's car, her mind racing with the revelations of the past few days. They had finally cracked open the secrets her father had buried, but the more they uncovered, the more tangled the web became. Marcus Reed had led them to Edward Mason, a name that now loomed like a dark cloud over their investigation. The connection to Blackwood Tech was undeniable, but one question still gnawed at her: What was Arabella Blackwood's role in all of this?

Shay's car navigated through the crowded streets, the headlights casting fleeting glances at the passing pedestrians. As they approached the Blackwood estate, the city's noise seemed to fade into the background, replaced by the ominous silence that surrounded the sprawling mansion. The estate loomed ahead, a fortress of glass and steel, its modern design both intimidating and uninviting.

"We need to be cautious," Shay said, breaking the silence. His voice was calm but carried an undercurrent of tension. "Arabella is powerful and well-connected. If she's involved, she'll be ready to protect her interests at any cost."

Emily nodded, her gaze fixed on the estate. "I know. But we need answers, and she might be the only one who can give them to us."

Shay pulled up to the estate's imposing gates, the sleek black metal reflecting the car's headlights. He reached out to press the intercom button, and after a moment's pause, a voice crackled through the speaker.

"Yes?"

"This is Shay Walsh and DI Emily Harper," Shay said, his tone steady. "We need to speak with Arabella Blackwood."

There was a brief silence, followed by the sound of the gates slowly swinging open. Shay drove through, the tyres crunching over the gravel driveway. As they approached the entrance, Emily couldn't shake the feeling that they were walking into a lion's den. The estate, with its sharp angles and towering glass walls, seemed to watch them with cold, indifferent eyes.

They stepped out of the car and made their way to the front door. A moment later, it swung open to reveal a woman in her early forties, her appearance as polished and sharp as the house she lived in. Arabella Blackwood stood before them, her expression a mask of calm control. Her dark hair was pulled back into a sleek ponytail, and her tailored suit emphasised her commanding presence.

"Mr Walsh, Detective Harper," Arabella greeted them, her voice smooth and composed. "To what do I owe the pleasure?"

"We're here to discuss your connection to Dr Robert Harper's research," Emily said, her tone direct but respectful. "We believe you may have information that could help us with our investigation."

Arabella's eyes narrowed slightly, though her expression remained neutral. "Of course, please, come in."

She led them through the grand foyer and into a spacious sitting room, where the walls were adorned with modern art and the furniture was minimalist yet luxurious. Arabella gestured for them to sit, and they took their seats on a sleek, low-slung couch. The atmosphere was thick with tension, the kind that comes from knowing everyone in the room is holding back something crucial.

Arabella sat across from them, crossing her legs with a fluid grace. "I'll be honest, Detective. I find this visit rather unexpected. I've already provided the police with all the information I have regarding your father's death."

Emily leaned forward, her gaze unwavering. "We've discovered some new information, Ms Blackwood. Information that suggests Blackwood Technologies has been involved in activities that go beyond the bounds of legal and ethical research. My father's work was at the centre of it."

Arabella's expression didn't falter, but Emily noticed the slightest twitch in her jaw. "I'm not sure what you're implying, Detective, but Blackwood Technologies operates within the strictest legal parameters. We're a leader in medical research, and Dr Harper's contributions were invaluable to our work."

Shay cut in, his voice steady. "We're not here to make accusations, Ms Blackwood. We're simply trying to understand what happened. Your company's involvement with Dr Harper's research puts you in a unique position to help us."

Arabella's eyes flicked to Shay, assessing him with a shrewd gaze. "And what exactly do you want to know?"

Emily took a deep breath, choosing her words carefully. "We believe that someone within Blackwood Tech was attempting to use my father's research for purposes he never intended. Specifically, we're looking into Edward Mason."

At the mention of Mason's name, Arabella's composure faltered ever so slightly. She quickly regained her poise, but not before Emily caught the flash of recognition—and perhaps fear—in her eyes.

"Edward Mason is a senior executive," Arabella said, her tone carefully measured. "He oversees several high-level projects, but I wasn't aware of any issues between him and your father."

"Marcus Reed mentioned that Mason was interested in weaponising my father's neural repair research," Emily pressed. "Is there any truth to that?"

Arabella's gaze hardened, her fingers tightening around the armrest of her chair. For a moment, it seemed as though she might deny everything. But then, with a resigned sigh, she leaned back, her shoulders sagging slightly as if the weight of her secrets had finally become too much to bear.

"Robert was a brilliant man," Arabella began, her voice softer now, tinged with something that almost sounded like regret. "But he was also deeply principled. He wanted his research to be used to heal, to improve lives. Mason…he saw another potential. Potential for control and power. There were arguments and disagreements that grew more intense as the project progressed. Robert refused to compromise, and that put him in Mason's crosshairs."

Emily felt a cold knot tighten in her stomach. "So Mason was behind my father's death?"

Arabella shook her head. "I don't know for certain. But I do know that Robert was increasingly worried in the weeks leading up to his death. He confided in me and told me he was being pressured to hand over certain data, data that Mason claimed was vital to the project's success. But Robert suspected that once he handed it over, it would be twisted into something he never intended."

Shay leaned forward, his eyes narrowing. "Why didn't you come forward with this information earlier?"

Arabella's expression darkened, guilt flickering across her features. "Because I was afraid. Mason is…dangerous. He has connections and power that go far beyond Blackwood Tech. If I had spoken out without evidence, it would have been my word against his, and I didn't have the strength to take that risk. I'm not proud of it, but I stayed silent."

Emily's mind raced. The pieces were finally starting to fit together, but the picture they formed was terrifying. Edward Mason had the motive, the means, and the opportunity to kill her father—and Arabella's silence had allowed it to happen.

"We need to bring this to light," Emily said; her voice resolute. "Mason can't get away with this."

Arabella met Emily's gaze, a flicker of hope in her eyes. "I'll help you, Detective. I'll do whatever it takes to make this right."

***

As they left the estate, the sun was beginning to set, casting long shadows over the driveway. Emily felt a sense of grim determination settle over her. They were closer than ever to uncovering the truth, but the danger was only growing. Edward Mason wasn't just a threat—he was a predator, lurking in the shadows, waiting to strike.

Shay walked beside her, his expression pensive. "Arabella's cooperation could be the break we need, but we can't trust her entirely. She's been complicit in this, even if only by her silence."

"I know," Emily replied, her voice steely. "But we need her. Mason is too powerful to take down without allies, and Arabella is our best shot at getting inside Blackwood Tech."

Shay nodded, his gaze distant as he mulled over their next move. "We need to tread carefully. One wrong step and Mason will know we're onto him."

They reached the car, and Emily paused, looking back at the estate. The towering structure seemed to loom even larger in the dimming light, a fortress guarding secrets that had already cost her father his life.

"We'll bring him down, Shay," Emily said quietly, more to herself than to him. "For my father, for everyone, Mason has hurt. We'll bring him down."

Shay placed a hand on her shoulder, a gesture of solidarity. "We will. But we need to be smart about it. Mason won't go down without a fight, and we need to be ready for whatever he throws at us."

As they drove away, the estate receded into the distance, swallowed by the night. But the shadows of the past still clung to Emily, a reminder that their fight was far from over. The connection had been made, the players revealed. Now, it was time to take the next step—and confront the darkness head-on.

Chapter 7
Confrontation at the Estate

The gravel crunched beneath their feet as Emily and Shay approached the massive iron gates of Edward Mason's estate. The imposing structure loomed ahead, a blend of old-world grandeur and modern luxury, nestled within acres of meticulously manicured grounds. The sun was setting, casting long shadows that stretched across the sprawling lawn, adding an air of foreboding to their mission.

Emily glanced at Shay, who was studying the estate with narrowed eyes. "This place feels like a fortress," she murmured, her voice tinged with apprehension.

Shay nodded, his expression grim. "Mason didn't get where he is by taking chances. He knows how to protect himself, and anyone who gets in his way." He paused, his gaze sharpening. "We need to be ready for anything."

They reached the gates, where a security camera swivelled to face them. After a moment, the intercom crackled to life. "State your business," a cold, detached voice demanded.

Shay stepped forward, his tone authoritative. "Shay Walsh and Detective Inspector Emily Harper. We have an appointment with Mr Mason."

There was a brief pause, followed by the heavy clank of the gates unlocking. The iron barriers slowly swung open, revealing a winding driveway lined with ancient oak trees. The mansion itself was a formidable sight—tall, with dark stone walls and narrow windows that gave it a fortress-like appearance. Emily couldn't help but feel a sense of unease as they made their way to the front entrance.

A man in a crisp black suit met them at the door. His expression was as emotionless as his voice had been. 'This way,' he instructed, leading them through the grand foyer and into a large study.

The room was decorated in dark wood and leather, exuding an air of wealth and power. A massive fireplace dominated one wall, its flames crackling quietly, casting flickering shadows across the room. In front of the fireplace, seated in a high-backed leather chair, was Edward Mason.

He rose as they entered, his presence commanding and intimidating. He was tall and broad-shouldered, with silver hair combed neatly back, and piercing blue eyes that seemed to dissect everything in their path. His tailored suit spoke of wealth and influence, but it was the cold, calculating gaze that sent a chill down Emily's spine.

"Mr Walsh, Detective Harper," Mason greeted them, his voice smooth and controlled. "To what do I owe the pleasure of this visit?"

Emily straightened, meeting his gaze head-on. "We're here about Dr Robert Harper's research. We have reason to believe that you were involved in efforts to misuse his work."

Mason's eyes narrowed slightly, but his expression remained impassive. "I'm not sure what you're implying, Detective, but all of Dr Harper's work was conducted with the full approval and oversight of Blackwood Technologies. I have nothing to hide."

Shay stepped forward, his voice calm, but firm. "We've spoken with Arabella Blackwood. She's given us some insight into what's been happening behind the scenes—specifically your interest in weaponising Dr Harper's research."

For the first time, a flicker of something crossed Mason's face—anger, perhaps, or annoyance—but it was gone in an instant. He took a measured step toward them, his gaze icy. "Arabella always was too soft-hearted for this business. She never understood the true potential of what we were working on."

Emily's heart pounded as she listened to Mason's words, the realisation dawning that this man was not only unrepentant but completely convinced of the righteousness of his actions.

"What exactly do you mean by 'potential'?" Emily asked; her voice steely.

Mason's lips curled into a thin, predatory smile. "Dr Harper's research was ground-breaking. The ability to repair and even enhance neural pathways has implications far beyond the medical field. Imagine soldiers with heightened cognitive abilities, spies who can retain and recall vast amounts of information, or leaders who can outthink their enemies at every turn. That's the future I'm interested in, Detective. Not just curing diseases, but advancing human capability to its absolute peak."

Emily felt a surge of anger and revulsion at Mason's words. "That's not what my father wanted," she said, her voice tight with emotion. "He was trying to help people, not create weapons."

Mason's expression hardened. "Your father was a brilliant man, but he lacked vision. He couldn't see the bigger picture, couldn't understand that progress sometimes requires difficult choices."

Shay stepped forward, his voice dangerously low. "Those 'difficult choices' got Robert killed."

For a moment, the tension in the room was palpable, the crackling of the fireplace the only sound. Mason's gaze flicked between Emily and Shay, his expression unreadable.

"I didn't kill Robert," Mason said finally, his tone cold and detached. "But I won't deny that I was interested in his research. Unfortunately, Robert was stubborn, and in the end, that stubbornness got him in over his head."

Emily's heart raced, her mind scrambling to make sense of Mason's words. "What do you mean by that? Who else was involved?"

Mason gave her a long, calculating look as if weighing how much to reveal. Finally, he spoke, his voice measured. "Robert was under pressure from multiple sides. There were...others who wanted his work, people who wouldn't take no for an answer. When he refused to cooperate, things escalated."

Emily exchanged a glance with Shay, her mind reeling. There were more players in this game than they had realised—more threats, more danger. But Mason was still holding back, and she needed to push him further.

"Who were they?" Emily demanded, stepping closer. "Who else wanted my father's research?"

Mason's eyes flicked to the door, a sign that their time was running out. "That's something you'll have to find out on your own, Detective. But I will give you one piece of advice—be careful who you trust. Not everyone is what they seem."

Before Emily could press him further, the man who had escorted them in reappeared at the door. "Mr Mason's time is up," he announced, his voice as cold and detached as before.

Mason nodded to the man, then turned back to Emily and Shay. "This conversation is over. I suggest you leave before you get yourselves into something you can't handle."

Emily opened her mouth to argue, but Shay placed a hand on her arm, stopping her. "We've heard enough," he said quietly, his gaze locked on Mason. "For now."

They turned and left the study, the tension following them out of the room and down the long hallway. As they stepped back into the cool evening air, Emily felt a mixture of frustration and dread. Mason was hiding something—something big—but they were running out of time to uncover it.

***

The ride back to the precinct was tense and silent, the weight of their encounter with Mason hanging heavily between them. Emily stared out the window, her mind replaying the conversation, searching for clues, for something that would give them the upper hand.

"We're missing something," she finally said, breaking the silence. "Mason knows more than he's letting on. And if there are others involved, we need to find out who they are."

Shay nodded, his expression thoughtful. "He's protecting himself, but he's also afraid. Whatever he's hiding, it's big enough to scare even someone like him."

Emily's thoughts drifted back to her father, to the last conversation they had shared before his death. He had been worried and on edge, but she had brushed it off as stress from his work. Now, she realised he had been trying to warn her, trying to protect her from something he couldn't face alone.

"We need to dig deeper," Emily said, her voice resolute. "We need to find out who else was involved in this, and we need to do it quickly. Mason's right about one thing—we're in over our heads."

Shay gave her a reassuring glance. "We'll figure it out, Emily. But we need to be smart about this. Mason's not going to go down without a fight, and we can't afford any mistakes."

As they pulled into the precinct's parking lot, Emily felt a renewed sense of purpose. The stakes were higher than ever, and the danger was closing in, but she wasn't going to back down. Her father's legacy—and her own life—depended on it.

They stepped out of the car, the night air crisp and cool against their skin. As they made their way inside, Emily couldn't shake the feeling that they were running out of time. But one thing was certain—they were closer than ever to the truth, and no matter what it took, they would uncover it.

Chapter 8
Breaking and Entering

The warehouse loomed before them, shrouded in darkness. Emily Harper, Shay Walsh, and Jamie Parker moved swiftly and silently through the shadows; their breaths barely audible in the still night air. The plan was clear—get in, find the evidence, and get out before anyone noticed. But as they approached the warehouse, Emily couldn't shake the feeling that they were stepping into something far more dangerous than they had anticipated.

"This place feels like a trap," Jamie whispered, her voice tense as they reached the side entrance. She knelt by the door, her fingers working quickly to disable the lock. "Mason's smart. He'd know we'd come for this."

Shay nodded, his eyes scanning the perimeter. "That's why we need to move fast. We're not the only ones interested in what's inside."

The door clicked open, and they slipped inside, the musty smell of decay and rust greeting them. The interior of the warehouse was vast and cavernous, filled with abandoned machinery and stacks of forgotten crates. The beams of their flashlights cut through the darkness, casting long shadows on the walls.

"We need to get to the office," Shay whispered, leading the way. "That's where we'll find anything worth taking."

They moved carefully through the warehouse, the silence oppressive. Every creak of the old floorboards echoed like a gunshot in the empty space. Emily's pulse quickened as they ascended a set of metal stairs that led to a small office overlooking the warehouse floor. The door was reinforced, just as they expected.

"Jamie, can you get us in?" Emily asked, her voice barely above a whisper.

Jamie nodded, setting to work on the lock. The minutes dragged on, the tension in the air thickening with each passing second. Finally, with a soft click, the door swung open, revealing a cluttered office filled with papers, filing cabinets, and an old computer.

"This is it," Shay murmured, stepping inside. "If Mason's hiding something, it'll be here."

They split up, each of them searching through the files and documents scattered around the room. Emily's hands trembled slightly as she rifled through a stack of papers, her breath catching when she found a file labelled 'Project Echelon.' She quickly opened it, scanning the pages, her heart sinking as she read the contents.

"Shay, Jamie," Emily whispered urgently, holding up the file. "This is it. This is what my father was working on."

Shay moved over to her, his eyes narrowing as he read over her shoulder. "Mason was trying to weaponise your father's research, just like we suspected. But it's more than that—he was planning on selling it to the highest bidder."

Jamie's face paled as she continued working on the computer. "I've found communications between Mason and several international clients. He was preparing to sell them prototypes—neural implants designed to control behaviour, alter memories…this is worse than we thought."

Before anyone could respond, the sound of a door creaking open downstairs sent a jolt of fear through Emily. Shay's hand immediately went to his gun and they all froze, listening intently. Heavy footsteps echoed through the warehouse, growing louder as they drew closer.

"We need to move," Shay whispered urgently. 'Now.'

They quickly gathered the files and shoved them into Jamie's backpack. As they turned to leave the office, another sound stopped them in their tracks—the unmistakable click of a gun being cocked.

"Not so fast," a cold voice said from the shadows.

Emily's heart leapt into her throat as a figure stepped out from the darkness, a gun aimed directly at them. The woman was tall, her face partially obscured by the low light, but her voice was unmistakably cold and controlled.

"Drop the bag," the woman commanded, her tone leaving no room for negotiation.

Jamie's grip tightened on the bag, her eyes darting to Emily and Shay. "We can't let them take this," she whispered, her voice trembling with fear.

Before anyone could react, the sound of a door slamming downstairs echoed through the warehouse, followed by hurried footsteps. The woman's gaze flicked to the stairs, and in that split second of distraction, Jamie made her move.

She tossed the bag towards Emily and lunged at the woman, trying to knock the gun out of her hand. The warehouse erupted into chaos. The woman fired her gun, the sharp crack echoing off the walls, and Jamie cried out as the bullet tore through her shoulder.

"Jamie!" Emily screamed, catching the bag as it skidded across the floor.

Shay rushed forward, his gun drawn, but the woman was already retreating, disappearing into the shadows as backup arrived. The sounds of more footsteps pounded through the warehouse, and Emily knew they were out of time.

"We have to go!" Shay shouted, grabbing Jamie as she collapsed, blood soaking through her shirt.

Emily clutched the bag tightly and sprinted for the side entrance, her heart hammering in her chest. Jamie's laboured breathing filled her ears as she glanced back, seeing the pained expression on her friend's face. She forced herself to focus—if they didn't get out now, they'd all be dead.

They burst through the side door into the night, the cool air hitting them like a shock. Shay half-dragged and half-carried Jamie as they raced towards the car parked at the edge of the lot. Emily threw open the door and jumped into the driver's seat, her hands shaking as she started the engine.

"Get in!" she yelled, her voice tight with panic.

Shay pulled Jamie into the backseat, slamming the door just as more gunshots rang out, hitting the side of the car. Emily floored the gas pedal, the tyres screeching as they sped away from the warehouse, bullets whizzing past them.

"Jamie, stay with us!" Shay shouted, pressing his hands against Jamie's wound to stem the bleeding.

Jamie's face was pale, her eyes fluttering as she fought to stay conscious. "I…I'm fine," she gasped, though the pain in her voice was unmistakable.

Emily's heart pounded in her chest as she sped through the deserted streets, her mind racing. They had the evidence, but Jamie was hurt—badly. The danger they had walked into was far greater than they had anticipated, and now it was clear that whoever was after them wouldn't stop until they were dead.

"Hang on, Jamie," Emily said, her voice shaking with emotion. "We're going to get you to a hospital."

As they drove through the city, the adrenaline began to wear off, replaced by a deep, gnawing fear. Jamie's breathing was laboured, and Emily could see the blood soaking through the towel Shay had pressed against her wound.

"We need to get her help, fast," Shay said, his voice tight with worry.

Emily nodded, her eyes scanning the streets for any sign of help. "There's a hospital nearby. We'll be there in five minutes."

The car screeched around a corner, and Emily's hands tightened on the steering wheel, her mind racing with what they had uncovered. Mason's plans, the betrayal by Arabella, and now Jamie's injury—it was all spiralling out of control.

As they neared the hospital, Emily's phone buzzed with an incoming call. She glanced at the screen and saw Arabella's name flash across it. Anger flared inside her, but she ignored the call, focusing instead on getting Jamie the help she needed.

Finally, they screeched to a stop outside the emergency entrance, and Shay jumped out, pulling Jamie from the backseat. 'Help!' he shouted, his voice filled with urgency.

Medical staff rushed out, grabbing a gurney and placing Jamie on it as Emily stumbled out of the car, her legs weak with fear. She watched helplessly as they wheeled Jamie inside, Shay following closely behind, his face a mask of worry.

Emily leaned against the car, her breath coming in shallow gasps as the enormity of the situation crashed down on her. They had the evidence, but at what cost? Jamie was hurt—seriously hurt—and Mason was dead. The enemy was closer than they realised, and now they were in a fight for their lives.

She glanced down at the phone in her hand, Arabella's name still flashing on the screen. The woman who had sent an assassin to kill Mason, the woman who had promised to help them, was now the person she trusted the least.

As the phone continued to buzz, Emily's resolve hardened. She would find out the truth behind Arabella's betrayal, and she would make sure that Jamie's sacrifice wasn't in vain. But first, she needed to make sure her friend survived the night.

With trembling hands, she pressed the button to silence the call, her mind already racing ahead to what they needed to do next. The fight was far from over, and now it was personal. Emily wasn't going to stop until she had taken down everyone responsible for her father's death—and for hurting Jamie.

As the night deepened, the lights of the hospital gleamed against the darkness, a beacon of hope in an increasingly dangerous world. Emily took a deep breath, steeling herself for what lay ahead. The situation was bigger, more complex than she had ever imagined, but she wasn't going to back down.

She couldn't. Not now. Not ever.

Chapter 9
A Desperate Night

The car sped through the dimly lit streets, its tyres screeching as Emily Harper gripped the steering wheel tightly, her knuckles white with tension. The city lights blurred past in a haze as she fought to keep her focus. In the backseat, Jamie Parker was slumped against Shay Walsh, her face pale and her breathing laboured. The bullet wound in her shoulder bled profusely, staining her clothes and the seat beneath her.

"Hang on, Jamie. Just hang on," Emily muttered under her breath, her voice trembling with a mixture of fear and desperation. The weight of the night's events pressed down on her like a suffocating blanket. They had gone to the warehouse for answers, but now they were running for their lives, with Jamie's condition worsening by the second.

"Emily, we need to get her to a hospital now," Shay urged, his voice filled with urgency. His hands were pressed against Jamie's wound, trying to stem the bleeding. "She's losing too much blood."

Emily's mind raced. A hospital was the logical choice, but it was also the most dangerous. If the people behind Mason's death—or the assassin herself—were watching, a hospital would be the first place they'd look. They couldn't risk walking into a trap, not with Jamie's life hanging by a thread.

"There's a clinic not far from here," Shay said suddenly, his tone shifting to one of cautious hope. "It's off the books, a place where they don't ask questions. We'll be safer there."

Emily hesitated for only a second before nodding. "Tell me where to go."

Shay quickly directed her through a series of turns, taking them deeper into the less trafficked parts of the city. The streets grew narrower and darker, the buildings older and more rundown. The sense of isolation heightened Emily's anxiety, but she forced herself to stay calm. They had no other choice.

"Jamie, stay with us," Shay said softly, his voice almost a plea. He glanced down at her, his expression a mixture of fear and determination. "We're almost there."

Jamie's eyes fluttered open briefly, her lips twitching as she tried to speak. "I...I'm fine," she whispered, but the pain in her voice was evident.

"You're going to be fine," Emily replied, her voice steady despite the panic clawing at her insides. "Just hold on a little longer."

Finally, they arrived at the clinic, a nondescript building nestled between a closed Laundromat and a boarded-up convenience store. The sign out front was faded and barely legible; the windows were dark. It looked abandoned, but Shay assured Emily that this was the place.

Emily parked the car, and they quickly helped Jamie out, supporting her as they rushed to the entrance. Shay knocked on the door with a rapid, urgent rhythm, glancing nervously over his shoulder as if expecting someone to appear from the shadows.

The door creaked open a moment later, revealing a middle-aged man with a weary expression and sharp, calculating eyes. He took one look at Jamie and nodded, stepping aside to let them in.

"Bring her this way," he said curtly, leading them down a narrow hallway into a small examination room. The space was cramped and dimly lit, with outdated medical equipment and a faint smell of antiseptic in the air. It wasn't much, but it would have to do.

The doctor—if he even was a doctor—immediately began working on Jamie, barking orders at Shay and Emily to hand him supplies and assist where they could. Emily felt a cold sweat break out across her skin as she watched him remove the bullet and tend to the wound. The entire time, Jamie was silent, her face twisted in pain but her eyes focused and determined.

"Will she be okay?" Emily asked, her voice barely above a whisper.

The man glanced at her, his expression unreadable. "I've seen worse," he said, his tone brisk. "She's lucky the bullet missed anything vital, but she'll need rest. Keep her here for the night, and I'll monitor her. After that, it's up to you."

Emily nodded, a small wave of relief washing over her. They had made it, but the danger was far from over. As the man continued to work on Jamie, Emily's mind raced. The assassin's words echoed in her head, "You shouldn't have betrayed Arabella." What had Arabella's role been in all of this? Had she orchestrated Mason's death from the start? And if so, what did that mean for them?

Shay seemed to sense her turmoil and placed a reassuring hand on her shoulder. "We need to regroup," he said quietly. "Once Jamie is stable, we need to figure out our next move."

Emily nodded, trying to steady her breathing. The reality of their situation was sinking in fast—they were up against forces far more powerful and connected than they had imagined. But she couldn't afford to lose her nerve now. Too much was at stake.

After what felt like hours, the doctor finally finished tending to Jamie and stepped back, wiping his hands on a towel. "She'll need to rest," he said, his tone softening slightly. "But she should make a full recovery if she's careful."

"Thank you," Emily said, her voice filled with genuine gratitude. She turned to Shay. "We need to keep her safe. We can't risk moving her until we know it's safe out there."

Shay nodded in agreement. "We'll stay here tonight, but we need to be ready to move if we have to."

As Jamie rested, Emily and Shay retreated to a small room next door, where they could keep an eye on her. The room was barely furnished, with only a couple of chairs and a small table, but it was enough. They sat in silence for a while, the weight of everything that had happened pressing down on them.

Finally, Emily spoke, her voice filled with determination. "We need to take down Arabella. She's behind this—behind everything."

Shay nodded his expression grim. "We need proof. The files we got tonight might be enough to connect her to Mason's death, but we need to be sure. We can't make a move without solid evidence."

Emily's thoughts raced as she considered their options. "We need to go through those files as soon as we can. If there's anything in there that ties her to the assassination, we call it in."

Shay's gaze was steady. "And if there's not?"

Emily met his eyes, her resolve hardening. "Then we find another way."

They sat in silence for a moment longer, the enormity of what lay ahead sinking in. The road they were on was dangerous, filled with unseen enemies and deadly secrets. But Emily knew one thing for sure—she wasn't going to back down.

As the night deepened and the city outside fell into a quiet lull, Emily kept watch over Jamie; her thoughts a whirlwind of plans and possibilities. The fight was far from over, and now it was personal. Arabella had betrayed them, and Jamie had nearly paid the price. Emily wouldn't let that go unanswered.

She would find the truth, no matter the cost. And when she did, she would make sure that those responsible faced justice.

The night stretched on, and Emily's resolve only grew stronger. They were in the middle of a storm, but they were still standing. And as long as they were, they would keep fighting—until the truth was finally revealed, and justice was served.

Chapter 10
Aftermath

The dawn light filtered through the cracked blinds of the small clinic room, casting a soft, golden hue over the plentiful surroundings. London was slowly coming to life, but within these walls, time seemed to stand still. Emily Harper sat slumped in a chair beside Jamie Parker's bed, exhaustion weighing heavily on her shoulders. The adrenaline that had fuelled her through the night had long since worn off, leaving her drained and emotionally raw.

Jamie lay on the narrow bed, her breathing steady but shallow, her face pale against the white sheets. The wound on her shoulder was bandaged, but the memory of the gunshot and the blood was still fresh in Emily's mind. She had almost lost her—Jamie, her closest friend, her confidante. The realisation hit her with a force that left her breathless.

Emily hadn't moved from Jamie's side all night. She'd kept vigil as the hours ticked by, her thoughts a tangled mess of fear, anger, and something deeper—something she hadn't fully acknowledged until now. She had always cared for Jamie and had always felt a deep connection with her, but this night had stripped away the barriers she had put up, leaving her feelings bare and undeniable.

A soft knock on the door pulled Emily from her thoughts. Shay Walsh stepped into the room, his expression weary but resolute. He had been up all night too, combing through the files they had risked so much to obtain. But now, his attention was focused on Emily, concern etched into the lines of his face.

"How's she doing?" Shay asked quietly, his voice barely above a whisper.

Emily looked up at him, her eyes heavy with worry. "She's stable," she replied, her voice hoarse from lack of sleep. "But she hasn't woken up yet."

Shay nodded, glancing at Jamie's still form. "She's tough. She'll pull through."

Emily wanted to believe him, but the fear gnawed at her. The thought of losing Jamie was unbearable, and the emotions she had tried to keep at bay all night threatened to overwhelm her. She stood abruptly, needing to move, to do something to keep herself from spiralling.

"I need some air," she muttered, brushing past Shay and heading for the door. The small room felt suffocating, and she needed space to think, to process everything that had happened.

Shay watched her go, his expression thoughtful but understanding. "I'll keep watch," he said gently.

Emily nodded, barely registering his words as she stepped into the narrow hallway. The clinic was quiet, the only sounds were the distant hum of the city and the occasional creak of the old building settling. She made her way outside, where the morning air was cool and crisp against her skin, a welcome contrast to the stifling warmth of the clinic.

She leaned against the rough brick wall, closing her eyes and taking deep breaths, trying to calm the storm of emotions swirling inside her. But it was no use—her thoughts kept returning to Jamie, lying there so vulnerable, so fragile. Emily's heart clenched with the realisation of how much Jamie meant to her, how much she had come to rely on her presence, her strength, her warmth.

The truth was undeniable now: Emily was in love with Jamie.

The thought was both exhilarating and terrifying. She had never allowed herself to think of Jamie in that way before, had never dared to hope for more than friendship. But the events of the night had stripped away her defences, leaving her feelings exposed and raw.

Emily wasn't sure when it had happened—when friendship had deepened into something more. Maybe it had been during one of their late-night stakeouts when Jamie's laugh had made the hours slip by effortlessly. Or maybe it had been in the quiet moments when they didn't need words to understand each other. But now, standing here alone in the cold morning air, Emily knew there was no turning back. She couldn't lose Jamie—not now, not ever.

Taking one last deep breath, Emily pushed herself off the wall and headed back inside. She had to be there when Jamie woke up. She needed to tell her—everything.

**

Back in the small room, the first thing Emily noticed was that Jamie's breathing had changed. It was deeper, more even, and as Emily approached the bed, she saw Jamie's eyes flutter open, blinking against the soft light of the room.

"Jamie," Emily whispered, relief flooding her voice as she rushed to her side. "You're awake."

Jamie's gaze focused on Emily, and a small, tired smile curved her lips. "Hey," she murmured, her voice weak but steady. "Guess I gave you a scare, huh?"

Emily let out a shaky laugh, her emotions too tangled to form a coherent response. She sank back into the chair beside the bed, her hand reaching out instinctively to grasp Jamie's. "You could say that," she replied, her voice thick with unshed tears. "You scared the hell out of me."

Jamie's smile faltered slightly as she noticed the strain in Emily's expression. "I'm sorry," she whispered, her fingers curling around Emily's hand. "I didn't mean to worry you."

"You don't have to apologise," Emily said, her voice breaking slightly. She squeezed Jamie's hand, her thumb brushing gently over her knuckles. "You were trying to protect us…to protect me."

Jamie's eyes softened a mixture of affection and concern in her gaze. "I'd do it again in a heartbeat," she said, her voice filled with quiet resolve.

Emily's heart swelled with emotion, the words she had been holding back all night threatening to spill over. She took a deep breath, trying to steady herself. "Jamie, I—" she began, but the words caught in her throat.

Jamie's brow furrowed slightly as she studied Emily's face. "What is it?" She asked gently.

Emily hesitated for a moment, searching Jamie's eyes for any sign of what she might be feeling. But all she saw was warmth, concern, and something that made her heart skip a beat—something that mirrored the emotions swirling inside her.

"I almost lost you last night," Emily said, her voice trembling with the weight of her emotions. "And I realised…I realised that I can't—I can't lose you, Jamie. I can't imagine my life without you."

Jamie's expression softened, her gaze never leaving Emily's. "You're not going to lose me," she said, her voice steady despite the weakness in her body. "I'm right here."

Emily shook her head, her grip on Jamie's hand tightening as if she was afraid to let go. "That's not what I mean," she whispered, her voice barely audible. "Jamie, I…I care about you. So much more than I ever let myself admit."

Jamie's eyes widened slightly, a flicker of surprise crossing her face. But then, slowly, a soft smile spread across her lips, and she gently tugged on Emily's hand, pulling her closer.

"Emily," Jamie said softly, her voice filled with warmth, "I've felt the same way for a long time. I just didn't want to make things complicated between us. But after last night…I can't keep pretending either."

Emily's breath caught as she stared into Jamie's eyes, seeing the truth in her words, the unspoken emotions that had been building between them for so long. Without thinking, she leaned in, her heart pounding in her chest as she gently pressed her lips to Jamie's.

The kiss was soft and tentative but filled with all the emotions they had been holding back—fear, relief, affection, and a deep, undeniable connection. When they finally pulled back, both of them were breathless, but the air between them felt lighter, charged with something new and beautiful.

Jamie's smile was radiant, her eyes shining with a mix of tears and joy. "I'm glad you finally figured it out," she teased, her voice playful despite the seriousness of their conversation.

Emily laughed, the sound filled with genuine happiness. "Took me long enough, didn't it?" She replied, her heart swelling with the realisation that she wasn't alone in this—that Jamie felt the same way.

For a moment, they simply held each other's gaze, the weight of the world slipping away as they basked in the warmth of their newfound understanding. But then reality crept back in, and Emily's smile faltered slightly.

"What happens now?" She asked quietly, the enormity of their situation settling back over them.

Jamie's smile softened, but her gaze remained steady. "We keep fighting," she said firmly. 'Together.'

Emily nodded, her resolve strengthening in the face of Jamie's determination. 'Together,' she agreed, knowing that whatever challenges lay ahead, they would face them side by side.

The road ahead was still uncertain, filled with danger and unknowns, but for the first time in a long time, Emily felt a sense of hope. She had Jamie by her side, and together, they were stronger than anything that might come their way.

As the morning sun continued to rise outside, casting its warm light over the clinic, Emily knew that they had turned a corner—both in their fight for justice and in their relationship. And no matter what the future held, they would face it together, their bond unbreakable, their love a source of strength that nothing could diminish.

Chapter 11
A New Mission

The morning after the chaos at the warehouse, Emily walked into the police station with a heavy heart. She knew there would be repercussions for her actions, and the weight of that knowledge pressed down on her like a physical burden. The station was abuzz with activity, but it seemed to quiet as she passed, officers and colleagues casting her furtive, curious glances.

As she approached her desk, she saw Detective Sergeant Mark Turner waiting for her, his expression a mix of concern and professionalism. "Emily, the Chief wants to see you. Now."

Emily nodded, trying to steel herself for what was to come. 'Thanks, Mark.' The walk to the Chief's office felt interminable, each step echoing her growing sense of dread. She knocked lightly on the door and waited for the terse 'Come in' from inside.

Chief Inspector Caldwell sat behind his desk, his stern expression doing little to mask his disappointment. He gestured for Emily to sit, his eyes never leaving her. "Detective Inspector Harper," he began, his voice cool and measured. "I've received reports about your unauthorised operation last night. Would you care to explain yourself?"

Emily took a deep breath, meeting his gaze. "Sir, I acted on a lead that was crucial to our investigation into Blackwood Tech and Edward Mason. I believed it was urgent to follow up immediately."

Caldwell's expression hardened. "And in doing so, you put yourself, Shay, and a civilian in grave danger. There were protocols you ignored and proper channels you bypassed. This is not how we operate."

Emily felt a surge of frustration. "With all due respect, sir, the situation demanded immediate action. Mason and his men were about to destroy evidence that could expose their illegal activities."

Caldwell leaned forward, his eyes narrowing. "And yet, because of your actions, we have an injured officer and a dead suspect who could have provided critical information. Do you understand the gravity of this, Harper?"

Emily's heart sank. "Yes, sir. I do."

He sighed, leaning back in his chair. "You're a good detective, Emily. But your impulsiveness and mistrust is a liability. Effective immediately, you're suspended pending an internal review. Hand over your badge and your weapon."

The words hit her like a physical blow. Emily reached for her badge and gun, placing them on the desk with a shaking hand. "Sir, please. We're so close to uncovering the truth."

Caldwell shook his head. "I'm sorry, Emily. But until this review is complete, you're off the case."

Emily stood, feeling numb. "Understood, sir."

As she walked out of the office, the reality of her suspension hit her hard. Her career, her father's legacy and everything she had been fighting for seemed to hang in the balance. She headed straight to the hospital, her thoughts racing, anger and frustration flowing through her.

***

Jamie was there, resting with a cup of tea, looking pale but determined. When she saw Emily, her eyes filled with concern. "Emily, what happened?"

Emily slumped into a chair, covering her face with her hands. "I'm suspended. The Chief thinks I acted recklessly, and now there's an internal review."

Jamie reached out, her hand gentle on Emily's arm. "I'm so sorry, Emily. But we're not giving up. We'll figure this out."

Emily looked up, her eyes brimming with tears. "How? I can't even work on the case anymore. They've taken everything from me."

Jamie's grip tightened. "They haven't taken us. We're still in this together. Shay and I will continue investigating, and we'll keep you in the loop. We're not stopping until we get justice for your father."

Emily nodded, drawing strength from Jamie's unwavering support. "Okay. We'll do this. Together."

Just then, Shay entered the hospital room, his expression grim. "I heard what happened. Emily, I'm sorry."

Emily forced a smile. "Thanks, Shay. But we need to stay focused. What's our next move?"

Shay glanced around, lowering his voice. "We need to dig deeper into Mason's connections. Sarah's intel mentioned a few key players we haven't looked into yet. We can start there."

Jamie nodded. "And we need to be careful. Whoever shot Mason is still out there, and they'll be watching us."

Emily took a deep breath, feeling a renewed sense of determination. "Right. Let's get to work."

Chapter 12
The Hunt Begins

Arabella Blackwood sat at the head of the long, polished conference table, her fingers tapping rhythmically on the surface. The morning sun streamed through the floor-to-ceiling windows of her corner office, casting a warm glow over the room. Outside, the city of London hummed with activity, but inside, the atmosphere was tense and expectant. Her senior team members sat around the table, their faces a mix of anticipation and apprehension.

"Let's get started," Arabella said; her voice crisp and commanding. She had an air of authority that demanded attention, her presence filling the room.

Marcus Reed sat to her right; his smug expression was replaced by one of unease when she sat. Arabella had been watching him closely, aware that his ambitious nature made him both a valuable asset and a potential threat.

"Marcus, where do we stand with the neural chip project?" She asked, her eyes fixed on him.

Reed cleared his throat, glancing at the papers in front of him. "We've made significant progress. The latest trials have shown promising results. However, there have been...complications."

Arabella's eyes narrowed. 'Complications?'

Reed hesitated and then continued, "There's been increased scrutiny from the police and other authorities. They're getting too close. We need to be cautious about our next steps. Edward was a good distraction but, with him dead, it may lead them closer to the truth."

Arabella leaned back in her chair, her fingers steepled in front of her. "Cautious? We can't afford caution, Marcus. We're on the brink of something monumental. You played your part well, but Mason's death was a necessity, he was too pompous, and an idiot. We can't let anything jeopardise the plan."

Reed nodded, but his eyes betrayed his fear. "I understand, Arabella. But the situation is volatile. We need to neutralise the threats before they become insurmountable."

Arabella's gaze swept across the room, taking in the faces of her top executives. Each of them owed their careers to her, and she knew they would follow her lead without question. "Our primary concern is Dr Harper's research. We need to secure all related data and ensure it's used as intended. No more delays, no more excuses."

One of the executives, a woman named Aria, leaned forward. "What about his daughter, Emily Harper? She's been digging around, and she's persistent. Should we consider…removing her from the equation?"

Arabella's lips curved into a cold smile. "Emily Harper is a minor inconvenience. She's been suspended from the force, which limits her reach. But we'll keep an eye on her. If she becomes a real threat, we'll deal with her accordingly."

Reed shifted uncomfortably in his seat. "And what about Shay Walsh? He's been a thorn in our side as well."

Arabella's smile faded, replaced by a look of disdain. "Shay Walsh is a relic of the past. His condition makes him less of a threat. However, we can't underestimate him. Ensure he's kept under surveillance. If he gets too close, we'll take necessary action."

The meeting continued, with each executive providing updates on their respective departments. Arabella listened intently, her mind constantly calculating, strategising. She had built Blackwood Tech from the ground up, and she wasn't about to let anyone or anything derail her vision.

As the meeting drew to a close, Arabella dismissed her team but motioned for Reed to stay behind. Once the room was empty, she fixed him with a piercing stare.

"Marcus, I need you to understand something," she said, her voice low and menacing. "We are on the cusp of greatness. Dr Harper's research is the key to unlocking a new era of technological advancement. But we must remain vigilant. Do not let your fear cloud your judgment."

Reed nodded, though his eyes remained wary. "I understand, Arabella. I won't let you down."

Arabella's expression softened slightly, but her gaze remained intense. "See that you don't. We've come too far to let anything slip through our fingers now."

***

Later that evening, Arabella sat in her private study, reviewing the latest data from the neural chip trials. The results were promising, but the risk of exposure was growing. She needed to tighten her grip on the situation and ensure that all loose ends were tied up.

Her phone buzzed, and she glanced at the screen to see a message from one of her operatives. It read: *"Walsh and Harper have obtained critical documents. They're planning to meet with an inside contact tonight."*

Arabella's eyes narrowed. She couldn't allow that meeting to happen. Picking up the phone, she made a quick call to her head of security.

"We have a situation," she said, her voice cold and precise. "I need you to intercept Walsh and Harper tonight. Ensure that they do not make contact with their informant. Use whatever means necessary."

A female voice crackled over the line, steady and professional. "Understood, Ms Blackwood. It will be done."

Arabella ended the call, a sense of satisfaction settling over her. She had taken every precaution and orchestrated every move. Her adversaries were closing in, but she was always one step ahead.

She poured herself a glass of wine and walked to the large window overlooking the city. The lights of London spread out before her like a sprawling tapestry, each flicker a reminder of her empire. She took a sip of the wine, savouring the taste of success mingled with the thrill of the hunt.

Her thoughts drifted to Robert Harper. They had shared a vision once, a dream of changing the world through technology. But he had been too idealistic, too focused on ethics and morality. When he realised the true potential of his research, he tried to pull back, to limit its scope. Arabella had known then that their paths would diverge.

She had done what was necessary, taken the steps he couldn't. And now, with his research firmly in her grasp, she would ensure it reached its full potential. The neural chip could reverse Alzheimer's and dementia, yes, but it could do so much more. The power to control minds, to shape thoughts and behaviours was within reach now. The possibilities were endless.

But first, she had to deal with the threats at hand. Emily Harper, Shay Walsh, and any other meddlesome figures would be handled. Arabella's smile returned as she contemplated the future. She had the resources, the intelligence, and the ruthlessness to see her vision realised.

As the night deepened, Arabella remained at the window, her mind a whirl of plans and contingencies. She would outmanoeuvre, outthink, and outlast anyone who stood in her way. Blackwood Tech was hers, and through it, she would reshape the world. Nothing would stop her.

The city lights blurred slightly as she took another sip of wine, the taste of victory lingering on her lips. Arabella Blackwood, queen of Blackwood Tech, would see her empire rise, no matter the cost. And those who dared to oppose her would learn the hard way that she was a force to be reckoned with.

Her thoughts returned to Edward Mason, her former right-hand man. Eliminating him had been a necessary but regretful step. Arabella's anger simmered beneath the surface. She had invested so much in him. But his removal had solidified her control, She felt more confident than ever now that her plan was coming together.

"To the future," Arabella whispered, raising her glass to the cityscape. And in her heart, she knew she would stop at nothing to claim it.

Chapter 13
A Shadowy Figure

The days following Emily's suspension were some of the hardest she had ever faced. The sting of being removed from the case and the uncertainty of the internal review weighed heavily on her. She spent her days trying to keep busy, but her thoughts constantly drifted back to the investigation and to Jamie, who was still recovering in the hospital.

Emily found solace in visiting Jamie. The hospital room had become a temporary refuge, a place where the two could find comfort in each other's presence. Today was no different; Emily walked into Jamie's room, carrying a bouquet of flowers she had picked up from a nearby shop.

Jamie looked up from her bed, her face lighting up with a smile. "Hey, Emily. Those are beautiful."

Emily smiled, placing the flowers in a vase on the bedside table. "I thought you'd like them. How are you feeling today?"

Jamie sighed, leaning back against the pillows. "Better. The doctors say I should be able to go home soon. But I'm more worried about you. How are you holding up?"

Emily sat down in the chair beside the bed, taking Jamie's hand. "I'm managing. It's been tough being side-lined, but Shay's been keeping me in the loop. We're still making progress, even if I can't be directly involved."

Jamie squeezed Emily's hand. "I know it's hard, but you're doing the right thing. We'll get through this together."

As they talked, Emily's phone buzzed with a message from Shay. She glanced at it, her heart skipping a beat as she read the text.

Shay:

'Got some information. Meet me at the cafe.'

Emily looked at Jamie, her eyes filled with determination. "Shay's got something. I need to go meet him."

Jamie nodded. "Go. I'll be here when you get back. And be careful."

Emily leaned down, kissing Jamie gently. 'I will. I promise.'

***

Emily arrived at the small café where she and Shay first talked. The place was quiet, a few patrons scattered at the tables, lost in their own conversations. She spotted Shay in a corner booth, a stack of papers and a laptop in front of him.

"Shay," Emily greeted as she slid into the seat across from him. "What's the news?"

Shay looked up, his eyes serious. "I've been digging through the information we got from Mason's operations. There's a lot to go through, but I found something that might interest you."

He handed her a document, and Emily scanned it quickly. It detailed a series of transactions linked to a shell company that Mason had been using to funnel money. More importantly, it mentioned several high-ranking officials within Blackwood Tech who were involved in the cover-up.

"This is huge," Emily said, her eyes widening. "If we can link these officials to the illegal activities, we can bring the whole operation down."

Shay nodded. "Exactly. But there's more. I've managed to get in touch with one of Sarah's contacts inside Blackwood Tech. They're willing to meet and provide us with additional information. It could be the break we need."

Emily's heart raced with a mixture of excitement and apprehension. "When and where?"

"Tonight, at a warehouse down by the docks," Shay replied. "It's risky, but we don't have much choice. If we're going to stop them, we need all the information we can get."

Emily took a deep breath. "I'm in. We need to move quickly and carefully."

Shay nodded. "Agreed. We'll meet there at 10 pm. Be ready for anything."

***

That night, Emily felt a familiar surge of adrenaline as she prepared for the meeting. Despite being officially off the case, her commitment to uncovering the truth and bringing justice for her father remained unwavering. She couldn't shake the feeling that this meeting could be a turning point in their investigation.

She arrived at the docks early, the cool night air biting through her jacket. The area was deserted, the faint sounds of the city a distant hum. She spotted Shay's car and made her way over, her senses alert for any signs of trouble.

"Ready?" Shay asked as she approached.

Emily nodded. "Let's do this."

They made their way to the warehouse, slipping inside through a side door. The interior was dimly lit, crates and equipment casting long shadows across the floor. As they moved deeper into the building, they saw a figure standing by a stack of crates, partially hidden in the shadows.

"Are you the contact?" Shay called out, his voice steady.

The figure stepped forward, revealing a middle-aged man with a nervous expression. "Yes. My name is Richard. I work in the IT department at Blackwood Tech. I've seen things...things that aren't right. I want to help."

Emily and Shay exchanged a glance and then approached Richard. "What can you tell us?" Emily asked, her voice filled with urgency.

Richard took a deep breath. "Mason was just the tip of the iceberg. There are others, high up in the company, they are manipulating Harper's research. They're planning something big, and it's happening soon. I have documents and files that can prove it."

Before he could say more, the sound of footsteps echoed through the warehouse. Emily's heart pounded as she realised they had been followed. "We need to get out of here," she whispered urgently.

But it was too late. Figures emerged from the shadows, guns drawn. Emily and Shay exchanged a quick, determined look, ready to fight their way out if necessary.

"Drop the documents and step away," a voice commanded, cold and authoritative.

Emily's mind raced. They couldn't let the evidence fall into the wrong hands. "Run!" she shouted to Richard, as she and Shay ducked behind a stack of crates.

Gunfire erupted, the warehouse filling with the deafening sound. Emily fired back, her heart pounding in her chest. They needed to get out, but the odds were against them.

Suddenly, one of the gunmen went down, taken out by a precise shot. Emily turned to see Richard, having grabbed a gun from a fallen assailant, covering their escape.

"Go!" Richard shouted, firing at the remaining attackers.

Emily and Shay didn't hesitate. They grabbed the documents and made a break for the exit, bullets whizzing past them. They burst through the door, sprinting towards Shay's car.

As they sped away, Emily glanced back at the warehouse, her heart aching for Richard, who had sacrificed himself to buy them time. She turned to Shay, her expression grim.

"We need to make sure his sacrifice wasn't in vain," she said, her voice shaken.

Chapter 14
Unlikely Allies

The sterile smell of disinfectant and the distant beeping of medical equipment filled the air as Emily and Shay walked through the hospital corridors, their steps echoing off the linoleum floor. They were heading to Jamie's room, carrying the evidence they had risked their lives to obtain. Emily's heart raced with anticipation and dread, the weight of their mission pressing heavily on her shoulders.

Jamie looked up as they entered, her face lighting up despite the bandages and the weariness in her eyes. 'Hey,' she greeted, her voice warm. "You made it out okay."

Emily smiled, though it didn't reach her eyes. "We did. And we've got something big." She held up a folder and a USB drive. "Blueprints and a complex code. We think it's connected to Blackwood Tech's operations and the neural chip project."

Shay nodded, setting the materials down on the small table beside Jamie's bed. "We need to go through this carefully. If we can decipher the code and understand the blueprints, we might be able to expose Arabella Blackwood and her plans."

Jamie shifted to sit up more comfortably, wincing slightly. "Let's get to it then. We don't have any time to waste."

They spread the blueprints out on the table, the intricate lines and notations forming a complex diagram. Emily frowned, her eyes scanning the details. "This looks like a facility layout, but I can't make out where it is."

Shay leaned in, studying the blueprints with a practised eye. "It's heavily encrypted. We'll need to cross-reference this with any known Blackwood Tech facilities. The code on the USB drive might help us narrow it down."

Jamie plugged the USB drive into her laptop, the screen lighting up with rows of encrypted data. "This is advanced stuff," she muttered, her fingers flying over the keyboard. "Whoever did this knew what they were doing."

As Jamie worked, Emily and Shay continued to analyse the blueprints. The layout showed a series of rooms and corridors, with annotations in a shorthand Emily didn't recognise. "This is beyond me," she admitted. "Shay, do you recognise any of this?"

Shay's eyes narrowed as he traced a line with his finger. "Some of these symbols are similar to ones used in military installations. It could be a secure research facility. Look at this section here—it's marked as 'Control Room.' That's likely where they're running their operations."

Emily's heart sank. "If this is where they're developing and testing the neural chip, we need to get in there and gather evidence. But we can't do it alone."

Jamie looked up from her laptop, her expression determined. "I'm getting somewhere with the code. It's a series of algorithms, likely used to control access to their systems. If I can crack it, we might be able to get more information on what they're doing."

The hours passed in a blur as they worked together, the hospital room becoming a makeshift war room. Jamie's laptop screen filled with lines of code; the blueprints spread out before them like a puzzle waiting to be solved.

Finally, Jamie let out a triumphant noise. "Got it! The code contains access protocols for a facility located on the outskirts of the city. It matches the layout of the blueprints."

Emily's eyes widened. "We have a location. Now we just need to figure out how to get in and gather the evidence we need."

Shay nodded, though his expression was tinged with concern. "We'll need to be careful. If Arabella and her team suspect we're coming, they'll tighten security. We need a plan."

As they discussed their strategy, Emily couldn't shake the feeling of urgency. "We need to act fast. Every moment we wait, they could be moving forward with their plans."

Jamie's face softened as she looked at Emily. "We'll do this together. But we need to be smart about it. Rushing in without a solid plan will only get us caught."

Shay rubbed his temples, a sign of the fatigue that was starting to show. "Jamie's right. We need to gather more intel; maybe get a team together. This isn't something we can handle alone."

Emily sighed, the weight of the situation pressing down on her. "You're right. Let's finish analysing what we have and then figure out our next steps."

They returned to the blueprints and code, dissecting every detail. As they worked, Shay's movements became slower, his focus wavering. Emily noticed but didn't comment, her own exhaustion creeping in.

Hours later, they had a clearer picture. The facility was a high-security research lab, with multiple checkpoints and surveillance. The code Jamie cracked provided them with access protocols, but they would need more than that to get inside undetected.

"We'll need disguises, forged IDs, and a distraction," Shay said, his voice showing signs of strain. "It's risky, but it's our best shot."

Emily nodded, though worry gnawed at her. "We'll need help. I can reach out to some of my contacts and see if they can provide us with what we need."

Jamie squeezed Emily's hand, offering a reassuring smile. "We'll make it work. Together."

As they continued to plan, Shay's condition worsened. He started to repeat himself, asking the same questions and losing track of their conversation. Emily's heart ached as she watched him struggle.

"Shay, maybe you should rest," Emily suggested gently. "You've been pushing yourself too hard."

Shay shook his head, frustration etched on his face. "No, we need to finish this. We're so close."

But it was clear that his Alzheimer's was taking its toll. He stumbled over his words, his hands shaking as he tried to focus. Emily and Jamie exchanged a worried glance.

"Shay, please," Jamie said softly. "We can handle this. You need to take care of yourself."

Shay's eyes filled with anger and despair. "I can't let you down. I promised Robert, I'd protect you and finish what he started."

Emily's throat tightened. "You've done so much, Shay. We wouldn't be here without you. But we need you to be okay. Please, take a break."

Shay opened his mouth to argue, but his legs gave out from under him. He collapsed to the floor, his body trembling. Emily and Jamie rushed to his side, panic surging through them.

"Shay!" Emily cried, cradling his head in her lap. "Stay with us."

Jamie pressed the call button for the nurse, her hands shaking. "We need help in here!"

Within moments, medical staff arrived, lifting Shay onto a gurney and rushing him out of the room. Emily and Jamie followed; their hearts in their throats. The sight of Shay, so strong and determined, now helpless and vulnerable, was almost too much to bear.

As they waited outside the emergency room, the silence was deafening. Emily paced back and forth, her mind racing with fear and guilt. "This is my fault," she whispered. "I pushed him too hard."

Jamie pulled her into a tight embrace. "No, it's not your fault. Shay wanted to help. He chose this."

Emily clung to Jamie, tears streaming down her face. "What if he doesn't make it? What if we lose him?"

Jamie's voice was steady, though her eyes were filled with tears. "We won't lose him. He's a fighter. And we'll keep fighting for him."

The minutes stretched into an eternity as they waited for news. Finally, a doctor emerged, his expression grave but not without hope.

"Shay is stable," he said, his voice calm. "He's had a severe episode, likely triggered by stress and exhaustion. He needs rest and monitoring, but he should recover."

Emily's legs nearly gave out from relief. "Can we see him?"

The doctor nodded. "Yes, but only for a few minutes. He needs to rest."

They entered Shay's room quietly, finding him pale and frail but awake. His eyes lit up as he saw them, a weak smile forming on his lips.

"Hey, old man," Jamie said softly, taking his hand. "You gave us quite a scare."

Shay chuckled weakly. "I'm not done yet."

Emily leaned down, her voice choked with emotion. "You need to rest, Shay. We need you. We'll take it from here."

Shay squeezed her hand. "You're not alone. You have each other. And I'll be back in the fight soon enough."

They stayed with him until he drifted off to sleep, the weight of the world momentarily lifting from their shoulders. As they left the room, Emily felt a renewed sense of determination. They had come too far to turn back now.

Back in Jamie's room, they sat down to finalise their plan. The blueprints and code were their key to exposing Arabella's plans, but they needed to be smart and cautious.

Chapter 15
The Betrayal

The sterile white walls of the hospital room were a stark contrast to the swirling memories in Shay Walsh's mind. As he lay in the hospital bed, the weight of his past pressed down on him, the line between past and present blurring. The soft beeping of the heart monitor became a rhythmic pulse that seemed to echo the beat of his life's journey, taking him back to his earliest memories, back to when he was Shay Tristan.

Shay and Robert Tristan had been inseparable as young boys. Living in a rundown orphanage on the outskirts of Manchester, they clung to each other for comfort and protection. At six years old, they were too young to understand why their parents had abandoned them, but old enough to feel the sting of rejection.

The orphanage was a cold, harsh place. The staff was overworked and underpaid, often resorting to harsh punishments for minor infractions. Shay, being the older of the two by just a few minutes, felt a fierce need to protect his brother. They shared everything—food, blankets, and whispered dreams of a better life.

But that life seemed impossibly far away.

One rainy afternoon, the brothers were playing in the muddy yard when they were called inside. A well-dressed couple stood in the foyer, speaking with the matron. Shay held Robert's hand tightly as they were led to the couple.

"Hello, boys," the woman said with a warm smile. "My name is Mrs Walsh, and this is my husband. We're here to meet you."

Shay glanced up at the couple, wary but hopeful. "Are you going to take us home?"

Mrs Walsh's smile faltered slightly, and she exchanged a glance with her husband. "We'd like to take you, Shay."

The words hung in the air, and Shay felt his heart drop. "What about Robert? We're a package deal."

Mr Walsh knelt down to Shay's level, his expression serious. "I'm sorry, son. We can only take one of you."

Tears filled Shay's eyes as he looked at his brother, who was clinging to his hand. "I won't go without Robert."

The matron stepped forward, her voice firm. "Shay, you need to go with Mr and Mrs Walsh. They can give you a good home."

Shay shook his head, pulling Robert closer. "No. We stay together."

But the decision was not his to make. The matron pried Robert's hand from Shay's, and despite his protests and tears, Shay was led away. He looked back to see Robert's tear-streaked face, his small frame shaking with sobs.

"Shay!" Robert cried out, reaching for his brother.

Shay struggled against the grip of the matron and Mr Walsh, but he was no match for their strength. "I'll come back for you, Robert! I promise!"

The car ride to the Walsh home was a blur of tears and confusion. Shay's heart ached with the loss of his brother, the guilt of leaving him behind an unbearable weight on his young shoulders. The Walshs tried to comfort him, but their words were hollow against the pain of separation.

The Walsh home was a stark contrast to the orphanage. It was a large, comfortable house with warm, inviting rooms. Shay was given his own room, filled with toys and books, but it all felt empty without Robert.

Days turned into weeks, and weeks into months. Shay struggled to adjust to his new life, haunted by the memory of his brother's cries. The Walshs were kind, but their love could not fill the void left by Robert's absence.

Shay's new parents were determined to help him adjust, enrolling him in school and encouraging him to make friends. But he remained distant, his thoughts always drifting back to the brother he had left behind.

One day, a year after his adoption, Shay received a letter from the orphanage. It was a brief note, informing him that Robert had been adopted by a family named Harper. Shay felt a mix of relief and sorrow. His brother had found a home, but it meant they were truly separated.

The Harper family provided Robert with a loving home, but the trauma of separation had left its mark. Robert was a quiet, introspective child, always yearning for the brother he had lost. The Harpers did their best to fill the void, but Robert never forgot Shay's promise to return.

Meanwhile, Shay's life with the Walshs was becoming increasingly difficult. Mr Walsh's initial kindness began to wane, replaced by frustration and anger at Shay's inability to let go of his past. The man who had once knelt down with kind eyes now wielded a harsh belt, punishing Shay for every perceived infraction.

Mrs Walsh tried to intervene, but her attempts were futile against her husband's growing temper. The home that had once seemed a refuge became another prison, and Shay's days were filled with fear and pain.

Shay found solace in books and stories of brave heroes who overcame great odds. He imagined himself as one of those heroes, fighting to find his way back to his brother. But as the years passed, the dream of reuniting with Robert seemed more and more distant.

The beatings grew more frequent and severe, and Shay's spirit began to harden. He learnt to hide his pain, to bury his emotions deep inside. He became a quiet, withdrawn teenager, focused on surviving each day.

When Shay turned eighteen, he saw an opportunity to escape. He enlisted in the army, seeking the structure and discipline that he hoped would provide a path to a better life. The military became his new family, offering him a sense of purpose and belonging that he had never known.

The years in the army were transformative. Shay excelled in training, his determination and resilience earning him the respect of his peers and superiors. He found a sense of camaraderie among his fellow soldiers, a bond that reminded him of the connection he had once shared with Robert.

But the memories of his brother never faded. Every letter he wrote, every phone call he made to the Harpers, went unanswered. The silence was a constant reminder of the promise he had failed to keep.

Shay's time in the army was marked by both triumph and tragedy. He served in various combat zones, facing the horrors of war and the loss of comrades. The experiences toughened him, shaping him into a man of strength and resolve.

After several years of service, Shay was honourably discharged. He returned to civilian life, determined to find his brother and fulfil the promise he had made so many years ago. Shay kept his last name, Walsh, as a symbolic break from his painful past, but he never forgot his true identity as a Tristan.

Chapter 16
The Pursuit

Shay Walsh had spent years in the army, honing skills that made him a formidable force. Yet, even after his honourable discharge, one mission remained unfinished: finding his brother, Robert. This quest for his brother became the driving force behind his decision to become a private detective. It was a path that would lead him to his first high-profile case, intertwining his fate with Marcus Reed.

***

After his discharge, Shay moved back to London, his home city and the last known whereabouts of his brother. He set up a small private investigation office in a modest neighbourhood, pouring his savings into the venture. Shay's reputation as a disciplined, meticulous investigator grew quickly, thanks to his army training and innate determination. He took on various cases, from infidelity to missing persons, all the while keeping an eye out for any information about Robert.

Shay's relentless search led him through a labyrinth of bureaucracy and dead ends. Every potential lead was a thread in a vast, tangled web. His frustration grew, it was during one of these seemingly fruitless days that a new client walked into his office, setting off a chain of events that would change everything.

***

The man was in his mid-forties, well-dressed, with a look of desperation in his eyes. He introduced himself as William Reed, a prominent tech executive. Shay offered him a seat and listened as he explained his predicament.

"My son, Marcus Reed, has been kidnapped," Harris said, his voice trembling. "He's an ethical hacker, very talented, but his skills have made him some dangerous enemies."

Shay leaned forward; his interest piqued. "Do you have any idea who might have taken him or why?"

Harris nodded, handing over a folder filled with documents. "Marcus was working on exposing a cybercrime ring. He found something big, something that scared them. He was taken three days ago, and I've received no ransom demands, just silence."

Shay flipped through the documents, his mind already forming a plan. "I'll take the case, Mr Harris. But I'll need full access to Marcus's files and any contacts he might have had."

Harris agreed; his relief palpable. "Thank you, Mr Walsh. Please, find my Son."

***

The investigation into Marcus Reed's kidnapping was unlike anything Shay had encountered before. It delved deep into the murky world of cybercrime and hacking, areas that were new to him. Shay immersed himself in the case, learning everything he could about Marcus's work and the enemies he had made.

Days turned into nights as Shay followed every lead, hacking into hidden networks, and meeting with informants in dark alleys. His efforts finally paid off when he discovered a connection between Marcus's work and a notorious cybercriminal known only as 'The Ghost.'

'The Ghost' was a shadowy figure in the hacking community, feared for his ruthlessness and skill. Shay's investigation revealed that Marcus had been on the verge of exposing The Ghost's real identity and operations, making him a prime target.

Shay's breakthrough came when he managed to intercept an encrypted message hinting at Marcus's location. The message was traced to an abandoned warehouse on the outskirts of the city. Shay knew it was a trap, but he also knew it was the only chance to save Marcus.

***

Armed and ready, Shay approached the warehouse with caution. The area was eerily quiet, the silence broken only by the distant hum of traffic. Shay's military training kicked in, and he moved silently through the shadows, his senses heightened.

Inside the warehouse, Shay found Marcus bound and gagged, guarded by two heavily armed men. Shay took them out with swift precision, his movements fluid and deadly. He freed Marcus, who was weak but unharmed.

"Thank you," Marcus whispered, his voice hoarse from disuse. "I thought I was done for."

Shay helped Marcus to his feet, scanning the area for any signs of more trouble. "We're not out of this yet. We need to move."

As they made their way out of the warehouse, Shay couldn't shake the feeling that they were being watched. His instincts proved correct when a figure stepped out of the shadows, blocking their path. It was The Ghost.

"You're persistent, Walsh," The Ghost said, his voice cold and mocking. "But you've interfered for the last time."

Shay's eyes narrowed, his grip tightening on his weapon. "Let us pass, or you'll regret it."

The Ghost laughed, a chilling sound. "I don't think so."

A fierce gunfight ensued; the air filled with the deafening sound of bullets. Shay moved with precision, protecting Marcus while taking down The Ghost's henchmen. The fight was brutal and intense, but Shay's determination and skill saw them through.

In the end, The Ghost lay dead, and Marcus was safe. Shay escorted him back to his father, who was overwhelmed with gratitude. The case had been a success, but it left Shay with a new understanding of the dangers and complexities of his chosen path. Shay's reputation as a private detective soared after the Reed case. He took on more high-profile cases, each one cementing his status as one of the best in the field.

Chapter 17
A Dangerous Game

The sterile environment of the hospital was a sharp contrast to the chaos that had engulfed Shay, Emily, and Jamie in their fight against Blackwood Tech. Shay's collapse had shaken them to the core, but as he lay in the hospital bed, his mind was a whirlpool of memories and realisations.

Emily and Jamie sat by his bedside, their concern for Shay palpable. They had managed to secure the evidence from their last mission, but the victory felt hollow with Shay's health in such a precarious state.

***

When Shay finally awoke, it was to the concerned faces of Emily and Jamie. The hospital room was filled with the soft hum of medical equipment, and the scent of antiseptic hung in the air.

"Shay," Emily said softly, relief flooding her voice. "You're awake."

Shay blinked, trying to focus. "Emily…Jamie…what happened?"

Jamie leaned in, her hand gently resting on his arm. "You collapsed, Shay. The doctors said it was a severe episode triggered by stress and exhaustion. You need to rest."

Shay closed his eyes, frustration mingling with his exhaustion. "I can't afford to rest. We're so close…"

Emily shook her head, her eyes filled with determination. "You need to take care of yourself, Shay. We can't do this without you."

Shay sighed, the weight of his condition pressing down on him. "I know. It's just…we've come so far."

Jamie squeezed his hand. "We have, and we'll continue. But we need to be smart about it. We can't lose you."

As they sat in silence, Shay's mind wandered back to Marcus. The realisation that Marcus had once been someone he had saved gnawed at him. There had to be a way to use that connection, to turn the tables.

"Emily, Jamie," Shay began, his voice weak but resolute. "We need to look into Marcus Reed. He's the key to understanding Arabella's plans."

Emily frowned. "Marcus? Why?"

Shay took a deep breath, his mind piecing together the fragments of his past. "Reed, he was an ethical hacker. When I first started as a PI, I he was a victim of a kidnapping. But, know he is working for Blackwood Tech. We need to understand his role in this."

Jamie nodded, her eyes lighting up with realisation. "If Marcus is with Blackwood Tech, we might uncover a weakness in Arabella's operation, if so, why lead us to Edward Mason."

Emily looked confused for a moment, and then it dawned on her. "We were led astray, to kill Mason, but in all the gunfight we couldn't get a clear shot and were more interested in arresting him. It wasn't in line with their motivation. So, the assassin kills him instead."

"That's our next move. Dig into Marcus's past, find his connection to Blackwood Tech, maybe there lies the connection to Robert's murder," Shay stated.

***

The next few days were a blur of activity. Emily and Jamie split their time between the hospital and their investigation, determined to piece together the puzzle that was Marcus Reed. Shay remained in the hospital, his condition closely monitored, but his mind was as sharp as ever, guiding Emily and Jamie through their next steps.

Using their contacts, they began to gather information on Marcus. They discovered that after his rescue by Shay, Marcus had continued his work as an ethical hacker, exposing cybercriminals and working to protect sensitive information. But something had changed along the way that caused him to go off the grid, leading him to align himself with Arabella Blackwood.

Jamie's skills with technology proved invaluable as she hacked into various databases, pulling up records and communications linked to Marcus. She found emails and messages that painted a picture of a man who had grown increasingly disillusioned with his work and the limitations it imposed.

***

"It looks like Marcus felt that the system was broken," Jamie explained one evening, as they pored over the data. "He started to believe that more drastic measures were needed to make real change."

Emily leaned back in her chair, a thoughtful expression on her face. "That could explain why he joined Blackwood Tech. Arabella's promises of revolutionising technology might have appealed to him."

Shay, who had been listening intently, nodded. "But it doesn't explain why he stayed. Arabella's methods are ruthless. Marcus must have seen that."

Jamie typed furiously on her laptop, pulling up more files. "Let's see if we can find any internal communications from Blackwood Tech. Maybe there's something that will give us a clue."

***

The breakthrough came late one night when Jamie managed to decrypt a series of emails between Marcus and Arabella. The emails revealed a complex relationship, filled with manipulation and promises of power.

"Listen to this," Jamie said, reading from one of the emails. Arabella writes, "*Your skills are unparalleled, Marcus. Together, we can reshape the future. Think of the possibilities.*"

Emily's eyes narrowed. "She played on his ambitions, his desire to make a real impact. But there's more to it. We need to find out what pushed him over the edge."

Jamie continued to dig through the emails, her eyes widening as she read one particularly damning message. Here's something. Marcus wrote, "*I can't keep doing this, Arabella. The cost is too high.*" And she responded, 'You've come too far to back out now. Remember what's at stake.'

Shay's brow furrowed. "What did she mean by that? What could be at stake that would keep Marcus in line?"

Emily shook her head. "We need to find out. If we can understand what Arabella is holding over him, we might be able to turn him."

***

Their investigation led them to Marcus's personal life. Jamie managed to hack into his social media accounts and emails, uncovering a side of Marcus that was more vulnerable and human. They discovered that Marcus had a younger sister, Lisa, who had been in and out of rehab for years, struggling with addiction.

"Look at this," Jamie said, showing Emily a series of messages between Marcus and Lisa. "He's been trying to help her for years. He's paid for her treatment, supported her financially."

Emily's eyes softened. "Arabella must have found out about Lisa and used her to control Marcus."

Shay's expression was grim. "If we can find proof of that, we might be able to use it to turn Marcus. He might be willing to help us if it means saving his sister."

They continued to dig, their efforts finally paying off when Jamie uncovered a series of financial transactions linking Arabella to Lisa's rehab payments. It was clear that Arabella had been using Lisa's treatment as leverage to keep Marcus in line.

"We've got her," Jamie said, a triumphant smile spreading across her face. "This is the proof we need."

Emily nodded, her mind already racing with the possibilities. "Now we need to find Marcus and confront him with this. If we can turn him, he could be our inside man."

Shay, despite his weakened state, felt a surge of hope. "It's a long shot, but it's our best chance. We need to act fast."

***

The plan was set in motion. They tracked Marcus's movements, discovering that he frequented a small café near Blackwood Tech's headquarters. Emily and Jamie decided to confront him there, while Shay remained at the hospital, providing support and guidance from afar.

The day of the confrontation dawned with a mix of tension and anticipation. Emily and Jamie arrived at the café early, positioning themselves at a corner table where they could observe Marcus without drawing attention.

Marcus entered the café a few minutes later, looking tired and worn. He ordered a coffee and sat down at a table by the window, staring out at the bustling street with a troubled expression.

Emily and Jamie exchanged a determined look before making their move. They approached Marcus's table, and Emily spoke first, "Marcus Reed?"

Marcus looked up, surprise and wariness in his eyes. "Yes? Who are you?"

Emily took a deep breath. "My name is Emily Harper. This is Jamie Parker. We need to talk to you about Arabella Blackwood and Blackwood Tech."

Marcus's eyes narrowed his posture tense. "I don't know what you're talking about."

Jamie placed a folder on the table, opening it to reveal the documents they had gathered. "We know about Lisa. We know Arabella is using her to control you."

Marcus's face went pale, his eyes darting to the documents. "How did you…?"

Emily leaned in, her voice gentle but firm. "We can help you, Marcus. But we need your help in return. Arabella is dangerous, and we need to stop her. You have the power to make a difference."

Marcus hesitated, his eyes filled with turmoil. "You don't understand. She'll hurt Lisa if I cross her."

Jamie reached out, placing a comforting hand on his arm. "We'll protect Lisa. We have resources and contacts. But we can't do it without you."

Marcus looked down at the documents, the weight of his decision pressing heavily on him. Finally, he looked up, his eyes filled with a mix of fear and determination. "What do you need me to do?"

Emily smiled, relief flooding her. "We need you to be our inside man. Give us information on Arabella's operations, help us gather the evidence we need to bring her down."

Marcus nodded slowly, the resolve building in his eyes. "I'll do it. For Lisa."

Jamie squeezed his hand. "Thank you, Marcus. You're making the right choice."

***

Back at the hospital, Shay listened to the updates from Emily and Jamie, a sense of hope and purpose filling him. They had a chance to turn the tide, to use

Marcus's knowledge and access to dismantle Arabella's operation from the inside.

"Good work, both of you," Shay said, his voice filled with pride. "This could be the break we need."

Emily's voice crackled over the phone, filled with determination. "We're not stopping until we bring Arabella down. For Robert, for Lisa, and for everyone she's hurt."

Jamie added, "We'll get through this, Shay. Together." As Shay lay back in his hospital bed, a sense of peace washed over him. The journey had been long and fraught with challenges, but they were closer than ever to uncovering the truth and bringing justice to those who had been wronged.

Chapter 18
Traps and Deceptions

Arabella's office was an imposing room filled with dark wood furniture and large windows that overlooked the city. The air was thick with the scent of expensive leather and faint hints of Arabella's signature perfume. Marcus took a deep breath, steeling himself for the conversation ahead as he knocked on her door.

"Come in," Arabella's voice called from within, smooth and controlled.

Marcus entered, closing the door behind him. Arabella was seated at her desk, her sharp eyes immediately locking onto his. She gestured for him to sit, her expression unreadable.

"Marcus," she began her voice icy. "I trust you have something important to report. You wouldn't come here unless it was urgent."

Marcus nodded, sitting down across from her. "I just met with Emily Harper and Jamie Parker."

Arabella's eyes narrowed slightly, but she remained composed. "Go on."

"They confronted me at the café," Marcus continued, choosing his words carefully. "They claimed to know about Lisa and how you've been using her to control me. They showed me documents, financial transactions linking you to her rehab payments."

Arabella's expression remained impassive, but Marcus could see the calculation in her eyes. "And what did you tell them?"

"I played along," Marcus said, his voice steady. "I pretended to be swayed by their information. I assured them I'd help in exchange for their protection for Lisa."

Arabella leaned back in her chair, her fingers steepled in front of her. "And do you believe they bought it?"

Marcus nodded. "They seemed convinced. But there's more. They're getting close to uncovering the link between you and Robert Harper's murder. They're determined to bring you down."

A flicker of annoyance crossed Arabella's face, but she quickly masked it. "I see. And what do you propose we do about this?"

Marcus hesitated for a moment, knowing the next words out of his mouth would be crucial. "We can use this to our advantage. Let them think I'm on their side. I can feed them false information and lead them astray. Meanwhile, we tighten our security and prepare for their next move."

Arabella studied him for a long moment, her eyes cold and assessing. "You're suggesting we play a double game, Marcus. That's a dangerous strategy."

Marcus met her gaze, his resolve firm. "It's our best shot at keeping them off balance. If they think they have an inside man, they'll be more likely to make mistakes."

Arabella's lips curved into a small, calculating smile. "Very well, but remember, Marcus, failure is not an option. If you betray me, there will be consequences."

Marcus nodded, the weight of her words settling heavily on him. "I understand. I won't let you down."

Arabella stood, walking around her desk to stand before him. She placed a hand on his shoulder, her grip firm. "Good. Now, tell me everything they said, every detail. We need to be prepared."

Marcus recounted the conversation with Emily and Jamie, sparing no detail. He told Arabella about their questions, their concerns, and their determination to expose the truth. As he spoke, Arabella's expression grew more thoughtful, her mind clearly working through the implications.

"They're getting too close," she said finally, her voice tinged with frustration. "We need to accelerate our plans. The neural chip project must be secured, and any loose ends tied up."

Marcus nodded. "What do you want me to do?"

Arabella's eyes narrowed a steely determination in her gaze. "Continue to play your part with them. Feed them just enough truth to keep them invested, but ensure they never get the full picture. Meanwhile, I'll take care of securing our operations. We can't afford any mistakes."

Marcus felt a knot of tension in his stomach. The double game he was playing was fraught with peril, but he had no choice. As he left Arabella's office, Marcus's mind raced with the implications of their conversation. He was walking a tightrope, with danger on all sides. One misstep and everything could come crashing down.

***

The next day, Marcus met with Emily and Jamie in a secluded park, far from prying eyes. They had chosen the location for its privacy, a place where they could talk openly without fear of being overheard.

Emily's eyes lit up with hope as Marcus approached. "Did you get anything?"

Marcus nodded his expression serious. "I've confirmed that Arabella is tightening security around the neural chip project. She knows you're close, and she's getting nervous."

Jamie frowned. "What about Lisa? Is she safe?"

Marcus hesitated, the weight of his lies pressing down on him. "I haven't been able to confirm her safety yet. Arabella is keeping her movements closely guarded. But I'm doing everything I can to find out."

Emily placed a reassuring hand on his arm. "We appreciate your help, Marcus. We'll do everything we can to protect Lisa. But we need to know more about Arabella's plans. What's her next move?"

Marcus took a deep breath, his mind racing to construct a believable narrative. "Arabella is accelerating the development of the neural chip. She's planning to move the project to a more secure location. If we can intercept it during the transfer, we might have a chance to gather the evidence we need."

Jamie nodded, her eyes filled with determination. "Do you know when and where the transfer will happen?"

Marcus shook his head. "Not yet. But I'm working on it. I'll let you know as soon as I have more information."

Emily smiled, a mix of gratitude and resolve in her eyes. "Thank you, Marcus. We're in this together."

As Marcus left the park, he couldn't shake the feeling of dread that had settled over him. The double game he was playing was becoming increasingly complex, and the stakes were higher than ever. One wrong move, and he could lose everything.

***

Back at his apartment, Marcus sat at his desk, staring at the documents and notes spread out before him. The path he had chosen was fraught with danger, but he couldn't back down now. He had to protect Arabella's plan, and the only way to do that was to stay one step ahead of Emily.

His phone buzzed with a message from Arabella: 'Progress update?'

Marcus typed a quick reply, keeping his tone neutral: "Emily and Jamie are convinced, they do not suspect that Lisa doesn't exist. Continuing to gather information. Will update with details on transfer soon."

Arabella's response was swift: 'Good. Keep them off balance. We can't afford any mistakes.'

Marcus set his phone aside, his mind racing. He had to find a way to turn the tide in their favour. But the line between truth and deception was becoming increasingly blurred, and he knew that one misstep could be fatal.

***

The following day, Marcus met with Emily and Jamie at a safe house they had established. The tension in the air was palpable as they gathered around a small table, the weight of their mission pressing down on them.

Emily looked at Marcus, her eyes filled with a mix of hope and apprehension. "What's the plan?"

Marcus took a deep breath, before laying out his idea. "Arabella is planning to transfer the neural chip project to a new location. If we can intercept it during the transfer, we might be able to gather the evidence we need to bring her down."

Jamie nodded her expression serious. "But how do we do that without tipping her off? She's already on high alert."

Marcus leaned forward, his voice steady. "We use the information we've gathered to create a diversion. We make her believe that we're targeting one location, while we move in on another. It's risky, but it might be our best shot."

Emily's eyes lit up with determination. "Then that's what we'll do. We'll gather our resources, create the diversion, and take her down."

Chapter 19
The Price of Power

Arabella Blackwood paced back and forth in her luxurious office at the top of Blackwood Tech's skyscraper. Her eyes scanned the sprawling cityscape of London below. To anyone looking in, she appeared the epitome of power and success: a formidable tech entrepreneur who had built an empire from nothing. But the journey that had led her here was paved with pain, betrayal, and an unrelenting drive to control her destiny.

***

Arabella's story began in a small village in Mexico, where poverty was a constant companion. She was born as Isabela Gomez, the youngest of five children. Her family struggled to make ends meet, but always managed to put food on the table. Her father was a farmworker, and her mother took on any odd jobs she could find, but it was never enough.

Despite the hardships, Isabela found solace in her family's love. But that fragile comfort was shattered when she was twelve. Her father died in a work-related accident, leaving the family even more vulnerable. Desperate to support her children, her mother made a heart-wrenching decision. She entrusted Isabela to a man who promised to take her to the United States for a better life. Instead, she was trafficked across the border and eventually to England.

The journey was a nightmare. Isabela and other girls like her were crammed into trucks, treated like cargo, and subjected to unimaginable horrors. They were beaten, starved, and abused by the men who controlled them. Isabela's spirit, however, refused to break. She clung to the hope that she could escape this hell and one day reclaim her life.

***

Her salvation came in the form of a young intelligence officer. The officer was part of an anti-trafficking unit that had been investigating the ring for years. When they finally raided the warehouse where Isabela was held, she was one of the few survivors. The officer took Isabela under her wing, promising to help her start a new life.

For the first time in years, Isabela felt a glimmer of hope. Isabela attended school and provided a safe place to live. The transition was difficult; Isabela had to learn a new language, adapt to a different culture, and deal with the trauma of her past. But she was determined to make the most of this chance.

The school became Isabela's refuge. She excelled in her studies, driven by a fierce desire to prove herself. She discovered a passion for science and technology, especially artificial intelligence and neural networks. She was fascinated by the potential of these technologies to change the world, to solve problems that seemed insurmountable.

But at the age of seventeen, Isabela's newfound stability was ripped away. The woman, who had become a surrogate mother to her, was abruptly reassigned. Without warning, Isabela found herself alone once again. The abandonment felt like a betrayal, and it reignited the anger and determination that had kept her alive during her darkest days.

***

Isabela poured herself into her studies, using her anger as fuel. She changed her name to Arabella Blackwood, shedding her past and creating a new identity. She was no longer the helpless girl who had been trafficked and abused; she was a survivor with a vision.

At university, Arabella delved deeper into AI and neural networks, captivated by their potential to not only understand but also influence human behaviour. She saw how these technologies could be used for good—curing diseases, improving lives—but she also recognised their darker applications. The power to control thoughts, emotions, and actions was a power she coveted. She vowed to master it, to never again be at the mercy of others.

After graduating with top honours, Arabella worked for several tech companies, gaining experience and building a network of contacts. Her intelligence and ruthlessness quickly set her apart. She understood that to achieve her goals, she needed to be in a position of absolute authority. So, at the age of thirty, she founded Blackwood Tech, a company dedicated to pushing the boundaries of AI and neural technology.

Blackwood Tech's rise was meteoric. Arabella's innovations attracted attention and investment, and soon the company was at the forefront of technological advancement. But behind the polished façade, Arabella's ambitions were far from benign. She used her technology to gather data, manipulate markets, and influence political outcomes. She was no longer content with merely succeeding; she wanted to reshape the world according to her vision.

***

Arabella's success, however, did not come without challenges. The more power she amassed, the more enemies she made. She dealt with each one ruthlessly, using every tool at her disposal to eliminate threats. It was during this time that she encountered Robert Harper and his ground-breaking work on neural chips. His research had the potential to revoluticnise the treatment of Alzheimer's and dementia, but Arabella saw a different potential: the ability to control minds.

Robert's ethical concerns were an obstacle, but Arabella knew how to manipulate people. She flattered him, funded his research, and gradually pushed him towards her vision. When he resisted, she used subtler forms of coercion, leveraging his desire to help humanity against him.

***

Sitting in her office, Arabella reflected on her journey. From the poverty-stricken village in Mexico to the heights of power in London, she had come a long way. She had endured unspeakable hardships and emerged stronger, more determined. But the scars of her past had shaped her into someone who trusted no one, who valued control above all else.

The recent developments with Emily Harper and Jamie Parker were troubling. They were getting too close, uncovering connections that threatened to unravel everything she had built. Arabella's eyes darkened with resolve. She would not let them succeed. She had faced and overcome greater challenges before, and she would do so again.

Chapter 20
Revelations

The days following Marcus Reed's meeting with Arabella Blackwood were a whirlwind of covert operations and calculated deceptions. Marcus played his role perfectly, feeding Emily and Jamie just enough information to make them believe they were on the verge of a breakthrough. Meanwhile, Arabella moved the neural chip project to a new, secure location, tightening her grip on her empire.

The night of the transfer, Marcus led Emily and Jamie to an abandoned warehouse on the outskirts of London. The air was thick with tension as they approached the building, the darkness swallowing the light from their flashlights.

"Are you sure this is the place?" Emily whispered, her eyes scanning the shadows.

Marcus nodded, his expression serious. "This is it. The transfer is happening inside. We need to move quickly."

Jamie tightened her grip on her gun, her heart pounding. "Let's do this." They entered the warehouse, their footsteps echoing off the concrete walls. The building was eerily silent, the only sound the distant hum of machinery. Marcus led them through a maze of corridors, his demeanour calm but focused.

As they reached a large, dimly lit room, Marcus turned to them, his face grim. "This is where the transfer is supposed to take place. Stay close."

Emily and Jamie exchanged a glance, their instincts on high alert. Something about the situation felt off, but they had come too far to turn back now. They followed Marcus into the room, their eyes scanning for any signs of the neural chip project.

Suddenly, the lights flickered on, blinding them momentarily. As their vision cleared, they realised they were surrounded. Armed guards emerged from the shadows, their guns trained on Emily and Jamie.

"Drop your weapons," a voice commanded, cold and authoritative.

Emily and Jamie reluctantly complied, their hearts sinking. Marcus stepped away, his expression apologetic. "I'm sorry," he murmured, a smirk played on his lips. "I had no choice."

Before they could react, the guards seized them, binding their hands and dragging them deeper into the warehouse. They were thrown into a small, windowless room, the door slamming shut behind them.

Emily struggled against her restraints, her mind racing. "What the hell is going on?"

Jamie shook her head, her face pale. "We've been set up. Marcus was playing us the whole time."

As they tried to free themselves, the door opened, and a figure stepped inside. The person was fully covered, their face hidden behind a mask. The assassin who had killed Edward Mason.

"Who are you?" Emily demanded, her voice steady despite the fear gnawing at her.

The assassin removed their mask, revealing the face of Sarah Bennett, Shay's contact. Emily and Jamie stared in shock, unable to comprehend the betrayal.

'Sarah?' Jamie whispered; her voice filled with disbelief. 'Why?'

Sarah's expression was cold, her eyes devoid of the warmth they had once held. "I'm sorry you had to find out this way," she said quietly. "But I have my reasons."

Emily's mind raced as she tried to piece together the puzzle. "You killed Edward Mason. Why? And why are you working with Arabella?"

Sarah sighed, rolled her eyes, and then started to grin. "It's complicated. Edward Mason was a threat to Arabella's plans. He was an imbecile and irritating. I was tasked with eliminating him."

Jamie shook her head, anger flaring in her eyes. "And what about us? Are you going to kill us too?"

Sarah's gaze softened slightly. "No. Arabella has other plans for you. She wants to use you as leverage against Shay."

Emily's heart pounded. "What do you mean?"

Sarah hesitated and then spoke. "Arabella knows how much you mean to Shay. She believes that by holding you captive, she can manipulate him into doing her bidding."

Jamie scoffed, her voice dripping with sarcasm. "So, we're just pawns in her game?"

Sarah's expression hardened again. "It's not that simple. After my time in British Intelligence, I realised how corrupt the system was. I saved her and she gave me a purpose, a reason to fight. I can't turn my back on her now."

The door opened again, and two guards entered, grabbing Emily and Jamie. "Time to go," one of them said gruffly.

As they were dragged out of the room, Emily glanced back at Sarah, her eyes pleading. "Please, Sarah. Help us."

Sarah's face remained impassive, but Emily saw a flicker of doubt in her eyes. Then the door closed, and they were led away.

They were taken to another part of the warehouse, where they were forced into separate cells. The cold, damp walls pressed in on Emily, and she felt a wave of despair wash over her. But she couldn't give up. She had to find a way to escape and warn Shay.

Time passed slowly in the cell, each minute feeling like an eternity. Emily's mind raced with plans and possibilities, but every idea seemed hopeless. She had no way of knowing what was happening to Jamie or what Arabella's next move would be.

Chapter 21
The Net Tightens

Sarah Bennett stared at her reflection in the bathroom mirror of a dilapidated apartment in East London. The face staring back at her was familiar, yet the eyes had seen more darkness than she ever thought possible. She adjusted the wig, ensuring that every strand was perfectly in place. Her undercover work as a government agent had led her to this moment, a pivotal chapter in her life that had shaped her into the person she was today.

***

Years ago, Sarah had been a bright-eyed graduate, eager to make a difference in the world. Her first assignment with the National Crime Agency had been exhilarating—she had joined a team focused on dismantling major drug trafficking operations in the UK. The mission was dangerous, but it was a challenge she welcomed.

Sarah's assignment was to infiltrate a notorious drug ring that was spreading its influence across London. The ring was ruthless and known for its violent enforcement methods and its ties to international cartels. Her mission was clear: gather intelligence, identify key players, and bring the operation down from the inside.

She assumed the identity of Sarah Williams, a small-time dealer looking to climb the ranks. The transformation was more than just a change of clothes and a new hairstyle; it required her to adopt a new persona entirely. She moved into a rundown apartment, frequented seedy bars, and made contacts within the drug community. The transition was gruelling, but Sarah's determination to succeed fuelled her every step.

***

One of her first major breakthroughs came when she managed to gain the trust of a mid-level dealer named Tony. Tony was a rough, burly man with a scar running down his cheek—a souvenir from a deal gone wrong. He was initially sceptical of Sarah, but her persistence and savvy eventually won him over.

"Sarah, you're not like the other girls," Tony had said one night, after a particularly successful deal. They were sitting in a dimly lit bar, the air thick with the smell of stale beer and cigarette smoke. "You've got guts. I like that."

Sarah smiled, taking a sip of her drink. "Just trying to survive, Tony. Same as everyone else."

Tony grunted in approval. "Stick with me, and you'll do more than just survive. There's a big deal coming up. If you play your cards right, you could be looking at a major promotion."

Sarah's heart raced with excitement. This was the opportunity she had been waiting for. "Count me in," she said, her voice steady.

***

The following weeks were a blur of clandestine meetings and dangerous encounters. Sarah learnt the ins and outs of the operation, memorising names, faces, and locations. She recorded everything in a small, hidden notebook, her lifeline to the outside world.

The more she delved into the organisation, the more she realised the complexity and scale of the operation. It wasn't just about drugs; there were arms deals, human trafficking, and money laundering schemes that extended far beyond the UK's borders. The web of crime was intricate, and Sarah knew that bringing it down would require more than just a few arrests.

Her suspicions about the operation's connections to high-ranking officials were confirmed one night when she overheard a conversation between Tony and his boss, a man known only as The Spider. The Spider was an elusive figure, his real identity a closely guarded secret.

"We need to move the shipment quickly," The Spider had said, his voice low and urgent. "The Senator is getting nervous. If we don't deliver on time, we could be looking at a major fallout."

Sarah's blood ran cold. A government official was involved. This revelation changed everything. She knew she had to tread carefully, but the stakes had never been higher.

***

Sarah's mission took a dangerous turn when she was summoned to a meeting with The Spider. It was an unexpected call and one that filled her with both dread and anticipation. She had been meticulous in covering her tracks, but the thought of coming face-to-face with the man behind the operation was daunting.

The meeting was set in an abandoned warehouse on the outskirts of the city. Sarah arrived early, her senses on high alert. The warehouse was a cavernous space, filled with the echoes of distant machinery and the faint scent of oil and rust. She took a deep breath, steeling herself for what lay ahead.

The Spider arrived with an entourage of heavily armed men. He was a tall, imposing figure, his face obscured by shadows. Sarah could feel his eyes on her, assessing, judging.

"Sarah Williams," The Spider said, his voice smooth but dangerous. "You've been making quite a name for yourself. I've heard good things."

Sarah forced a smile, keeping her voice steady. "Just trying to do my job."

The Spider chuckled, a sound that sent chills down her spine. "Indeed. But I have to wonder, why is someone as smart as you content with small-time deals? Surely, you have bigger ambitions."

Sarah's mind raced, searching for the right words. "I do. But I know I need to prove myself first. Show that I'm loyal, that I can be trusted."

The Spider nodded, seemingly satisfied with her answer. "Loyalty is important. And it's something that is in short supply these days."

He stepped closer, his eyes piercing through the dim light. "I have a task for you, Sarah. Succeed, and you'll be rewarded handsomely. Fail, and…well, let's just say failure is not an option."

Sarah's heart pounded in her chest. "What do you need me to do?"

The Spider handed her a sealed envelope. "Inside, you'll find details of a shipment that needs to be moved discreetly. Ensure it reaches its destination without any interference. Do this, and you'll have a place by my side."

Sarah took the envelope, her mind already planning her next move. "I won't let you down."

The Spider's smile was cold and calculating. "See that you don't."

***

Back at her apartment, Sarah opened the envelope with trembling hands. Inside were detailed instructions for moving a large shipment of drugs and weapons across the city. The shipment was scheduled to take place in three days, giving her little time to plan.

She knew she couldn't handle this alone. Sarah contacted her handler at the National Crime Agency, a seasoned agent named Michael who had been her lifeline throughout the operation.

"Sarah, this is huge," Michael said, his voice filled with urgency. "We need to move quickly. If we can intercept this shipment, we'll have enough evidence to take down The Spider and his entire operation."

Sarah nodded, her resolve hardening. "I'll make sure everything goes according to plan. Just be ready to move in."

The next few days were a blur of preparation and tension. Sarah meticulously followed The Spider's instructions, ensuring that every detail was perfect. She couldn't afford any mistakes.

On the night of the shipment, Sarah arrived at the designated location—a deserted dockyard under the cover of darkness. The air was thick with anticipation as she oversaw the loading of the shipment onto a series of trucks.

Her heart pounded as she gave the signal for the trucks to move out. Everything seemed to be going smoothly, but Sarah knew that danger lurked around every corner.

As the convoy made its way through the city, Sarah's phone buzzed with a message from Michael. "We're in position. Wait for my signal."

Sarah's nerves were on edge as she watched the trucks disappear into the night. She followed them at a distance, her mind racing with thoughts of what was to come.

Finally, Michael's signal came through. 'Move in. Now.'

Sarah's pulse quickened as she sped towards the rendezvous point. She could see the flashing lights of police cars and hear the distant sounds of sirens. The trap had been sprung.

As the police moved in to intercept the shipment, chaos erupted. Shots were fired, and the night was filled with the sounds of shouting and the screech of tyres. Sarah's heart pounded as she fought to maintain her cover while ensuring the operation's success.

In the midst of the chaos, Sarah spotted The Spider's men attempting to flee. She knew she had to act quickly. Drawing her gun, she pursued them through the maze of containers and crates.

Her training kicked in as she confronted the fleeing men, her shots precise and deadly. The confrontation was intense, but Sarah's determination and skill saw her through.

When the dust finally settled, the police had successfully intercepted the shipment, and The Spider's operation lay in ruins. Sarah felt a surge of relief and triumph, but she knew the fight was not over.

***

Back at the police station, Sarah debriefed with Michael and the rest of the team. The evidence they had gathered was overwhelming, and it was clear that The Spider's operation had been dealt a significant blow.

But there was one final piece of the puzzle that needed to be addressed: the involvement of the government official.

Michael's expression was grim as he laid out the evidence. "We've traced the connections back to Senator Thompson. He's been orchestrating the entire operation from behind the scenes."

Sarah's mind raced as she processed the information. Senator Thompson was a powerful and influential figure, someone she had never suspected.

"We need to move carefully," Michael continued. "Thompson has connections and resources. If he gets wind of this, he'll try to cover his tracks."

Sarah nodded, her resolve hardening. "We need to take him down. This is our chance to dismantle the entire operation."

The team worked tirelessly, gathering evidence and building their case against Thompson. It was a race against time, but Sarah's determination never wavered.

***

The day of the arrest came, and Sarah felt a mix of anticipation and dread. They had managed to gather enough evidence to secure a warrant for Thompson's arrest, but she knew that bringing him in would be a dangerous task.

The operation was meticulously planned, with agents positioned at strategic points around Thompson's estate. Sarah was part of the team assigned to enter the house and apprehend him.

As they moved in, the tension was palpable. The front door was kicked open, and agents flooded into the house, their weapons drawn.

Sarah's heart pounded as she made her way through the opulent rooms, her eyes scanning for any signs of Thompson. She found him in his study, a look of shock and anger on his face.

"Senator Thompson, you're under arrest," she said, her voice steady.

Thompson's eyes flashed with rage. "You have no idea what you're doing. This will ruin everything."

Sarah's expression was resolute. "You've already ruined enough lives. It's time for you to face justice."

As Thompson was led away in handcuffs, Sarah felt a surge of triumph. The operation had been a success, and a major blow had been dealt to the drug ring.

***

In the aftermath of the operation, Sarah was hailed as a hero. Her bravery and determination had been instrumental in dismantling one of the most dangerous criminal organisations in the country.

But the victory came at a cost. The mission had taken a toll on her, and the betrayal of Senator Thompson left her with a lingering sense of distrust. She had seen the darkest sides of humanity, and it had changed her.

Sarah continued her work with the National Crime Agency, but her experiences had hardened her. She became more cautious, more guarded, always aware of the shadows that lurked around her.

Chapter 22
The Lion's Den

Arabella Blackwood stood in her private office at Blackwood Tech, her mind racing with the complexities of the tasks ahead. Her gaze drifted across the panoramic view of the city, a sprawling testament to her success and ambition. The room was bathed in the warm hues of the setting sun, casting long shadows that seemed to echo the weight of her thoughts.

A soft knock on the door pulled her from her reverie. She turned to see Sarah Bennett standing in the doorway, a mixture of determination and uncertainty on her face. It had been years since they had seen each other, and the journey that had brought them to this moment was filled with both triumph and betrayal.

"Come in, Sarah," Arabella said, her voice cool and composed.

Sarah stepped inside, closing the door behind her. She walked to the centre of the room, hesitating for a moment before speaking. "Arabella, it's been a long time."

Arabella nodded, her eyes narrowing slightly. "Yes, it has. Fifteen years, to be exact."

Sarah sighed, her expression softening. "I never intended to leave without saying goodbye. I thought it was for the best."

Arabella's gaze hardened, memories flooding back. "You left me when I needed you the most. I had just started to feel safe, to trust someone, and then you disappeared."

Sarah's eyes filled with regret. "I know. And I'm sorry. But there were reasons I couldn't explain back then. The operation to shut down the trafficking ring was more complex than I realised, and my superiors decided it was safer for you if I disappeared."

Arabella leaned back in her chair, studying Sarah. "And now? Why come back now?"

Sarah took a deep breath, her resolve strengthening. "Because we have unfinished business. Because you need me, and I need you. Together, we can achieve something extraordinary."

Arabella raised an eyebrow, intrigued but cautious. 'Go on.'

Sarah approached the desk, her eyes locked on Arabella's. "Your vision for Blackwood Tech, for using AI and neural networks to control emotions and reshape human behaviour—it's ground-breaking. But it's also dangerous. We need to be careful and precise. And for that, we need the best minds in the field."

Arabella's lips curled into a small smile. 'Robert Harper.'

Sarah nodded. "Exactly. His work on neural chips for treating Alzheimer's and dementia is unparalleled. If we can bring him on board, we can leverage his expertise to develop a technology that not only treats brain diseases but also enhances human capabilities."

Arabella's eyes gleamed with ambition. "And how do you propose we get him to join us? Robert is known for his integrity and ethical stance. He won't agree to anything that doesn't align with his moral compass."

Sarah's expression turned serious. "We present him with a version of the truth. We tell him we're developing a neural chip to help people with brain diseases, which is true. We just don't mention the full extent of our plans."

Arabella leaned forward, her mind already calculating the possibilities. "And once he's on board, we can subtly guide his research to align with our goals. He'll be the face of our project, legitimising it in the eyes of the public and the scientific community."

Sarah nodded a determined glint in her eyes. "Exactly, but we need to be careful. Robert is intelligent and perceptive. If he suspects anything, it could jeopardise everything."

Arabella stood, walking around the desk to stand beside Sarah. "Then we need to make sure he doesn't suspect a thing. We'll offer him resources, funding, and the promise of a breakthrough that could change the world. And all the while, we'll keep our true intentions hidden."

Sarah met Arabella's gaze, a silent understanding passing between them. They were in this together, bound by a shared vision and a history that had forged an unbreakable bond.

***

The plan to bring Robert Harper into the fold began to take shape. Arabella and Sarah worked tirelessly, crafting a proposal that would be impossible for him to refuse. They emphasised the potential of his research to revolutionise the treatment of Alzheimer's and dementia, painting a picture of a brighter future where his work could save millions of lives.

Arabella made the initial contact, reaching out to Robert through a mutual acquaintance. She arranged a meeting at Blackwood Tech, ensuring that every detail was meticulously planned to impress and reassure him.

When the day of the meeting arrived, Robert entered Blackwood Tech's headquarters with a mix of curiosity and caution. He had heard of Arabella Blackwood's reputation as a visionary in the tech industry, but he was also aware of the rumours that surrounded her methods.

Arabella greeted him warmly, her demeanour professional yet approachable. "Dr Harper, thank you for coming. It's an honour to meet you."

Robert smiled politely, shaking her hand. "Thank you for inviting me, Ms Blackwood. I'm intrigued by what you have to offer."

Arabella led him to a sleek conference room, where Sarah was already seated. Robert's eyes widened slightly at the sight of her. "Sarah Bennett. I didn't expect to see you here."

Sarah smiled her expression warm but guarded. "It's good to see you, Robert. I've recently joined Blackwood Tech to help with some exciting new projects."

Robert took a seat, his curiosity piqued. "I'm listening."

Arabella launched into the presentation, detailing their vision for a neural chip that could revolutionise the treatment of brain diseases. She spoke passionately about the potential to improve millions of lives, emphasising the ethical and humanitarian aspects of the project.

Robert listened intently, his interest growing with each passing minute. The proposal was impressive, and the resources Blackwood Tech offered were unparalleled. But a part of him remained cautious.

"This is incredible," Robert said, leaning back in his chair. "But I have to ask, what's in it for you? Why is Blackwood Tech interested in this particular project?"

Arabella smiled, her eyes sincere. "Blackwood Tech is committed to pushing the boundaries of technology to create a better world. We believe that your research has the potential to make a profound impact, and we want to support you in achieving that."

Sarah added, "We've seen too many people suffer from diseases like Alzheimer's and dementia. This project is about more than just technology; it's about making a real difference in people's lives."

Robert nodded, feeling reassured. "I appreciate your support and your vision. I'm interested, but I'll need time to review the proposal in detail."

Arabella stood, extending her hand. "Of course, take all the time you need. We're here to answer any questions you may have."

As Robert left the meeting, Arabella and Sarah exchanged a satisfied glance. The first step of their plan was complete. Now, they just had to ensure that Robert remained unaware of the full scope of their ambitions.

***

In the weeks that followed, Robert became increasingly involved with Blackwood Tech's project. He was provided with state-of-the-art facilities and a team of brilliant researchers to assist him. Arabella and Sarah monitored his progress closely, ensuring that he stayed on track while subtly guiding his research towards their ultimate goal.

Arabella's mind often wandered back to the past, to the moment when Sarah had saved her from the trafficking ring. It had been a turning point in her life, the moment when she had realised the power of control and the importance of being the one to wield it.

One evening, Arabella and Sarah sat in Arabella's office, discussing the progress of the project. The room was dimly lit, the soft glow of the city lights casting long shadows.

"Do you ever think about the past?" Arabella asked her voice contemplative.

Sarah looked up, her eyes reflecting a mix of emotions. "All the time. Saving you from that ring was one of the hardest and most rewarding things I've ever done."

Arabella nodded, her gaze distant. "It changed everything for me. It made me realise that I needed to be in control, to never let anyone else dictate my fate."

Sarah reached across the desk, placing a hand on Arabella's. "And look at what you've accomplished. You've built an empire, and now we have the chance to change the world."

Arabella smiled, a rare warmth in her eyes. "We do. But we have to be careful. Robert is smart, and if he discovers our true intentions, everything could fall apart."

Sarah's expression turned serious. "We'll make sure he doesn't. We've come too far to let anything stand in our way."

As they sat in silence, the weight of their shared history and their ambitious plans hung heavily in the air. They were bound together by a vision of a future where they held the reins of power and where they could reshape humanity according to their will.

***

Robert's work on the neural chip progressed rapidly. The initial results were promising, and the potential applications for treating brain diseases were groundbreaking. Arabella and Sarah kept a close eye on his research, ensuring that it aligned with their broader goals.

One afternoon, as Robert was working in the lab, Arabella and Sarah visited him. The lab was filled with the hum of advanced machinery and the soft glow of computer screens.

"Robert, how's the progress?" Arabella asked, her tone genuinely interested.

Robert looked up, a hint of excitement in his eyes. "It's going well. We're seeing significant improvements in memory retention and cognitive function in our test subjects. This could be a real breakthrough."

Arabella smiled, her eyes gleaming. "That's wonderful news. Your work is truly inspiring, Robert."

Sarah added, "We're proud to have you on board. This project has the potential to change so many lives."

Robert nodded, feeling a sense of pride and accomplishment. "Thank you. I couldn't have done it without the support of Blackwood Tech."

As Arabella and Sarah left the lab, they exchanged a knowing look. Robert was fully immersed in the project, unaware of the broader implications of his work. They were one step closer to achieving their vision.

***

That evening, Arabella and Sarah sat in Arabella's office, discussing the next steps. The room was filled with an air of anticipation and determination.

"We need to ensure that Robert remains focused on the therapeutic applications of the neural chip," Arabella said, her voice steady. "He must not suspect that we're also developing it for more...advanced purposes."

Sarah nodded. "Agreed We'll continue to support him and provide the resources he needs. But we'll also need to start working on the next phase of our plan."

Arabella leaned back in her chair, her eyes gleaming with ambition. "The AI integration. Once we have the neural chip perfected, we can begin to incorporate AI to enhance and control human behaviour."

Sarah's expression turned serious. "It's a delicate balance. We need to ensure that the AI is sophisticated enough to achieve our goals but subtle enough to go undetected."

Arabella nodded, her mind already racing with ideas. "We'll start with small-scale trials, refine the technology, and then gradually expand its applications. We must be patient and precise."

Sarah reached across the desk, her eyes filled with determination. "We'll make it happen, Arabella. Together."

Arabella smiled, a rare warmth in her eyes. 'Together.'

***

As the weeks turned into months, Robert's work continued to progress. The neural chip showed incredible promise in treating Alzheimer's and dementia, and the scientific community began to take notice. Articles were published, and accolades poured in, further legitimising Blackwood Tech's project.

Behind the scenes, Arabella and Sarah began to implement the next phase of their plan. They worked with a team of AI specialists, developing algorithms that could subtly influence human emotions and behaviour. The technology was complex and required meticulous testing, but they were driven by their shared vision.

One evening, as Arabella and Sarah reviewed the latest AI developments, Arabella's mind drifted back to the moment when Sarah had saved her. She remembered the fear, the pain, and the overwhelming sense of helplessness. But she also remembered the determination that had driven her to seize control of her destiny.

"Sarah," Arabella said quietly, her voice tinged with emotion. "I never properly thanked you for what you did for me. You gave me a second chance at life."

Sarah looked up, her eyes reflecting a mix of warmth and resolve. "You don't need to thank me, Arabella. You've done more with that second chance than anyone could have imagined. You've built something incredible."

Arabella smiled, a rare vulnerability in her eyes. "And we're just getting started. Together, we'll create a future where we hold the power, where we can shape the world according to our vision." Sarah nodded, her expression determined. "We will. And nothing will stand in our way."

Chapter 23
The Cost of Truth

Arabella was deep in thought, contemplating the progress of the neural chip project and the delicate balance she had to maintain with Robert Harper when there was a soft knock on the door. 'Come in,' she called, her voice steady.

The door opened, and Robert Harper stepped inside. He looked tired but determined, his eyes lighting up as they met Arabella's.

"Good evening, Robert," Arabella said, her tone warm. "How's the project coming along?"

Robert smiled, closing the door behind him. "Evening, Arabella. The project is progressing well. We're seeing some remarkable results with the neural chip."

Arabella gestured for him to sit, her eyes never leaving his. "That's wonderful news. Please, take a seat."

Robert took the chair across from her desk, placing a folder of documents in front of him. "I've brought some reports for you to review. I think you'll be pleased with the advancements we've made."

Arabella leaned forward, her interest piqued. "Show me."

Robert opened the folder, spreading out the reports and data charts. As he explained the latest findings, Arabella listened intently, her mind racing with possibilities.

"These results are extraordinary, Robert," she said, her voice filled with genuine admiration. "Your work is truly ground-breaking."

Robert looked up, a hint of pride in his eyes. "Thank you, Arabella. I couldn't have done it without your support and resources."

Arabella smiled, her gaze softening. "We're a team, Robert. And I believe in your vision."

There was a moment of silence, charged with unspoken emotions. Arabella felt a growing connection with Robert, a bond that went beyond their professional collaboration. She had always admired his intellect and dedication, but there was something more—something that drew her to him on a deeper level.

"Robert," she began, her voice gentle, "I was wondering if you'd like to join me for dinner tonight. We can discuss the project further and get to know each other better."

Robert hesitated for a moment, then nodded. "I'd like that, Arabella."

***

Dinner was held at an exclusive restaurant in the heart of London. The atmosphere was elegant and intimate, with soft lighting and quiet music setting the perfect backdrop for their evening.

As they sat across from each other, Arabella felt a mixture of excitement and nervousness. She had invited Robert with the intention of discussing their work, but she couldn't ignore the growing attraction she felt towards him.

The conversation flowed easily, transitioning from professional topics to more personal ones. They talked about their backgrounds, their passions, and their dreams for the future. Arabella found herself opening up to Robert in a way she hadn't with anyone else.

"Tell me more about your childhood," Robert said, his eyes filled with curiosity. "You've mentioned it briefly, but I'd like to know more."

Arabella took a deep breath, her gaze distant. "I grew up in a small village in Mexico. It was a difficult life, filled with hardship and struggle. My family was poor, and we often went without basic necessities."

Robert listened intently, his expression empathetic. "That must have been incredibly tough."

"It was," Arabella admitted. "But it also made me strong. It taught me to fight for what I wanted and to never give up. When I was trafficked to England, I thought my life was over. But then, someone saved me and gave me a second chance."

Robert's eyes widened in surprise. "You were trafficked?"

Arabella nodded, her voice steady. "Yes. It was a dark time in my life, but it shaped who I am today. The person, who saved me, Sarah Bennett, became a mentor to me. She showed me that I could rise above my circumstances and make a difference."

Robert reached across the table, taking her hand in his. "I'm so sorry you went through that, Arabella. But I'm glad you found your strength and your purpose."

Arabella felt warmth spread through her at his touch. "Thank you, Robert. Your support means a lot to me."

The evening continued with more shared stories and laughter. Arabella felt a growing sense of intimacy with Robert, a connection that went beyond their professional relationship.

As the night drew to a close, Arabella hesitated before speaking. "Robert, would you like to come to my place for a nightcap? I have a beautiful view of the city from my terrace."

Robert smiled, his eyes reflecting the same attraction she felt. "I'd love to."

***

Arabella's house was a modern marvel, perched on a hill with panoramic views of London. The interior was sleek and sophisticated, filled with contemporary art and luxurious furnishings.

As they entered, Arabella led Robert to the terrace, where they were greeted by a breath-taking view of the city lights. She poured them both a glass of wine, handing one to Robert.

"To new beginnings," she said, raising her glass.

Robert clinked his glass against hers. "To new beginnings."

They stood in silence for a moment, taking in the view and the shared sense of possibility. Arabella felt a magnetic pull towards Robert, a desire that she could no longer ignore.

"Robert," she said softly, turning to face him. "There's something I need to tell you."

He looked at her, his eyes filled with curiosity and anticipation. "What is it, Arabella?"

She took a deep breath, gathering her courage. "I've developed feelings for you. This connection we have—it's more than just professional for me. I don't know where it will lead, but I can't deny it any longer."

Robert's eyes softened, a smile playing at the corners of his lips. "I've felt the same way, Arabella. There's something special between us, something that I can't ignore either."

Arabella took a step closer, her heart pounding. "Then let's not ignore it."

Robert reached out, cupping her face in his hands. "I've wanted to do this for a long time."

Their lips met in a gentle kiss, the world around them fading away. The kiss deepened, filled with a longing and passion that had been building for months.

Arabella led Robert inside, their kisses growing more urgent. They moved through the house, shedding their inhibitions along with their clothes. By the time they reached her bedroom, the air was charged with desire.

They fell onto the bed, their bodies entwined. Arabella felt a rush of emotions as Robert's hands roamed over her skin, his touch sending shivers down her spine. She responded with equal fervour, exploring his body with a hunger that matched his own.

The night was a blur of passion and intimacy, each touch and kiss drawing them closer together. Arabella felt a sense of completeness with Robert, a connection that transcended words.

As they lay together in the aftermath, their breaths mingling, Arabella felt a deep sense of contentment. She knew that their relationship would face challenges, but for now, she was grateful for this moment of closeness and understanding.

"Thank you, Robert," she whispered, her voice filled with emotion. "For being here, for being you."

Robert kissed her forehead, his arms tightening around her. "And thank you, Arabella. For letting me in, for trusting me."

As they drifted off to sleep, Arabella felt a sense of peace she hadn't known in years. She had found someone who understood her, who shared her dreams and her passion. Together, they would face whatever the future held, united by their love and their vision.

***

The following days brought a new dynamic to Arabella and Robert's relationship. They continued to work closely on the neural chip project, their professional collaboration now infused with a deeper, more personal connection.

Arabella found herself looking forward to their late-night meetings and shared moments of intimacy. She felt a renewed sense of purpose and excitement, driven by both their shared vision and their growing love for each other.

One evening, as they sat in Arabella's office reviewing the latest data, Robert reached out and took her hand. "I've been thinking about our conversation the other night," he said softly. "About your past and how it's shaped who you are."

Arabella looked at him, her heart swelling with affection. "What about it?"

Robert's eyes were filled with admiration. "You're one of the strongest people I've ever met. Your determination and resilience inspire me. I want to be a part of your journey, to support you in every way I can."

Arabella felt a lump in her throat, touched by his words. "Thank you, Robert. Your support means more to me than you know."

He smiled, leaning in to kiss her gently. "Together, we can achieve anything."

Their relationship continued to deepen, each day bringing new moments of connection and discovery. Arabella found herself opening up to Robert in ways she never thought possible, sharing her fears, her hopes, and her dreams.

Chapter 24
Alliances Tested

Sarah's eyes were fixed on the conference doors. She was waiting for Arabella, and her mind was racing with a mixture of concern and frustration. Beside her, Edward Mason and Marcus Reed shared her unease. The three of them had been Arabella's closest allies, but recent developments had left them feeling side-lined and worried.

Arabella's growing relationship with Robert Harper was diverting her focus from their master plan, and it was time to address it. The stakes were too high to let personal matters interfere with their mission.

The door finally opened, and Arabella walked in, her expression unreadable. She glanced at her three associates, sensing the tension in the room.

'Good evening,' she said, her voice calm. "What's this about?"

Sarah stepped forward, her eyes locking onto Arabella's. "We need to talk, Arabella. It's about Robert."

Arabella raised an eyebrow, her demeanour still composed. "What about him?"

Edward Mason crossed his arms, his face stern. "Your relationship with him. It's becoming a distraction, and it's diverting you from our plan."

Arabella's eyes narrowed slightly, a hint of defiance in her gaze. "My relationship with Robert is personal. It doesn't affect our work."

Marcus Reed shook his head, his voice filled with concern. "But it does, Arabella. You've been spending more time with him, and it's impacting our progress. We need you to stay focused."

Sarah took a deep breath, trying to keep her tone steady. "We're worried, Arabella. The neural chip project is crucial, and we can't afford any distractions. Robert is important to the project, but your relationship with him is complicating things."

Arabella's expression hardened, her eyes flashing with anger. "You're questioning my commitment to this project? After everything we've done together?"

Edward stepped forward, his voice firm. "We're not questioning your commitment. We're concerned about the impact this is having on our progress. We've worked too hard to let anything jeopardise our plan."

Arabella looked at each of them in turn, her anger simmering beneath the surface. She knew they had a point, but the accusation stung. Her relationship with Robert had become important to her, and she resented the implication that it was a weakness.

"Robert's work is integral to our success," she said, her voice cold. "And my relationship with him ensures his loyalty and commitment to the project."

Marcus frowned, his concern evident. "But at what cost, Arabella? We can't lose sight of our goals. The AI integration, the control we've planned—it's all at risk if we let emotions cloud our judgment."

Sarah stepped closer, her tone softening. "Arabella, we're not trying to undermine you. We're trying to protect our vision. Please, consider the bigger picture."

Arabella felt a surge of conflicting emotions. She valued her team's loyalty and their shared ambition, but she also valued the connection she had found with Robert. She took a deep breath, trying to find the balance between her personal desires and their collective goals.

'Fine,' she said finally, her voice steely. "I understand your concerns. I'll ensure that my relationship with Robert doesn't interfere with our work. But make no mistake—Robert is crucial to our success, and I won't jeopardise that."

Edward nodded, his expression softening slightly. "That's all we're asking, Arabella. We need to stay focused and united."

Arabella glanced at Sarah, Marcus, and Edward, seeing the determination in their eyes. She knew they were right, but it didn't make the decision any easier.

"I appreciate your loyalty and your honesty." she said, her tone more measured. "We have a vision to realise, and we can't let anything stand in our way."

Sarah stepped back, a sense of relief washing over her. "Thank you, Arabella. We're with you, every step of the way."

As they left the conference room, Arabella's mind was a whirlwind of thoughts. She knew she needed to keep her personal feelings in check, but the connection she had with Robert was strong. Balancing her professional ambitions and her personal desires would be a challenge, but she was determined to find a way.

***

Later that evening, Arabella was staring at a picture on her desk, the only remaining photograph that she had of her family. It helped calm her nerves, thinking about a time when things were simpler. The confrontation with Sarah, Edward, and Marcus had left her feeling unsettled. She knew she had to refocus, to ensure that her relationship with Robert didn't derail their plans.

A soft knock on the door pulled her from her thoughts. "Come in," she called, her voice steady.

The door opened, and Robert stepped inside, a concerned look on his face. "Arabella, is everything alright? You seemed distant during our last meeting."

Arabella sighed, motioning for him to sit. "There are some concerns among my team about our relationship, Robert. They're worried it's affecting my focus."

Robert frowned; his eyes filled with worry. "I don't want to be a distraction, Arabella. Your work is too important."

She reached out, taking his hand. "You're not a distraction, Robert. You're important to me. But I need to find a balance. Our work on the neural chip is critical, and we can't afford any setbacks."

Robert squeezed her hand, his expression determined. "I understand. We'll find a way to make this work, Arabella. Together."

Arabella felt a surge of affection for him. His support and understanding meant the world to her. She leaned in, kissing him gently. "Thank you, Robert. Your support means everything to me."

***

The following days were a whirlwind of activity. Arabella and her team worked tirelessly to keep the project on track. She made a conscious effort to maintain a professional demeanour around Robert, ensuring that their relationship didn't interfere with their work.

Despite the challenges, their bond continued to grow. Arabella found solace in Robert's presence, his support and understanding providing a refuge from the pressures of her ambition.

One evening, after a particularly gruelling day, Robert suggested they have dinner at her place. Arabella hesitated, aware of the scrutiny from her team, but she agreed. She needed the comfort and connection that only Robert could provide.

As they arrived at her house, the tension of the day began to melt away. The warmth of the setting sun, bathed the terrace in a golden light, creating a serene atmosphere.

Arabella poured them both a glass of wine, handing one to Robert. "To finding balance," she said, raising her glass.

Robert clinked his glass against hers. "To finding balance."

They sat on the terrace, the city lights twinkling below them. The conversation flowed easily, transitioning from work-related topics to more personal ones. Arabella felt a sense of peace, a rare moment of tranquillity amidst the chaos of her life.

As the night grew darker, Robert reached out, taking her hand. "Arabella, I want you to know that I'm here for you, no matter what. We'll face whatever challenges come our way together."

Arabella felt a lump in her throat, touched by his words. "Thank you, Robert. Your support means more to me than you know."

Robert leaned in, his lips meeting hers in a soft, tender kiss. What started as a gentle caress quickly evolved into something deeper, a kiss filled with the pent-up longing and passion that had been building between them the past week. Arabella felt a surge of emotions, a profound desire to be close to him, to share every part of herself with him.

Their kisses became more urgent as they moved inside, shedding the day's stresses along with their inhibitions. Arabella led Robert to her bedroom, and as they entered, the atmosphere shifted, charged with a palpable desire that seemed to electrify the air.

Clothes were discarded with a sense of urgency, each piece falling away to reveal bare skin and unspoken need. They fell onto the bed, and Arabella felt a rush of emotions wash over her. Robert's touch was both gentle and insistent, sending shivers down her spine as his hands roamed her body. His kisses ignited a fire within her, a burning need that she met with equal fervour.

The night unfolded in a blur of passion and intimacy. Every touch, every kiss, every whispered word drew them closer together, forging a connection that transcended the physical. Arabella felt a sense of completeness with Robert, a bond that went beyond mere words. Their bodies moved in harmony, each responding to the other's needs and desires with a natural, instinctive rhythm.

As they lay together in the aftermath, their breaths mingling, Arabella felt a deep sense of contentment. She knew that their relationship would face challenges, but for now, she was grateful for this moment of closeness and understanding.

"Thank you, Robert," she whispered, her voice filled with emotion. "For being here, for being you."

Robert kissed her forehead, his arms tightening around her. "And thank you, Arabella. For letting me in, for trusting me."

***

The following weeks brought intense focus and collaboration among Arabella, Sarah, Marcus, and Edward. They worked tirelessly to advance Project Echelon, a secret side project that used Robert's technology to control people's minds and emotions. The tension between Arabella and her colleagues was palpable, as each had their own vision for the project's future.

One evening, as they were deep in discussion, Sarah raised a critical point. "Arabella, we need to consider the long-term implications of Project Echelon. This technology could be incredibly dangerous if it falls into the wrong hands."

Arabella nodded her expression serious. "You're right, Sarah. We need to establish strict protocols and safeguards to prevent misuse. Our goal is to enhance people's lives, not control them."

Edward added, "We must ensure full cooperation when using the device."

Marcus leaned back in his chair, a thoughtful look on his face. "If Robert finds out about Project Echelon and tells Shay then the fallout will be an impossible mess. Robert has to be kept in the dark, Arabella; if he gets a whiff of your idea, your relationship is over."

The words weighed down on Arabella, her project was so close to becoming a reality, but it was getting so complicated; her feelings had changed. Once she would have manipulated Robert without a second thought, but now she didn't know if she could take lying to him anymore.

***

Throughout the intense development period, Arabella and Robert's relationship remained a source of strength and solace. Despite the ethical complexities and pressures of their work, they found comfort in each other's company, sharing moments of quiet intimacy that balanced the intensity of their professional lives.

One night, as they reviewed the latest data in Arabella's office, Robert looked at her, his eyes filled with determination. "Arabella, we're on the brink of something truly ground-breaking. But we need to ensure that our work is used for the right purposes."

Arabella nodded, her eyes reflecting the same concern. "I know. We need to establish clear guidelines and protocols to ensure that our technology is used ethically and responsibly. We can't afford to let it fall into the wrong hands."

Robert reached out, taking her hand. "I believe in us, Arabella. Together, we can navigate these challenges and create something truly revolutionary."

Arabella felt a swell of pride and affection for Robert. "I believe in us too. We have the opportunity to change the world, and I know that we can do it."

As the project continued to progress, the tension within the team grew. Sarah, Edward, and Marcus had differing opinions on how to proceed, and the ethical dilemmas they faced weighed heavily on them. Arabella found herself at the centre of these conflicts, trying to balance their ambitions with the need for caution and responsibility.

One evening, as Arabella and Robert took a walk to clear their minds, Robert spoke softly, his voice filled with affection. "Arabella, I want you to know how much you mean to me. You've changed my life in so many ways, and I can't imagine doing this without you."

Arabella felt her heart swell with emotion. "You mean the world to me, Robert. I never thought I'd find someone who understands me the way you do. Together, we can achieve anything."

They stopped by a park, sitting on a bench and watching the city lights twinkle in the distance. The world felt vast and full of possibilities, and Arabella felt a deep sense of gratitude for the journey they were on.

Chapter 25
The Final Piece

Shay Walsh lay in his hospital bed, his mind a whirlwind of worry and frustration. He had been recovering slowly, his body healing from the collapse that had taken him out of the fight temporarily. But his spirit remained unbroken, driven by the need to protect Emily and Jamie.

The sterile smell of the hospital room had become all too familiar, and the constant beeping of machines was a reminder of his current limitations. He hated feeling helpless, knowing that Emily and Jamie were out there, potentially in danger, without him to watch their backs.

His thoughts were interrupted by a nurse entering the room, carrying a small, nondescript package. "Mr Walsh, this came for you," she said, placing the package on the table beside his bed.

Shay frowned, confused. "Who sent it?"

The nurse shrugged. "There's no return address. Just your name on it."

As the nurse left, Shay reached for the package, his heart pounding with a sense of foreboding. He tore open the plain brown paper, revealing a stack of photographs inside. His breath caught in his throat as he flipped through the images, each one more horrifying than the last.

Emily was chained up, her face bruised, and her expression filled with pain and defiance. The images were clearly taken in some kind of warehouse, the surroundings dim and industrial. Shay's heart pounded in his chest, his mind racing with a mixture of fear and anger.

He had to rescue them. There was no other option.

***

Shay wasted no time in preparing for the rescue mission. He called in a few favours from old contacts, gathering intel on potential warehouse locations that matched the background in the photographs. His mind was focused, every thought directed towards getting Emily out safely.

Ignoring the doctor's orders, Shay checked himself out of the hospital. His body protested with each movement, but he pushed through the pain, driven by sheer determination. He gathered his gear, including a concealed weapon and lock-picking tools, and headed towards the location his contacts had identified as the most likely hideout.

The warehouse was in a secluded part of the city, surrounded by empty lots and abandoned buildings. Shay approached cautiously, his senses on high alert. He scanned the area for guards or any signs of activity, his military training kicking in as he planned his approach.

***

Inside the warehouse, Emily lay on the cold concrete floor, her wrists chafing against the metal chains. She had been trying to stay strong, but the fear and uncertainty were taking their toll. She didn't know where Jamie was or what had happened to her. The thought of Shay, still recovering in the hospital, was her only comfort.

The sound of the warehouse door creaking open made her heart leap. She strained to see who it was, her pulse quickening with a mixture of hope and dread. Footsteps echoed through the cavernous space, growing closer with each step.

"Emily!" Shay's voice was a whisper, filled with urgency.

"Shay!" Emily's voice broke, relief flooding through her.

Shay hurried to her side, quickly assessing the chains that bound her. "I'm getting you out of here," he said, his voice firm.

He used his lock pick to work on the chains, his hands steady despite the adrenaline coursing through him. The locks clicked open, and Emily collapsed into his arms, tears of relief streaming down her face.

"Thank you, Shay," she whispered, her voice trembling.

"We're not safe yet," Shay replied, helping her to her feet. "We need to get out of here."

As they moved towards the exit, Shay's instincts screamed a warning. He pushed Emily behind him just as Marcus Reed stepped out of the shadows, a cold smile on his face.

"You really think you can just waltz in here and take her?" Marcus sneered, his voice dripping with contempt.

Shay's eyes narrowed, his body tensing for a fight. "I'm not leaving without her."

Marcus lunged at Shay, and the two men clashed in a brutal fistfight. The warehouse echoed with the sounds of punches and grunts of pain as they grappled, each trying to gain the upper hand.

Shay's military training gave him an edge, but Marcus fought with a desperate ferocity. They exchanged blows, their movements quick and ruthless. Shay ducked a swing from Marcus and landed a solid punch to his gut, making Marcus double over in pain.

Marcus recovered quickly, slamming his fist into Shay's jaw. Shay staggered back, but he refused to go down. He focused on Marcus, his mind clear despite the pain.

With a final surge of strength, Shay tackled Marcus to the ground, pinning him with a knee to his chest. He pulled out a pair of handcuffs, securing Marcus's wrists with a swift, practised motion.

"You're under arrest," Shay said, his voice cold and unwavering.

Marcus struggled, but he was no match for Shay's iron grip. "You think this changes anything?" He spat. "Arabella will come for you. She'll come for all of you."

Shay tightened the cuffs, ensuring they were secure. "We'll see about that."

With Marcus subdued, Shay turned his attention back to Emily. "Are you alright?" He asked, his voice softening.

Emily nodded, her eyes filled with gratitude. "I am now, thanks to you."

Shay helped her to her feet, supporting her as they made their way out of the warehouse. The night air was cool and refreshing, a stark contrast to the tension that had filled the warehouse.

"We need to find Jamie," Emily said, her voice filled with determination.

Shay nodded, his mind already working on the next steps. "We will. But first, we need to get you to safety."

Chapter 26
Confronting the Enemy

The sterile corridors of the police station buzzed with activity, the hum of voices and the clatter of footsteps creating a backdrop to the tension Emily Harper felt as she walked towards the internal review room. After the ordeal in the warehouse and her subsequent rescue by Shay, Emily knew she would have to face the consequences of her actions. Her heart pounded with a mix of dread and resolve as she approached the door, her mind racing with thoughts of the impending review.

Inside the room, Chief Inspector Caldwell sat at the head of a long table, flanked by two senior officers and a representative from the department's internal affairs unit. Emily took a deep breath, straightened her posture, and stepped inside, closing the door behind her.

"Detective Inspector Harper, please take a seat," Chief Inspector Caldwell said, his voice calm but authoritative.

Emily nodded and sat down, her hands resting on the table in front of her. She met Caldwell's gaze, her eyes steady and determined.

"Detective Harper," Caldwell began, "we're here to review your recent actions, particularly regarding the unauthorised operation at the warehouse and the events leading up to it. This review is to determine whether your actions were justified and to assess any potential disciplinary measures."

Emily took a deep breath, preparing herself to explain and defend her decisions. She knew the stakes were high, but she also believed in the righteousness of her actions.

"Thank you, sir," she said, her voice steady. "I understand the gravity of the situation, and I'm prepared to provide a full account of my actions."

Caldwell nodded, gesturing for her to begin. "Let's start with the events that led to the warehouse operation. Can you explain why you felt it necessary to act without prior authorisation?"

Emily recounted the sequence of events, starting with the initial investigation into Blackwood Tech and the discovery of Arabella Blackwood's connections to Robert's murder and the broader conspiracy. She explained how the situation escalated, leading to her capture and subsequent rescue by Shay.

"I acted on the information I had at the time, sir," Emily said, her voice unwavering. "My primary concern was the safety of my colleagues and the urgency of stopping Blackwood Tech's illegal activities. I believed that waiting for formal authorisation would have jeopardised the operation and potentially led to more harm."

One of the senior officers, Detective Superintendent Davis, leaned forward, his expression sceptical. "And what about your personal involvement with Shay Walsh? How did that influence your decisions?"

Emily's eyes flickered with determination. "My relationship with Shay did not cloud my judgment. In fact, it strengthened my resolve to act swiftly and decisively. I knew the risks, but I also knew that we had a limited window of opportunity to gather critical evidence and ensure the safety of those involved."

The representative from internal affairs, Inspector Thompson, interjected, his tone measured. "Detective Harper, there are concerns about the lack of communication and coordination with your team. Acting independently can lead to significant risks and unintended consequences."

Emily nodded, acknowledging the validity of the concern. "I understand that, Inspector Thompson. In hindsight, I realise that better communication and coordination would have been beneficial. However, the urgency of the situation left me with little choice. My priority was to act quickly and decisively to prevent further harm."

Caldwell exchanged a glance with the other officers, his expression thoughtful. "Detective Harper, your commitment to the case and your willingness to take risks are commendable. However, we must also consider the potential ramifications of acting outside established protocols."

Emily felt a surge of anxiety, but she remained composed. "I understand, sir. My actions were driven by the need to protect and serve, even if it meant bending the rules. I take full responsibility for my decisions and their outcomes."

The room fell silent for a moment as the officers deliberated. Emily's heart pounded in her chest, each passing second stretching into an eternity. Finally, Chief Inspector Caldwell spoke.

"Detective Harper, your actions have raised serious concerns about procedural adherence and operational safety. However, your dedication to the case and your successful efforts in disrupting Blackwood Tech's operations are also noteworthy. Therefore, we have decided on the following course of action."

Emily held her breath, her eyes fixed on Caldwell.

"You will receive a formal reprimand for acting without authorisation and failing to communicate effectively with your team," Caldwell continued. "Additionally, you will be required to undergo additional training to reinforce the importance of protocol and coordination. However, considering the circumstances and your overall contributions, you will retain your position as a detective inspector."

Relief washed over Emily, her shoulders relaxing slightly. "Thank you, sir. I accept the reprimand and the additional training. I will ensure that future operations are conducted with the utmost regard for protocol and team coordination."

Caldwell nodded, his expression firm but not unkind. "See that you do, Detective Harper. Your skills and dedication are valuable assets to this department. We expect you to continue making meaningful contributions while adhering to the standards and procedures that ensure the safety and effectiveness of our operations."

Emily stood, her resolve renewed. "I will, sir. Thank you for this opportunity."

***

Back at her desk, Emily reflected on the review and the lessons she had learnt. She knew that her passion for justice and her willingness to take risks were strengths, but they needed to be balanced with respect for protocol and teamwork. She resolved to work closely with her colleagues, ensuring that future operations were conducted with the highest standards of professionalism and coordination.

Her thoughts were interrupted by a knock on her office door. She looked up to see Shay standing there, a supportive smile on his face.

"How did it go?" He asked, stepping inside.

Emily sighed, her expression a mix of relief and resolve. "I received a formal reprimand and have to undergo additional training, but I'm keeping my position."

Shay nodded; his eyes filled with admiration. "You did the right thing, Emily. You acted to protect others and stop a dangerous operation. I'm proud of you."

Emily felt a surge of gratitude, her confidence bolstered by Shay's support. "Thank you, Shay." Shay stepped closer, taking her hand, the way her father used too. "We'll face whatever comes next together. We're a team, and we'll make sure we do things the right way."

Emily squeezed his hand, feeling a renewed sense of purpose. 'Together,' she echoed, her voice filled with determination. But she also felt lost, Jamie had been taken and the thoughts of what potentially could be happening to her, haunted Emily's mind.

Chapter 27
A Twist in the Tale

The interrogation room at the police station was cold and sterile, the harsh fluorescent lights casting a stark glow on Marcus Reed's face. He sat at the metal table, his hands cuffed in front of him, a smirk playing at the corners of his lips. Across from him, Shay and Emily stood, their expressions a mix of determination and frustration.

Emily stared at Marcus; her eyes narrowed. "You've got one chance to make this easy on yourself, Marcus. Tell us about Arabella's plans."

Marcus leaned back in his chair, his smirk widening. "Oh, Emily, you think you can scare me into talking? How adorable."

Shay stepped forward; his fists clenched. "This isn't a game, Marcus. People's lives are at stake. Tell us what we need to know."

Marcus shrugged, his demeanour casual. "And why would I do that? You've got nothing on me. Besides, even if I did talk, Arabella would make sure it's the last thing I ever did."

Emily's patience was wearing thin. "You're already in deep trouble, Marcus. Cooperate, and maybe you'll have a chance at a lighter sentence."

Marcus chuckled, shaking his head. *"Nice try, Harper. But I'm not afraid of you or your threats. Arabella is ten steps ahead of you, and there's nothing you can do to stop her."*

Shay slammed his fist on the table, making Marcus flinch slightly. "Stop playing games, Marcus. We know you're involved in something big. Give us the information we need."

Marcus's smirk faded, replaced by a look of cold defiance. "You think you're so righteous, don't you? You're just as ruthless as Arabella, but you hide behind your badge. You're no better than us."

Emily's eyes flashed with anger. "We're trying to stop a dangerous operation that's putting innocent lives at risk. You're just a pawn in Arabella's game."

Marcus leaned forward, his voice low and taunting. "And what about you, Shay? How does it feel to be the hero, knowing that you can't save everyone? Knowing that Arabella is out there, doing whatever she wants while you're stuck here, playing by the rules?"

Shay's jaw tightened, but he refused to rise to the bait. "We'll find a way to stop her. And we'll do it without stooping to your level."

Marcus laughed, the sound hollow and mocking. "Good luck with that. Arabella is untouchable. You're wasting your time."

Emily and Shay exchanged a frustrated glance. It was clear that Marcus wasn't going to give up any useful information willingly. They would have to find another way to uncover Arabella's plans.

Shay gently touched Jamie's face, his eyes filled with anguish. "Hang on, Jamie. We're going to get you help."

As the medical team arrived and began to tend to Jamie, Emily and Shay exchanged a look of grim determination. Arabella had crossed a line, and they knew they had to act fast to save their friend and stop her sinister plans.

Chapter 28
The Betrayal Unmasked

Sarah ran through the Blackwood Techs building, turning heads as she flew past the lobby. Running straight into the elevator, repeatedly pressing the penthouse office button. As the doors slid closed, she started to pace, trying to figure out what was the best course of action with the situation that had arisen.

Sarah flung open the door to Arabella's office and stepped inside, her face a mask of concern. Arabella turned to face her, her eyes narrowing slightly as she took in Sarah's tense demeanour.

"Arabella," Sarah began, her voice filled with underlying tension, "we have a problem. Marcus has been taken into police custody."

Arabella's expression hardened, her eyes flashing with anger. "I expected as much. Marcus was always a weak link. He should have known better than to let himself get caught."

Sarah nodded, her face reflecting the gravity of the situation. "What do we do now? They'll try to extract information from him. He knows too much."

Arabella paced the length of her office, her mind racing with possibilities. "Marcus won't talk. He's a smart kid and hates Shay. But we can't take any chances. We need to ensure that our plans remain secure."

Sarah stepped closer, her voice low and urgent, "What about Jamie? We can initiate Project Echelon. We could use her to destroy any evidence they might have gathered."

A cold smile curved Arabella's lips. "Yes, Jamie. She's the perfect tool for the job. Her connection to Shay and Emily will make it all the more impactful."

Sarah's eyes gleamed with a mix of determination and concern. "But we need to be careful. If they suspect that we're using Jamie, they'll find a way to counter it. We need to ensure that she acts convincingly."

Arabella nodded, her mind already forming a plan. "We'll program Jamie to seek out and destroy any evidence they've collected. She'll appear confused and desperate, which will make her actions seem more believable."

Sarah frowned, her concern evident. "And what if she resists? What if she remembers who she is and tries to warn them?"

Arabella's eyes hardened her voice cold and unyielding. "She won't. The neural chip is too powerful. And if she does try to resist, we'll deal with her accordingly."

Sarah took a deep breath, her resolve strengthening. "Then we need to act quickly. The longer Marcus is in their custody, the greater the risk."

Arabella nodded; her expression determined. "Prepare Jamie for her mission. Ensure that she's programmed to destroy any evidence and leave no trace. We can't afford any mistakes."

Sarah turned to leave; her mind focused on the task at hand. As she reached the door, she paused, looking back at Arabella. "What about Shay and Emily? They won't stop until they've uncovered the truth."

Arabella's smile was cold and calculating. "Let them try. By the time they realise what's happening, it will be too late. We'll have already moved on to the next phase of our plan."

Sarah nodded a sense of unease lingering in her mind. She trusted Arabella's vision, but the stakes were higher than ever. One misstep could unravel everything they had worked for.

As she left the office, Sarah couldn't shake the feeling that they were walking a dangerous tightrope. But she knew that they had come too far to turn back now. They had to see this through to the end, no matter the cost.

***

Arabella watched Sarah leave, her mind a whirlwind of thoughts and calculations. She knew that the next few days would be critical. Marcus's capture was a setback, but it was not insurmountable. They had faced challenges before and emerged stronger. This would be no different.

She turned back to the window, her eyes scanning the city below. The lights of London twinkled like stars, a reminder of the power and influence she wielded. She had built an empire, and she would not let anyone tear it down.

With Jamie under her control and their plans set in motion, Arabella felt a renewed sense of determination. The game was far from over, and she was ready to play her hand to the very end.

As the night settled over the city, Arabella's thoughts turned to the future. She had always known that power came with a price, and she was willing to pay it. The stakes were higher than ever, but so were the rewards. With a final glance at the city below, Arabella turned away from the window, her mind focused on the first time she met Marcus.

***

In a hidden underground facility, Sarah stood over Jamie, her expression cold and calculating. Jamie was strapped to a metal table, her body bruised and battered from the relentless torture she had endured. Sarah's eyes gleamed with cruel satisfaction as she prepared the neural chip for implantation.

"Your friends think they can stop Arabella," Sarah said, her voice dripping with contempt. "But they have no idea what I'm capable of."

Jamie's eyes were filled with pain and defiance. "They'll come for me. They'll stop you all."

Sarah smirked, her fingers deftly working to implant the neural chip into Jamie's head. "Let them try. By the time they find you, you'll be under my control. And you'll lead them right into my trap."

Jamie's body convulsed as the neural chip was activated, her screams echoing through the room. Sarah watched with a twisted sense of satisfaction as the chip took hold, manipulating Jamie's mind and body.

"Welcome to the new world, Jamie," Sarah whispered, her eyes gleaming with malice. "You belong to Blackwood now."

***

Hours later, Jamie stumbled her way into the police station, her body bloody and bruised. Her movements were jerky and uncoordinated, her eyes vacant and filled with pain. The officers at the front desk rushed to her side, their faces filled with shock and concern.

"Jamie! What happened?" One of the officers exclaimed, trying to support her.

Jamie's lips moved, but no sound came out. She collapsed into their arms, her body limp and unresponsive. The officers quickly called for medical assistance; their voices filled with urgency.

Emily and Shay burst into the room, their faces pale with horror as they saw Jamie's condition. They rushed to her side, their hearts pounding with fear and desperation.

"Jamie, can you hear me?" Emily cried, her voice shaking.

Chapter 29
Closing In

Jamie Parker's mind was a foggy mess as she sat in her lab at the police station. The normally bustling environment around her felt distant and surreal, her thoughts clouded by an overwhelming sense of confusion and disorientation. She stared blankly at the computer screen in front of her, the lines of code and files blurring together.

She knew she was supposed to be doing something important, but the specifics eluded her. All she could focus on was the persistent, nagging voice in her head, urging her to delete the files. Her fingers moved mechanically over the keyboard, deleting data with a detached precision.

The door to the lab creaked open, and Chief Inspector Caldwell stepped inside. He observed Jamie for a moment, his brow furrowing in concern. 'Jamie,' he called out gently, "how are you holding up?"

Jamie looked up, her eyes glassy and unfocused. "I'm fine, sir," she replied, her voice distant. "Just trying to catch up on some work."

Caldwell approached her desk, his curiosity piqued. "I was wondering how you managed to escape from Arabella's clutches. Can you tell me what happened?"

Jamie's mind struggled to form a coherent response. She knew she needed to say something, but the details were hazy. "I...don't remember much," she said slowly. "There was a lot of confusion. I managed to get away somehow."

Caldwell's concern deepened as he watched Jamie. Something about her behaviour seemed off, but he couldn't quite put his finger on it. "If you need to talk or take a break, don't hesitate to let us know. You've been through a lot."

Jamie nodded absently, her focus already drifting back to the task at hand. "Thank you, sir. I'll keep that in mind."

Caldwell lingered for a moment longer, his instincts telling him that something wasn't right. But he knew pressing Jamie further wouldn't be productive, so he left the lab, making a mental note to keep an eye on her.

As soon as Caldwell was gone, Jamie's actions became more frantic. She pulled out a stack of physical files from a drawer, the ones they had received from the whistle-blower who had sacrificed himself. The files contained crucial information about Arabella's operations and evidence that could bring her down.

Her movements were jerky and uncoordinated as she gathered the files, her mind screaming at her to destroy them. With a determined effort, she climbed out of the lab's window, clutching the files tightly to her chest. The cold night air hit her face, momentarily clearing some of the fog in her mind, but the voice in her head remained insistent.

***

Caldwell walked down the hallway, his mind occupied with thoughts of Jamie's odd behaviour. He spotted Emily and Shay talking in the break room and decided to join them.

"Emily, Shay," he greeted, his expression serious. "We need to talk about Jamie."

Emily's eyes widened with concern. "What's wrong? Is she okay?"

Caldwell shook his head slightly. "I'm not sure. I just checked on her in the lab, and she seemed…off. Distracted and vague. She couldn't even remember how she escaped from Arabella."

Shay frowned, his protective instincts kicking in. "That doesn't sound like Jamie. She's always sharp and focused."

Caldwell nodded. "Exactly. I think we need to keep a close eye on her. Something's not right, and I don't want to take any chances."

Emily exchanged a worried glance with Shay. "We'll check on her. Make sure she's okay."

Shay's jaw tightened with resolve. "And if something's wrong, we'll find out what it is and help her."

Caldwell placed a hand on Emily's shoulder, his expression earnest. "I trust you both. Jamie's been through a lot, and she needs all the support she can get right now."

***

Jamie moved through the shadows, her mind a battleground of conflicting thoughts. She knew she needed to destroy the files, but a part of her fought against the compulsion. She found a secluded spot behind the station, her hands trembling as she fumbled with the files.

As she prepared to set them on fire, a voice in her head screamed in protest. She hesitated, her mind a swirling storm of confusion and fear. The neural chip's control was strong, but Jamie's willpower fought to break free.

Suddenly, she heard footsteps approaching. Panicked, she stuffed the files back into her bag and tried to climb back through the window. Her movements were clumsy, and she fell to the ground, scraping her hands and knees.

Breathing heavily, Jamie managed to climb back inside just as Emily and Shay entered the lab. They saw her dishevelled state and rushed to her side, their faces filled with concern.

"Jamie, what happened?" Emily asked, helping her to her feet.

Jamie looked at them, her eyes filled with a mix of fear and confusion. "I...I don't know. Everything's so foggy."

Shay gently took her hand, his voice soothing. "It's okay, Jamie. We're here to help you. We'll figure this out together."

As they led Jamie to a chair, Emily noticed the blood on her hands and the scraped knees. Her worry deepened, but she forced herself to stay calm. "Jamie, can you tell us what you were doing outside?" Jamie shook her head, tears welling up in her eyes.

"I don't remember. I just...I felt like I had to do something, but I don't know what." Emily and Shay exchanged a worried glance. It was clear that something was very wrong, and they needed to get to the bottom of it.

Jamie moved through the shadows, her mind a battleground of conflicting thoughts. She knew she needed to destroy the files, but a part of her fought against the compulsion. She found a secluded spot behind the station, her hands trembling as she fumbled with the files.

"We're going to take care of you, Jamie," Emily said gently. "We're going to find out what's going on and make sure you're safe."

Jamie's eyes narrowed suddenly, a flash of anger crossing her face. "No, Emily. You don't get it. You don't get to decide what's best for me. You've always tried to control everything, but you can't control this."

Emily was taken aback, her voice softening with concern. "Jamie, I'm not trying to control you. I just want to help."

Jamie stepped back, her hands clenched into fists. "Help? You think you can help me? You're the reason I'm in this mess! You dragged me into this nightmare with Arabella. I should have never listened to you."

Shay tried to intervene, his voice calm. "Jamie, that's not fair. Emily has always had your best interests at heart."

But Jamie's anger was like a dam that had finally burst. "Fair? You think any of this is fair? I'm done, Emily. I can't be around you anymore. Every time I look at you, I see everything that's gone wrong in my life."

Tears welled up in Emily's eyes. "Jamie, please, don't say that. We need to stick together. We can get through this."

But Jamie was already backing away, her face a mask of pain and anger. "No, Emily. I'm done. I'm done with all of this. Stay away from me."

With that, Jamie turned and bolted out of the lab, leaving Emily and Shay stunned in her wake.

"Jamie, wait!" Emily cried, starting to run after her.

Shay held her back gently. "Let her go, Emily. She needs time. We'll find her when she's ready."

Emily's shoulders slumped, her heart breaking. "I just wanted to help her."

Shay nodded, his expression filled with understanding. "I know. We'll get her back, Emily. We won't give up on her."

As they stood in the empty lab, the weight of Jamie's words hung heavily in the air. The strain on their relationship was palpable, but Emily knew that they couldn't leave her out there.

Chapter 30
The Final Confrontation

Shay Walsh stood in his modest apartment, staring at the papers strewn across his desk. The room was dimly lit by the early-morning light filtering through the blinds, casting long shadows that seemed to mirror the confusion in his mind. He rubbed his temples, trying to will away the fog that had settled over his thoughts.

The past few days had been a whirlwind of activity and emotion. The confrontation with Marcus, Jamie's disappearance, and the looming threat of Arabella had all taken their toll. Shay's determination to find Jamie and stop Arabella remained unwavering, but he couldn't deny the creeping fear that something else was slipping away from him: his own mind.

He picked up a report from the desk, squinting at the words that seemed to swim before his eyes. The letters blurred and shifted, refusing to come into focus. Frustration gnawed at him, and he tossed the paper aside, running a hand through his hair.

"Come on, Shay," he muttered to himself. "Get it together."

But the truth was becoming harder to ignore. The moments of forgetfulness, the lapses in concentration, the names and faces that slipped through the cracks of his memory—they were all signs that his Alzheimer's was advancing.

He needed to focus, to push through the fog. Jamie's life depended on it.

***

Later that morning, Shay met with Emily at the police station. They had planned to go over the latest developments in their search for Jamie and their efforts to dismantle Arabella's operation. Emily greeted him with a concerned smile, her eyes searching his face for signs of how he was holding up.

"Morning, Shay," she said softly. "How are you doing?"

Shay forced a smile, trying to mask the growing anxiety. "I'm fine, Emily. Let's get to work."

As they sat down in the briefing room, Emily began to outline their strategy. Shay listened intently, but he found it increasingly difficult to follow the thread of her words. His mind kept drifting, fragments of past conversations and memories intruding on the present.

"Shay, did you get that?" Emily asked, looking at him expectantly.

Shay blinked, realising he had missed a crucial part of her plan. He nodded, trying to cover his lapse. "Yeah, I got it. We, uh, we need to focus on the—"

Emily's expression softened with concern. "Shay, are you sure you're okay? You seem a bit…distracted."

He clenched his fists under the table, frustration boiling inside him. "I'm fine, Emily. Just tired, that's all. Let's keep going."

Emily hesitated, clearly worried, but she continued with the briefing. Shay made a conscious effort to stay focused, but the fog in his mind persisted. He scribbled notes on his pad, hoping that writing things down would help him remember.

***

As the day wore on, Shay's struggles became more apparent. He found himself losing track of conversations, misplacing important documents, and forgetting details that he had known only moments before. Each lapse was a dagger to his pride and his determination to stay in control.

In the afternoon, Emily and Shay headed out to follow up on a lead about Jamie's whereabouts. They drove through the city in silence, the weight of their unspoken concerns hanging heavily in the air.

At one point, Shay missed a turn, and Emily gently corrected him. "Shay, it's the next right."

He nodded, embarrassment flushing his cheeks. "Sorry, I guess I'm just a bit off today."

Emily didn't press the issue, but her worry was palpable. She knew that Shay was struggling, and it pained her to see him this way. She wanted to help him, but she also knew that he needed to feel capable and strong, especially now.

***

That evening, Shay returned to his apartment, the day's events weighing heavily on him. He sat at his desk, staring at the photos of Jamie and the notes he had taken. His mind felt like a jumbled puzzle, with pieces that no longer fit together.

He reached for a photo of Jamie, her face a reminder of what he was fighting for. "Hang on, Jamie," he whispered. "I'm not giving up on you."

But as he tried to focus on the task at hand, his thoughts drifted again. He found himself staring at the wall, lost in memories that he couldn't quite grasp. The fog was thickening, and he felt a growing fear that he might not be able to keep it at bay much longer.

A knock on the door startled him, and he blinked, trying to shake off the haze. He opened the door to find Emily standing there, her eyes filled with concern.

"Shay, can we talk?" She asked, stepping inside.

He nodded, closing the door behind her. "Sure, what's on your mind?"

Emily took a deep breath, her expression serious. "Shay, I know you're struggling. I can see it. And I want you to know that you're not alone. We're in this together."

Shay looked away, his fists clenching at his sides. "Emily, I can't afford to be weak right now. Jamie needs us. We need to stop Arabella. I can't let this...this disease slow me down."

Emily stepped closer, placing a hand on his arm. "Shay, it's not about being weak. It's about being honest with yourself and letting us help you. We can find a way to manage this, but you have to let us in."

Tears of frustration and fear welled up in Shay's eyes. He had always been the strong one, the protector. Admitting his vulnerability felt like a betrayal of everything he stood for.

"I don't want to be a burden," he whispered, his voice breaking.

Emily's grip on his arm tightened. "You're not a burden, Shay. You're a friend, a partner. And we need you. Jamie needs you. We'll find a way to get through this together."

Shay took a deep breath, trying to steady himself. "I don't know how much longer I can keep it together, Emily. The fog...it's getting worse."

"We'll figure it out," Emily said firmly. "One step at a time. But we can't do it without you."

Chapter 31
A Last Stand

Emily Harper was staring blankly at the screen in front of her. The hum of the police station around her felt distant and surreal, a backdrop to the chaos inside her mind. She had spent countless hours in this room, poring over case files and piecing together evidence, but today, everything felt different. Today, she felt lost.

Jamie was missing. The thought echoed in her mind, a constant reminder of her failure to protect her friend. The guilt weighed heavily on her shoulders, a burden she couldn't shake. Emily had always prided herself on her ability to remain composed under pressure and to find solutions even in the darkest of times. But now, the darkness seemed impenetrable.

She glanced at the clock on the wall. Only an hour had passed since she had last checked, but it felt like an eternity. Time dragged on, each minute a reminder of Jamie's absence.

Emily's thoughts were interrupted by the sound of footsteps approaching her desk. She looked up to see Chief Inspector Caldwell standing there, his expression a mix of concern and determination.

"Emily, any updates on Jamie?" He asked, his voice gentle.

Emily shook her head, her eyes filled with frustration and despair. "No, sir. We've followed every lead, but there's been no sign of her. It's like she vanished into thin air."

Caldwell nodded, his gaze steady. "I know this is hard, Emily. But we can't give up. We'll find her."

Emily forced a smile, but it didn't reach her eyes. "I know, sir. I'm not giving up. I just…I don't know where else to look."

Caldwell placed a reassuring hand on her shoulder. "Take a deep breath, Emily. We'll get through this. Remember, you're not alone."

As Caldwell walked away, Emily tried to focus on the files in front of her, but her mind kept drifting back to Jamie. She replayed their last conversation over and over, analysing every word, every gesture. Jamie had been so angry, so hurt. Emily couldn't shake the feeling that she had let her down.

Her phone buzzed, pulling her out of her thoughts. It was a message from Shay, checking in on her. Emily typed a quick response, assuring him that she was fine, even though she didn't feel fine at all. She appreciated Shay's concern, but she couldn't help but feel a growing sense of isolation. The people around her wanted to help, but they couldn't understand the depth of her guilt and fear.

Emily stood up, needing to escape the confines of her office. She walked through the station, the familiar faces of her colleagues blurring together. She felt like an outsider, disconnected from the world around her. Her trust in the people she worked with was waning, her mind filled with doubts and suspicions.

She found herself in the forensic lab, staring out the window at the bustling city below. The noise of traffic and the distant chatter of people seemed to mock her, a reminder that life went on even as her world crumbled.

Emily's thoughts were a whirlwind of emotions. Anger at Arabella for what she had done. Fear for Jamie's safety. Guilt for not being able to protect her. And an overwhelming sense of helplessness. She had always been the one to find answers, to solve problems. But now, she felt powerless.

She clenched her fists, her nails digging into her palms. "I have to find her," she whispered to herself. "I have to bring her back."

***

As the sun began to set, casting long shadows across her desk, Emily's phone buzzed again. This time, it was a message from Shay, asking if she wanted to meet for dinner. Emily hesitated, her instinct to withdraw and isolate herself warring with her need for support.

She took a deep breath and typed a response, agreeing to meet him. She knew she couldn't do this alone, no matter how much she wanted to retreat into her own world. Shay and her colleagues were her allies, and she needed them now more than ever.

***

Later that evening, Emily sat across from Shay. The familiar surroundings of the cafe and Shay's presence provided a small measure of comfort. They talked about the case, about Jamie, and about their fears and hopes.

Shay reached across the table, taking her hand. "Emily, we'll find her. I know it's hard, but we have to believe that we will."

Emily nodded, tears welling up in her eyes. "I know, Shay. I just feel so…helpless."

Shay's hand trembling squeezed her hand, his gaze steady. "You're not helpless, Emily. You're one of the strongest people I know. And we'll get through this together."

Chapter 32
The Truth Revealed

The morning light filtered through the blinds, casting a soft glow across the police station. Emily Harper sat at her desk, sipping on a lukewarm cup of coffee. She had barely slept, her mind racing with thoughts of Jamie. The weariness clung to her like a heavy fog, but she knew she couldn't afford to slow down. Jamie was still out there, and every moment counted.

Emily's phone buzzed, jolting her from her thoughts. It was a message from Shay.

Shay:

'Any leads on Jamie? Let's meet in my office.'

Emily took a deep breath and replied, then gathered her files and headed towards Shay's office. Her steps were quick and purposeful, a stark contrast to the turmoil within her.

When she reached Shay's office, she found him already deep in thought, a map spread out on his desk with various notes and markers. He looked up as she entered, offering a tired but determined smile.

"Morning, Emily. I was just going over some potential hideouts we might have missed," Shay said, gesturing to the map.

Emily nodded, setting her files on the desk. "Any promising leads?"

Shay ran a hand through his hair, a look of frustration crossing his face. "A few possibilities, but nothing concrete. I thought we could brainstorm together, see if we can come up with something we haven't considered yet."

Emily appreciated Shay's relentless determination. Despite the struggles with his Alzheimer's, he continued to push forward, driven by the same need to find Jamie that she felt. They spent the next few hours poring over the map, cross-referencing with their files, and discussing potential locations where Jamie might be.

As they worked, Emily couldn't shake the nagging feeling of doubt and mistrust that had been plaguing her since Jamie's disappearance. She wanted to believe in the people around her, but Arabella's reach was long, and the fear of betrayal loomed large.

"Shay, have you noticed anything off with the team?" Emily asked suddenly, breaking the silence.

Shay looked up; his expression thoughtful. "What do you mean?"

"I don't know," Emily admitted, struggling to articulate her feelings. "I just…I feel like we can't trust anyone completely. Arabella has already manipulated so much. What if she has people on the inside?"

Shay nodded slowly. "It's possible. We've seen how far she's willing to go. But we can't let that paralyse us, Emily. We have to keep moving forward, one step at a time."

Emily sighed, knowing he was right. "I know. It's just hard to shake the feeling."

"We'll figure it out," Shay said firmly. 'Together.'

***

Later that day, Emily and Shay decided to visit a few of the potential locations they had identified. They moved quickly through the city, their eyes and ears alert for any sign of Jamie. Each empty warehouse and abandoned building they searched brought a mix of hope and disappointment.

As they approached the last location on their list, an old factory on the outskirts of town, Emily felt a strange sense of déjà vu. The building was dilapidated, its windows shattered, and its walls covered in graffiti. It seemed like an unlikely place for Arabella to hide Jamie, but they couldn't afford to leave any stone unturned.

Shay led the way, his hand resting on the grip of his gun. Emily followed closely; her senses heightened. They moved silently through the building, checking each room carefully. The air was thick with dust and the smell of decay, and the only sound was the echo of their footsteps.

"Shay, over here," Emily whispered, motioning towards a door that appeared to lead to the basement.

Shay nodded, and they approached the door cautiously. Emily tried the handle, finding it locked. Shay produced a set of lock-picking tools and began working on the lock. Within moments, the door clicked open, and they descended the stairs into the darkness below.

The basement was a maze of rooms and corridors, each one more foreboding than the last. As they moved deeper into the building, Emily's heart pounded in her chest. She felt a mix of fear and determination, knowing that they were getting closer.

Finally, they reached a large room at the end of the corridor. The door was slightly ajar, and a faint light flickered inside. Emily and Shay exchanged a glance, then pushed the door open and stepped inside.

The room was empty, save for a single chair in the centre and a small table with various tools and equipment. Emily's eyes scanned the room, her heart sinking. There was no sign of Jamie.

"Damn it," Shay muttered under his breath, his frustration palpable.

Emily approached the table, her eyes catching on a piece of paper partially hidden under some tools. She picked it up, her eyes widening as she read the hastily scrawled note.

Emily

If you're reading this, it means I'm not here. I'm sorry for everything.

Arabella's control is stronger than I anticipated.

There's something bigger at play here, something I need to figure out. Please, don't stop looking for me. I need you to believe in me.

Jamie

Emily's hands shook as she read the note, tears welling up in her eyes. "She's alive, Shay. She's trying to fight it."

Shay placed a reassuring hand on her shoulder. "We will find her, Emily. And we'll bring her back."

Chapter 33
The Aftermath

Emily's hands wrapped around a cup of coffee that had long since gone cold. The room was filled with her colleagues, all of whom shared the same tense, determined expressions. Shay was at her side, his gaze fixed on Chief Inspector Caldwell, who stood at the front of the room, addressing the assembled officers.

"Thank you for coming on such short notice," Caldwell began, his voice steady. "I know you're all aware of the urgency and complexity of our situation. Arabella Blackwood remains at large, and while we have gathered significant evidence of her involvement in various illegal activities, there are legal obstacles that prevent us from making an immediate arrest."

Emily leaned forward; her frustration palpable. "Sir, with all due respect, we've seen first-hand what Arabella is capable of. We can't just sit back and do nothing while she continues to manipulate and harm people."

Caldwell nodded, his expression serious. "I understand your frustration, Detective Harper. But the reality is that the evidence we have, while compelling, is not yet sufficient to secure a warrant for Arabella's arrest. We need concrete, irrefutable proof that directly links her to criminal activities. Without it, any arrest would be premature and could jeopardise our entire case."

Shay spoke up, his voice filled with resolve. "What about the neural chip? We know she's been using it to control people, including Jamie. Isn't that enough to bring her in?"

Caldwell sighed, running a hand through his hair. "The problem is proving it beyond a reasonable doubt. The neural chip technology is complex, and while we have testimony and circumstantial evidence, we need hard, scientific proof that Arabella is the one behind its creation and implementation. We need the smoking gun."

Emily felt a surge of frustration. "So, what do we do in the meantime? Just let her continue her operations while we gather more evidence?"

"We continue our investigation," Caldwell said firmly. "We need to be methodical and precise. Any misstep could give Arabella the chance to destroy evidence or manipulate the situation further. We need to ensure that when we move, we have an airtight case that will stand up in court."

Detective Superintendent Davis, who had been quietly observing, added, "We also have to consider the political and social ramifications. Arabella has a lot of influence and powerful allies. Any action we take against her will be heavily scrutinised. We need to be absolutely sure that our case is bulletproof."

Emily nodded reluctantly, understanding the gravity of the situation. "I get it. But it's hard to sit back and watch her get away with this."

"We won't let her get away with it," Caldwell assured her. "But we have to be smart about how we proceed. We need more concrete evidence, and that means continuing to follow leads, gathering data, and staying vigilant."

Shay leaned in closer to Emily, his voice low and reassuring. "We'll get her, Emily. We just need to be patient and keep pushing forward."

Emily took a deep breath, trying to quell the frustration and anxiety that churned within her. She knew Shay was right, but the thought of Jamie still out there, possibly suffering under Arabella's control, was almost unbearable.

Caldwell continued, "In the meantime, we need to ensure that our own operations are secure. Arabella has shown that she's willing to go to great lengths to protect herself and her interests. We need to be on guard for any attempts to undermine our investigation."

Detective Inspector Thompson, the internal affairs representative, spoke up. "We also need to keep a close eye on our own team. Arabella has already demonstrated her ability to manipulate people. We can't rule out the possibility that she has informants or allies within our ranks."

The room fell silent as everyone absorbed the weight of Thompson's words. The sense of mistrust and paranoia that had been simmering beneath the surface now felt more pronounced.

Caldwell nodded. "Agreed. We'll need to conduct internal reviews and ensure that our communication and security protocols are airtight. This is a delicate situation, and we can't afford any leaks or compromised information."

Emily felt a heavy sense of responsibility settle over her. The stakes were higher than ever, and the path forward was fraught with challenges. But she also felt a renewed sense of determination. They couldn't afford to fail.

As the meeting concluded and her colleagues began to disperse, Emily remained seated, deep in thought. Shay placed a comforting hand on her shoulder.

"We'll get through this, Emily," he said quietly. "We'll find Jamie, and we'll bring Arabella to justice. We just need to stay focused and keep pushing forward."

Emily nodded, drawing strength from Shay's words. "I know. And we will. One step at a time."

Chapter 34
A New Beginning

The early-morning light filtered through the high windows of the police station, casting long shadows across the floor. Emily had barely slept, her mind racing with thoughts of Jamie and Arabella's looming threat. She walked through the prison, a fresh cup of coffee in hand, hoping the caffeine would help clear the fog of exhaustion.

As she approached Marcus's cell, she noticed an unusual amount of activity. Officers were clustered around, their expressions a mix of shock and urgency. Emily quickened her pace, her heart pounding with a sense of foreboding.

"What's going on?" She asked, pushing her way through the gathered officers.

Detective Superintendent Davis turned to face her, his face pale and grim. "It's Marcus Reed. He's...he's dead."

Emily's heart sank. "What? How?"

Davis shook his head, his voice low. "We don't know yet. It looks like it could be suicide, but we're not ruling anything out."

Emily pushed past him, her mind racing. She had to see for herself. As she reached Marcus's cell, the sight before her confirmed Davis's words. Marcus lay on the floor, his body lifeless. There was a makeshift noose around his neck, fashioned from the bed sheets.

For a moment, Emily just stood there, staring at Marcus's body. The man who had been a crucial link to Arabella, the man who could have provided the evidence they needed, was now gone. The frustration and despair she had been feeling intensified, mingling with a sense of betrayal and anger.

Shay arrived moments later, his expression mirroring Emily's shock. "Damn it," he muttered, taking in the scene. "This complicates everything."

Emily nodded, her eyes still on Marcus's body. "We need to find out exactly what happened here. This can't be a coincidence."

Davis stepped forward; his tone sombre. "I've already called for the coroner and forensic team. We'll conduct a thorough investigation. But if this was a setup, we need to find out who was behind it and how they managed to get to Marcus."

Emily's mind raced with possibilities. "Arabella," she whispered. "She must have had a hand in this. She knew Marcus could implicate her."

Shay nodded. "It makes sense. We need to check the security footage, talk to the guards and see if anyone noticed anything unusual."

As the forensic team arrived and began their work, Emily and Shay made their way to the security office. The footage from the prison would be crucial in determining what had happened. They sat in the dimly lit room, watching the grainy video feed.

Hours passed as they combed through the footage, their eyes straining from the constant focus. Finally, they saw something. In the early hours of the morning, the lights in Marcus's cell flickered. Moments later, a shadowy figure appeared at the door of the cell, manipulating the lock with practised ease.

Emily's heart raced as she watched the figure enter the cell and approach Marcus. There was a brief struggle, and then the figure left, leaving Marcus to his fate. The entire incident had taken less than five minutes.

"Who the hell is that?" Shay muttered, his eyes narrowing as he tried to discern the figure's identity.

Emily shook her head. "I don't know, but we need to find out. We need to enhance this footage, and see if we can get a clearer image of the intruder."

As they worked on enhancing the video, Emily's mind raced. Arabella's reach was extensive, and she had clearly gone to great lengths to silence Marcus.

The enhanced footage provided a clearer image of the intruder, but the figure was still obscured by shadows. However, they did catch a glimpse of a distinctive tattoo on the intruder's wrist.

Emily leaned closer to the screen, her eyes narrowing. "We need to find out who has that tattoo. Check our records; see if we can match it to anyone with known connections to Arabella."

Shay nodded, already typing commands into the computer. "On it."

As they waited for the results, Emily felt a surge of frustration and anger. Arabella had struck a significant blow, but she had also made a mistake. The tattoo was a lead, and they would follow it relentlessly.

***

Hours later, the computer beeped, signalling a match. Emily and Shay leaned in, reading the report. The tattoo belonged to a known associate of Arabella's; a man named Leo Vargas. He had a criminal record that included burglary, assault, and ties to organised crime.

Emily's eyes blazed with determination. "We need to bring him in. He could be the key to uncovering Arabella's operations."

Shay nodded, already reaching for his phone to coordinate with their team. "Let's move quickly. We can't let him slip through our fingers."

As they prepared to leave, Emily took one last look at the cell where Marcus had died. The fight against Arabella was far from over, but this latest development could be the smoking gun that they needed to bring down Arabella and her empire.

Chapter 35
Hidden Agendas

The early-morning sun was just beginning to rise, casting a soft glow over the city. Emily Harper sat in the passenger seat of Shay Walsh's car, her mind focused on the task ahead. They had been tailing Leo Vargas for several days, and today, they had finally pinpointed his location. Leo was a crucial link in their investigation into Arabella Blackwood's network, and capturing him could provide the breakthrough they desperately needed.

Shay navigated the car through the quiet streets, his expression grim and determined. Despite the toll that his Alzheimer's was taking on him, he remained committed to the mission. Emily could see the strain in his eyes but admired his unwavering resolve.

"He's holed up in an old warehouse on the outskirts of town," Emily said, breaking the silence. "We need to move quickly before he slips away again."

Shay nodded, his grip on the steering wheel tightening. "Let's make sure we get him this time."

They pulled up a few blocks away from the warehouse, parking in a secluded spot to avoid drawing attention. Emily checked her weapon, ensuring it was loaded and ready. Shay did the same, his movements steady despite the tremor in his hands.

"Ready?" Emily asked, looking at Shay.

"Ready," he replied, his voice firm.

They exited the car and moved swiftly through the shadows, approaching the warehouse with caution. The building was old and decrepit, its windows boarded up and the paint peeling from the walls. Emily signalled to Shay, and they positioned themselves near the entrance, listening for any signs of movement inside.

Hearing nothing, Emily gestured for Shay to cover her as she carefully picked the lock on the door. Within moments, the lock clicked open, and they slipped inside, their footsteps silent on the dusty floor.

The warehouse was dimly lit, the only light coming from the cracks in the boarded-up windows. They moved through the building, checking each room methodically. Finally, they reached a large open area where Leo Vargas was sitting at a makeshift table, examining some documents.

"Leo Vargas," Emily called out, her voice echoing through the space. "You're under arrest."

Leo looked up, his eyes widening in surprise. He sprang to his feet, knocking over the table and scattering the documents. "You think you can take me?" He sneered, reaching for a gun tucked into his waistband.

Before he could draw his weapon, Shay fired a warning shot into the air. "Don't even think about it, Leo."

Leo hesitated, glancing between Emily and Shay. Realising he was outnumbered, he slowly raised his hands in surrender. "Alright, alright. No need to shoot."

Emily moved quickly, securing Leo's hands behind his back with handcuffs. "You're coming with us."

Chapter 36
Unfinished Business

Leo Vargas slouched in the cold chair in the interrogation room, his hands stretched out in front cuffed to the metal table. The room was stark and sterile, the harsh fluorescent lights casting a cold glow over everything. Emily stood on one side of the table, Shay on the other, both of them focused intently on Leo.

"You know why you're here," Emily began, her voice steady. "We have questions, and you have answers. The sooner you cooperate, the better it will be for you."

Leo leaned back in his chair, a smirk playing at the corners of his lips. "I don't know what you think you have on me, but you're wasting your time. I don't know anything."

Shay stepped forward, his eyes narrowing. "Don't play games, Leo. We know you're involved with Arabella Blackwood. We know you're part of her network. You can either help us, or you can go down with her."

Leo's smirk faded slightly, but he maintained his defiant posture. "Arabella who? I don't know what you're talking about."

Emily placed a file on the table and opened it, revealing photos and documents linking Leo to Arabella's operations. "These say otherwise. We have evidence connecting you to several of Arabella's illegal activities, smuggling, money laundering and even kidnapping. Do you really want to go down for all of that?"

Leo's eyes flicked over the photos, his confidence wavering for a moment. "You can't prove any of that. It's all circumstantial."

"Maybe," Shay said, leaning in closer. "But we can make your life very difficult while we gather more evidence. Or, you can help us now and maybe cut a deal for yourself."

Leo hesitated, his eyes darting between Emily and Shay. "What's in it for me if I talk?"

Emily crossed her arms, her expression serious. "That depends on what you give us. We need information on Arabella's operations, locations, names and plans. If you help us, we can talk to the DA about a reduced sentence."

Leo seemed to consider this for a moment and then shook his head. "I don't know anything that can help you. I'm not risking my neck for nothing."

Shay sighed, glancing at Emily. They had anticipated resistance, but Leo's defiance was frustrating. Shay took a deep breath, trying to keep his focus despite the cloudiness creeping into his mind.

"Leo," Shay said, his voice calm but firm, "you're already in a lot of trouble. Arabella won't protect you. The sooner you realise that the better off you'll be."

Leo's eyes hardened. "You think I'm afraid of her? I've survived worse than Arabella."

Emily leaned forward, her tone sharp. "And you'll survive a lot worse if you don't start talking. We have ways to make you talk."

For a moment, there was a tense silence in the room. Leo's defiance wavered, and he seemed to weigh his options. Finally, he leaned forward, lowering his voice.

"Alright," he said reluctantly. "I'll tell you what I know. But you have to promise me protection. Arabella's not someone you mess with lightly."

Emily nodded. "You have our word. Start talking."

Leo took a deep breath, glancing around the room as if making sure no one else could hear. "There's a hidden facility outside the city. That's where she conducts her more secretive operations. It's heavily guarded, and not many people know about it."

Shay exchanged a glance with Emily, his mind racing. This was the breakthrough they needed.

"Where is this facility?" Shay asked, his voice urgent.

Leo hesitated, then provided an address. "That's all I know. I swear. Arabella keeps her circle tight. If she finds out I told you this, I'm dead."

Emily jotted down the address, her heart pounding with anticipation. "You did the right thing, Leo. We'll make sure you're protected."

As they left the interrogation room, Emily felt a surge of determination. They had a lead, and now they needed to act on it. The hidden facility could hold the key to bringing down Arabella and rescuing Jamie.

Shay followed her out, his expression resolute despite the weariness in his eyes. "We need to move quickly. Arabella won't hesitate to cover her tracks."

Emily nodded. "Let's gather the team and make a plan. We're one step closer to ending this."

With renewed purpose, they headed to the briefing room, ready to take the next steps in their mission. The road ahead was dangerous and uncertain, but Emily knew they were on the right path. They would find Jamie, stop Arabella, and bring justice to those who had been wronged. The fight was far from over, but they were ready to face whatever came next.

Chapter 37
The Reckoning

Emily stared at the ceiling, the silence of the early morning enveloping the police station. The dim light from her desk lamp cast long shadows on the walls, creating a sombre atmosphere. She rubbed her temples, trying to ease the pounding headache that had been her constant companion since Jamie's disappearance. The note Jamie had left haunted her thoughts, and Emily couldn't shake the feeling that there was something more to it.

With a deep breath, Emily pulled the note out of her drawer. She had read it countless times, hoping to find a clue that might have been overlooked. The words were etched in her memory.

Jamie

Emily studied the note again, her eyes narrowing as she scrutinised every word, every letter. There was a nagging feeling at the back of her mind; a sense that Jamie had left a hidden message, a clue that was just out of reach.

She decided to take a different approach. Grabbing a piece of blank paper, she wrote down the first letter of each sentence in Jamie's note:

E
I
A
T
S
J

Emily frowned, the letters forming a seemingly random sequence. She stared at the paper, willing the letters to reveal their secret. Minutes passed, and frustration began to set in. She leaned back in her chair, closing her eyes and taking a deep breath. There had to be a pattern, a code that she was missing.

Suddenly, an idea struck her. What if the message wasn't in the letters themselves, but in their positions? Emily quickly grabbed a fresh sheet of paper and wrote down the positions of each letter in the alphabet:

E (5)
I (9)
A (1)
T (20)
S (19)
J (10)

She rearranged the numbers, hoping for a breakthrough. As she wrote them down, a realisation hit her. The numbers seemed to form coordinates, but they were too long for standard coordinates. What if they represented something else?

Emily's eyes widened as she connected the dots. The numbers could be referencing pages and lines in Jamie's personal notebook, which she had left behind in the safe house. She grabbed the notebook from her drawer and flipped to the fifth page. Her heart raced as she counted down to the ninth line and began reading.

The line read: *'The key is hidden within.'*

Emily's pulse quickened as she flipped to the next page indicated by the sequence. On the first page, the twentieth line, she found: 'Follow the light.'

Her excitement grew with each page she turned, following the numbers Jamie had cleverly embedded in her note. Nineteenth page, tenth line: 'Safe house—trust no one.'

Emily sat back, piecing together the clues Jamie had left. The message was clear: there was something hidden in the safe house, and she had to find it without drawing attention.

***

Later that day, Emily and Shay drove to the safe house on the outskirts of the city. The small, nondescript building had been their base of operations before everything had gone wrong. It felt eerie returning there, knowing what had transpired.

As they approached the safe house, Shay glanced at Emily, his expression a mix of determination and concern. "Are you sure about this? What if it's a trap?"

Emily shook her head, her resolve unwavering. "Jamie left this message for a reason. She knew we'd come looking for her. We have to trust her."

They entered the safe house cautiously, their senses on high alert. The place was untouched, a time capsule of their previous operations. Emily made her way to Jamie's makeshift workstation, her eyes scanning the room for any signs of a hidden clue.

"The key is hidden within," she murmured, recalling the first part of the message. "Follow the light."

She looked around, her gaze landing on a small desk lamp in the corner. It seemed out of place, its position slightly off from where it had been the last time they were there. Emily approached the lamp and examined it closely. As she twisted the base, it clicked, revealing a hidden compartment underneath.

Inside the compartment was a small flash drive. Emily's heart pounded as she retrieved it, her mind racing with possibilities. This had to be what Jamie had hidden, the key to understanding Arabella's plans.

"Shay, look at this," Emily called, holding up the flash drive.

Shay joined her, his eyes widening. "Jamie was always one step ahead. Let's see what's on it."

They quickly set up Jamie's old laptop and plugged in the flash drive. The screen flickered to life, displaying a series of encrypted files. Emily's fingers flew over the keyboard, using the decryption codes Jamie had taught her. After a tense few moments, the files opened, revealing detailed schematics and documents outlining Arabella's neural chip project.

"These are the plans," Shay said, awe in his voice. "Jamie found everything."

Emily nodded, her eyes scanning the documents. "This is what we needed. Proof of Arabella's plans, the technology she's using, and the people involved. This could be our breakthrough."

As they continued to review the files, they discovered a list of names—individuals who had been implanted with the neural chip. Among the names was someone unexpected: Leo Vargas.

"Leo was part of this all along," Emily muttered. "No wonder he was so scared."

The pieces of the puzzle were starting to come together. With this information, they had the leverage they needed to bring down Arabella and her operation. But they also knew that time was of the essence. Arabella would stop at nothing to protect her plans, and they had to act quickly.

"We need to get this to Caldwell," Shay said, his voice filled with urgency. "And we need to make sure Jamie is safe."

Chapter 38
Secrets Unravelled

The sun dipped below the horizon, casting long shadows over the city. Emily sat in the passenger seat of the unmarked car, her eyes scanning the street through a pair of binoculars. The warehouse where they had last seen Leo Vargas was quiet, the only movement coming from the occasional stray cat or passing car.

Next to her, Shay Walsh sat behind the wheel, his fingers tapping rhythmically on the steering wheel. Despite his Alzheimer's, Shay's instincts were as sharp as ever, his determination unwavering. The information they had uncovered from Jamie's hidden message had led them to this moment—a stakeout that could finally give them the evidence they needed to bring down Arabella Blackwood.

"Anything yet?" Shay asked his voice low and steady.

Emily shook her head, lowering the binoculars. "Nothing so far. But if Leo's involved with Arabella, he's bound to show up sooner or later."

They had been sitting in the car for hours, taking turns watching the warehouse and monitoring the surrounding area. The stakeout required patience and vigilance, both of which were tested by the long, uneventful hours.

Emily glanced at Shay, noticing the lines of fatigue etched on his face. "You okay, Shay? You can take a break if you need to."

Shay shook his head, his gaze fixed on the warehouse. "I'm fine. We can't afford to miss anything."

Emily admired Shay's resolve, even as she worried about his health. She knew how much this mission meant to him, how deeply he cared about finding Jamie and stopping Arabella. But she also knew that the strain was taking its toll on him.

As the night wore on, the streets grew quieter. Emily adjusted the radio to a secure channel, listening for any updates from their team members who were stationed nearby. The minutes ticked by, each one feeling like an eternity.

"Do you ever wonder how we got here?" Emily mused, breaking the silence. "*All the cases, all the risks. Sometimes it feels like we're in a never-ending battle.*"

Shay glanced at her, a small smile tugging at his lips. "It's who we are, Emily. We fight because we have to. Because if we don't, who will?"

Emily nodded, appreciating Shay's perspective. "You're right. We can't back down now."

Just as she finished speaking, movement near the warehouse caught her eye. She raised the binoculars again, focusing on a figure emerging from the shadows. It was Leo Vargas, his posture tense and alert. He looked around, clearly nervous, before heading towards the entrance of the warehouse.

"Shay, it's Leo," Emily whispered, her pulse quickening. "He's going inside."

Shay's expression hardened. "Let's see what he's up to."

They watched as Leo disappeared into the warehouse, the door closing behind him. Emily and Shay exchanged a glance, knowing that this could be their opportunity to gather critical information.

"We need to get closer," Emily said, her voice determined.

Shay nodded, and they exited the car, moving stealthily towards the warehouse. They kept to the shadows, using the cover of darkness to their advantage. As they approached the building, they could hear muffled voices coming from inside.

Emily found a narrow window and carefully peered inside. Leo was talking to another man, someone Emily recognised from the files they had uncovered—one of Arabella's key associates.

"They're discussing something," Emily whispered to Shay. "I can't make out the details, but it sounds important."

Shay motioned for her to continue listening while he scanned the perimeter for any signs of additional guards or surveillance. Emily focused on the conversation, straining to catch every word.

"—shipment is delayed," the associate was saying. "Arabella won't be pleased. We need to expedite the process."

Leo nodded his expression anxious. "I know, but security has been tighter. We can't risk getting caught."

"We don't have a choice," the associate replied. "Arabella's orders are clear. We need to move the equipment to the new facility by the end of the week."

Emily's heart raced. This was exactly the kind of information they needed—confirmation of a new facility and a timeline for their operations. She motioned for Shay to join her, and they both listened intently.

The conversation continued, revealing more details about the facility's location and the logistics of the upcoming shipment. Emily took mental notes, knowing that this information could be crucial in their efforts to dismantle Arabella's network.

As the conversation wrapped up, Leo and the associate began to move towards the exit. Emily and Shay quickly retreated to a safe distance, watching as the two men emerged from the warehouse and parted ways.

"We need to follow Leo," Emily said, her voice urgent. "He might lead us to more information."

Shay nodded, and they resumed their surveillance, tailing Leo as he made his way through the city. They kept a safe distance, ensuring that they wouldn't be detected.

Leo's path took him to a small, nondescript building on the outskirts of town. He entered the building, and Emily and Shay took up positions nearby, ready to observe any further activity.

Hours passed, and the quiet of the night settled in around them. Emily's mind raced with the implications of what they had learnt. The new facility, the shipment, the timeline—these were all pieces of the puzzle that could help them bring down Arabella once and for all.

As dawn began to break, Emily and Shay decided to regroup and plan their next steps. They returned to their car, exhausted but knowing they were on the brink of a breakthrough.

"We got what we needed," Emily said, her voice filled with a mix of relief and anticipation. "Now we need to act on it."

Shay nodded, his eyes reflecting the same determination. "Let's get back to the station and update Caldwell. We have a lot of work to do."

As they drove back to the station, Emily couldn't help but feel the weight of the information they had gathered. They were getting closer to Arabella, but the stakes were higher than ever. As they navigated the early-morning traffic, a sense of unease settled over her. They were running out of time, and one wrong move could cost them everything.

Returning to the station, they were greeted by the early-morning hustle of officers starting their shifts. Emily and Shay made their way to Chief Inspector Caldwell's office, where they found him already at his desk, reviewing reports.

"Caldwell, we have important information," Emily said, stepping inside. "We need to discuss our next steps."

Caldwell looked up, his expression serious. "Come in. Tell me everything."

Emily and Shay detailed their findings from the stakeout, including the location of the new facility and the timeline for the shipment. Caldwell listened intently, his face growing graver with each piece of information.

"This is significant," Caldwell said, leaning back in his chair. "We need to act fast. I'll mobilise a team to start planning a raid on the facility."

Emily nodded. "We need to be thorough. If we miss anything, Arabella will slip through our fingers again."

Caldwell agreed, his eyes meeting theirs with determination. "We'll make sure everything is in place. Good work, both of you. Now let's bring her down."

Chapter 39
The Shadow of Doubt

The room was dimly lit, the heavy drapes drawn to keep the outside world at bay. Arabella Blackwood sat behind her ornate wooden desk, her fingers steepled as she listened to Sarah Bennett. Sarah's voice was calm but insistent, her eyes reflecting a cold determination that matched Arabella's own.

"Robert Harper is a liability," Sarah said, her tone measured. "He's too close to uncovering everything. If we don't eliminate him now, he will bring everything crashing down."

Arabella's mind raced. Robert Harper had been a trusted associate, a brilliant mind whose work on the neural chip had been invaluable. But Sarah was right. Robert had grown increasingly uneasy about the project, his moral qualms threatening to expose their operation. Arabella couldn't afford to let sentimentality cloud her judgment.

"Are you sure there's no other way?" Arabella asked, her voice steady despite the turmoil inside her.

Sarah shook her head, her expression resolute. "No He's too dangerous. He knows too much, and his conscience will lead him straight to the authorities. You can't control him anymore."

Arabella took a deep breath, feeling the weight of the decision pressing down on her. She had always prided herself on being a leader who could make the tough choices, who could do what was necessary for the greater good. But this was different. This was personal.

"Very well," Arabella said finally, her voice firm. "Make the arrangements. Ensure that it's clean and leaves no traces back to us."

Sarah nodded, a hint of satisfaction in her eyes. "I'll take care of it."

As Sarah left the room, Arabella leaned back in her chair, her mind swirling with conflicting emotions. She thought back to the early days when Robert had been brought in for his technology. But, now Project Echelon wasn't her only goal, Robert had become so much more to her. Her emotions had gotten the better of her and distracted her from her goal.

Arabella stood and walked to the window, pulling the drapes aside to gaze out at the city below. The lights of London twinkled in the distance, a reminder of the power and influence she wielded. She had built an empire, and she wasn't about to let anyone tear it down. Sarah, Marcus and Edward had been right; she could not maintain a relationship and achieve her dream…not with Robert anyway.

***

The night of Robert's death, Arabella found herself alone in her Victorian-style house, the grandeur of the surroundings doing little to comfort her. The house was filled with the echoes of the past, memories of a time when things had been simpler; when her ambition hadn't required such sacrifices.

She poured herself a glass of wine, the rich aroma filling the air as she took a sip. The plan for Robert's death had come through earlier, to be delivered with the clinical precision she had come to expect from Sarah. It was done. Robert was gone.

Arabella felt a pang of sorrow, a small part of her mourning the loss of a friend and colleague. But she couldn't afford to dwell on it. There was too much at stake, too many lives depending on the success of their project. She had to stay focused, to keep moving forward.

Her thoughts were interrupted by a soft knock on the door. Arabella turned to see Sarah standing in the doorway, her expression unreadable.

"It's done," Sarah said simply.

Arabella nodded, her face a mask of calm. "I know. Thank you, Sarah."

Sarah stepped inside, closing the door behind her. "This was the right thing, Arabella. Robert would have destroyed everything we've worked for."

"I know," Arabella replied, her voice tinged with sadness. "But it doesn't make it any easier."

Sarah crossed the room and placed a hand on Arabella's shoulder, her touch surprisingly gentle. "You're a strong leader. Sometimes that means making hard choices. But in the end, it's all for the greater good."

Arabella nodded, her resolve hardening. "Yes, it is. We can't let anything or anyone stand in our way."

As Sarah left, Arabella returned to her desk, her mind already turning to the next steps. The neural chip project had to succeed, and she would do whatever it took to ensure that it did. She couldn't afford to let emotions cloud her judgment, not when the stakes were so high.

***

The days that followed were a blur of activity. Arabella threw herself into her work, determined to push the project forward. She oversaw the final stages of development, her mind focused on the potential of the neural chip and the plan for complete control. But beneath her professional façade, a storm of emotions raged.

She thought of Robert often, his memory haunting her in quiet moments. She remembered the way his eyes had sparkled with excitement when they first discussed the project, his unwavering belief in their vision. It had been that passion, that idealism that had drawn her to him in the first place. But it had also been his downfall.

Arabella knew she couldn't dwell on the past. She had to look to the future, to the possibilities that lay ahead. The neural chip was just the beginning. With it, they could unlock the secrets of the human mind and achieve things that had once seemed impossible. And she would be at the forefront, leading the charge.

But there were times, late at night when the world was quiet, that Arabella allowed herself to feel the weight of her choices. She thought of the people she had left behind, the sacrifices she had made in the name of progress. She wondered if, in the end, it would all be worth it.

As she sat in her office, the shadows lengthening around her, Arabella made a silent promise to herself. She would see this project through to the end, no matter what it took. She owed it to Robert, to herself, and to all the people who would benefit from their work.

Chapter 40
In the Crosshairs

The tension in the air was palpable as Emily and Shay drove through the deserted streets towards the safe house. The coded message hidden in Jamie's note had led them here, and both knew the importance of whatever they might find. The safe house was located in a quiet, almost forgotten part of the city, its surroundings a mix of decaying industrial buildings and overgrown lots.

Shay parked the car a few blocks away, and they approached the safe house on foot, sticking to the shadows. The building itself was nondescript, blending seamlessly into its neglected surroundings. Emily scanned the area for any signs of surveillance or activity but found none.

"Ready?" Shay asked, his voice barely above a whisper.

Emily nodded, gripping her flashlight tightly. "Let's do this."

They moved quickly but cautiously, reaching the door and finding it locked. Emily knelt and began to pick the lock, her hands steady despite the rush of adrenaline coursing through her veins. After a few tense moments, the lock clicked open, and they slipped inside.

The interior of the safe house was dimly lit, dust motes floating in the air. It had been some time since anyone had been here. The furniture was sparse and functional, a small table, a couple of chairs, and a desk in the corner. Emily's eyes immediately went to the desk, where several papers and notebooks were scattered.

"This must be Jamie's workstation," she said, moving towards it.

Shay nodded, his eyes scanning the room for any signs of danger. "Let's hope she left us something useful."

Emily began to sift through the papers, her heart racing. The notes were detailed, filled with Jamie's meticulous handwriting. There were schematics, research papers, and lists of names. But what caught Emily's attention was a small, leather-bound journal. She picked it up and flipped it open, her eyes widening as she read the first entry.

"Shay, look at this," she said, handing him the journal.

Shay took the journal and read the entry, his expression growing more serious with each word. "This is it. This is what we needed."

The journal detailed Jamie's findings on Arabella's neural chip project, including its development and potential uses. But more importantly, it contained information about a hidden facility where the most sensitive operations were conducted. Emily scanned the entries, noting the urgency in Jamie's writing.

"We need to find this facility," Emily said, her voice resolute. "It's our best chance to uncover Arabella's entire operation."

Shay nodded, his eyes reflecting the same determination. "Agreed. But we need to be careful. If Arabella realises we're onto her, she'll tighten security and make it even harder to get inside."

Emily continued to read through the journal, her mind racing with possibilities. The facility was located outside the city, in a remote area that would make it difficult to approach undetected. Jamie had included maps and coordinates, as well as detailed notes on the security measures in place.

"Jamie was thorough," Emily said; her admiration for her friend growing. "She knew exactly what we would need."

Shay placed a reassuring hand on Emily's shoulder. "We'll find her, Emily. And we'll stop Arabella."

They spent the next few hours combing through Jamie's notes, piecing together the information they would need to plan their infiltration. As they worked, the gravity of their task became clear. The facility was heavily guarded, with advanced security systems and armed personnel. It would take careful planning and precise execution to get inside and gather the evidence they needed.

As dawn began to break, casting a pale light through the dusty windows, Emily and Shay knew they had to move quickly. They packed up the most critical documents and prepared to leave the safe house.

"We need to get this information to Caldwell," Emily said, her voice firm. "He'll know how to mobilise the team and plan the operation."

Shay nodded his expression serious. "Let's get back to the station. We've got a lot of work to do."

As they exited the safe house and made their way back to the car, Emily couldn't shake the feeling of unease that had settled over her. They were walking into a dangerous situation, and the stakes had never been higher. But with Jamie's notes in hand and Shay by her side, she knew they had a fighting chance.

Returning to the station, they were greeted by the early-morning hustle of officers starting their shifts. Emily and Shay made their way to Chief Inspector Caldwell's office, where they found him already at his desk, reviewing reports.

"Caldwell, we have important information," Emily said, stepping inside. "We need to discuss our next steps."

Caldwell looked up, his expression serious. "Come in. Tell me everything."

Emily and Shay detailed their findings from the safe house, including the location of the hidden facility and the information about the neural chip project. Caldwell listened intently, his face growing more grave with each piece of information.

"This is significant," Caldwell said, leaning back in his chair. "We need to act fast. I'll mobilise a team to start planning a raid on the facility." Emily nodded. "We need to be thorough. If we miss anything, Arabella will slip through our fingers again."

Chapter 41
The Enemy Within

The briefing room at the police station was filled with tense energy. Maps and blueprints were spread across the large table, along with photographs and documents gathered from Jamie's notes. Chief Inspector Caldwell stood at the head of the table, addressing the assembled team. Emily and Shay were among them, their focus unwavering despite the weight of the task ahead.

"Listen up, everyone," Caldwell began, his voice commanding attention. "We have a critical operation ahead of us. Thanks to the information provided by Detectives Harper and Walsh, we have identified two hidden facilities where Arabella Blackwood is conducting her most secretive operations. Our objective is to infiltrate both facilities one after the other, gather evidence, and apprehend key personnel involved in the neural chip project."

He gestured to the maps and blueprints on the table. "The first facility is located outside the city, in a remote area. It's heavily guarded with advanced security systems and armed personnel. This will not be an easy mission, but it's our best chance to bring down Arabella's entire operation."

Emily scanned the faces around the table, a sea of rookies and veterans. Despite the difference in experience, they all had the same look of determination in her colleagues' eyes. They were all aware of the risks, but they were ready to face them head-on, one of their own had been taken.

Caldwell continued, outlining the specifics of the operation. "We will approach the facility under the cover of darkness. A small, specialised team will infiltrate the perimeter and disable the security systems. Once inside, we will secure the evidence and apprehend any personnel we find. Timing and coordination are crucial."

Shay leaned over to Emily, his voice low. "This is going to be tough, but we can do it."

Emily nodded, her resolve firm. "We have to. For Jamie, and Robert."

Caldwell wrapped up the briefing. "Any questions?"

A hand went up. It was Detective Thompson, known for his meticulous attention to detail. "What about backup? In case things go south, we need a contingency plan."

Caldwell nodded. "Good point. We'll have a secondary team on standby, ready to move in if needed. We'll also have aerial support to monitor the situation. We're covering all our bases."

Satisfied with the plan, the team dispersed to prepare for the mission. Emily and Shay stayed behind, reviewing the blueprints one last time.

"This facility is like a fortress," Emily said, tracing a path on the map with her finger. "We need to be precise. One mistake and we could lose everything."

Shay placed a reassuring hand on her shoulder. "We've been through worse. We can handle this."

Emily smiled weakly, appreciating Shay's confidence. But she couldn't ignore the gnawing worry in the pit of her stomach. They were walking into a lion's den, and the stakes had never been higher.

***

As night fell, the team gathered at the designated rendezvous point, a secluded area near the facility. The moon was obscured by clouds, providing the cover of darkness they needed. Emily adjusted her gear, ensuring everything was in place. Shay did the same, his face a mask of concentration.

Caldwell gave a final briefing, his voice steady. "Remember, this is a covert operation. We go in, get the evidence, and get out. Stay focused, stay together, and we'll get through this."

The team moved out, approaching the facility with practised stealth. They reached the perimeter, crouching in the shadows as they assessed the security measures. Emily pointed to a camera mounted on a nearby pole.

"I'll disable the cameras," she whispered. "Shay, you take out the guards."

Shay nodded, slipping silently into the darkness. Emily worked quickly, hacking into the security system and temporarily disabling the cameras. Moments later, she heard the faint sounds of a scuffle as Shay neutralised the guards.

"All clear," Shay whispered, re-joining her.

They moved forward, reaching the entrance to the facility. Emily used the codes Jamie had provided to unlock the door, and they slipped inside, their senses on high alert. The interior was dimly lit, with sterile white walls and high-tech equipment lining the corridors.

"Remember the plan," Emily whispered. "We split up and search for the main control room and any documentation related to the neural chip project. We meet back here in fifteen minutes."

Shay gave a curt nod, and they separated, each taking a different path through the facility. Emily's heart pounded as she moved silently down the hallway, her flashlight cutting through the darkness. She reached a door marked 'Control Room' and carefully opened it, slipping inside.

The room was filled with monitors and servers, the hum of machinery filling the air. Emily approached the main console, her fingers flying over the keyboard as she accessed the system. She downloaded files onto a flash drive, her eyes scanning the information for anything that could be used against Arabella.

As she worked, the sound of footsteps echoed in the corridor outside. Emily's heart raced, and she quickly hid behind a large server rack, holding her breath. The door creaked open, and a guard entered, his flashlight sweeping the room.

Emily waited her muscles tensed, ready to strike if necessary. The guard's light passed over her hiding spot, and he continued his patrol, leaving the room and closing the door behind him. Emily exhaled slowly, her pulse still racing.

She finished downloading the files and slipped out of the control room, making her way back to the rendezvous point. Shay was already there, holding a folder filled with documents.

"Got what we needed?" He asked.

Emily nodded, holding up the flash drive. "This has everything. Let's get out of here."

They moved quickly and quietly through the facility, avoiding guards and security measures. Just as they reached the exit, an alarm blared, the sound piercing the silence. Emily's heart sank.

"We've been made," Shay said, urgency in his voice. "We need to move, now."

They sprinted towards the perimeter, the sounds of guards shouting and footsteps growing closer. Emily's mind raced, calculating their next move. They had to reach the extraction point before they were overwhelmed.

They burst through the door, the cold night air hitting their faces as they ran towards the rendezvous point. The backup team was already in position, and as they reached the extraction point, they were quickly ushered into waiting vehicles.

"Go, go, go!" Caldwell shouted, and the vehicles sped away, leaving the facility behind.

Chapter 42
A Fragile Alliance

The early-morning light was barely creeping over the horizon as Emily and Shay, along with their team, they had new the next facility was on high alert, but the quicker they hit it, the less time the enemy had to prepare. The cold air was heavy with anticipation, each breath visible in the frosty dawn. The team moved with practised precision, their expressions grim and focused.

The facility loomed ahead, a stark contrast to the surrounding wilderness. It was a fortress of modern design, its sleek, metallic exterior betraying nothing of the secrets it held within. The perimeter was surrounded by high fences topped with barbed wire, and surveillance cameras dotted the landscape, their lenses sweeping methodically.

"Remember the plan," Emily whispered her voice barely audible over the hum of the approaching day. "We move in, secure the control room, and gather as much evidence as we can. No unnecessary risks."

Shay nodded, his eyes scanning the area. "Understood. Let's make this quick and clean."

The team split into smaller units, each tasked with disabling a specific aspect of the facility's security. Emily and Shay moved towards the main entrance, their footsteps silent on the dew-covered ground. The tension was palpable, the knowledge of what lay ahead weighing heavily on their minds.

Emily reached the main gate and quickly accessed the control panel, using the codes Jamie had provided. The gate clicked open, and they slipped inside, their movements synchronised and efficient. The interior of the facility was as high-tech as the exterior, with sleek corridors and state-of-the-art equipment lining the walls.

"Control room is this way," Emily whispered, leading Shay through the maze of hallways. The facility was eerily silent; the only sound was the soft hum of machinery and their own measured breathing.

They reached the control room without incident, the door marked with a digital lock. Emily quickly bypassed the security measures and pushed the door open, revealing a room filled with monitors and servers. The walls were covered with schematics and blueprints, evidence of the intricate planning that had gone into Arabella's operation.

"Start downloading everything," Emily instructed, moving to the main console. "We need to get as much information as we can."

Shay nodded, plugging in a flash drive and beginning the data transfer. As the files downloaded, Emily scanned the room, her eyes narrowing at the sheer volume of information. There were documents detailing the neural chip's development, lists of test subjects, and plans for future expansions of the project.

"Look at this," Shay said, holding up a folder filled with handwritten notes. "These are Arabella's personal notes. This could be the smoking gun we need."

Emily's eyes widened as she took the folder, quickly flipping through the pages. The notes were detailed, outlining Arabella's vision for the neural chip and its potential applications. There were mentions of influential figures involved in the project, including names they hadn't encountered before.

"This is it," Emily said, her voice filled with a mix of awe and determination. "This is the evidence we need to take her down."

Suddenly, the room was filled with a loud, piercing alarm. Red lights flashed, and a voice over the intercom announced an intruder alert. Emily's heart sank. They had been discovered.

"Finish the download," Emily ordered her voice urgent. "We need to get out of here, now."

Shay worked quickly, his fingers flying over the keyboard as the data transfer was completed. The door burst open and armed guards flooded into the room, their weapons raised. Emily and Shay dove for cover, returning fire as the room erupted into chaos.

"Go, go, go!" Emily shouted, grabbing the flash drive and the folder. They fought their way through the guards, their movements swift and precise. The corridors were a blur of motion and noise, the alarm blaring incessantly.

They reached the exit, the cold air a stark contrast to the heat of the fire fight. The rest of their team was waiting, covering their retreat as they sprinted towards the extraction point. The sound of gunfire echoed through the early-morning air, a reminder of the danger they were leaving behind.

As they reached the vehicles, Emily glanced back at the facility, the red lights still flashing. They had the evidence, but the cost had been high. The team piled into the vehicles, and they sped away, leaving the facility and its secrets behind.

***

Back at the police station, the atmosphere was tense as Emily and Shay reviewed the evidence they had gathered. The data on the flash drive was extensive, providing a detailed account of Arabella's operation. The notes from the folder added a personal touch, revealing her ambitions and the extent of her influence.

Chief Inspector Caldwell stood behind them, his expression grave. "This is more than we could have hoped for. With this, we can finally take action against Arabella."

Emily nodded, her eyes scanning the files. "We need to move quickly. The longer we wait, the more time she has to cover her tracks."

Caldwell agreed, his voice firm. "I'll start the process for arrest warrants and coordinate with other agencies. This ends now."

As the team worked to compile the evidence and prepare for the next steps, Emily felt exhausted. They had achieved a significant victory, but the fight still felt far from over, they had learnt so much about the circumstances surrounding her father's murder and yet she felt no closer to arresting the killer. Arabella would not go down without a fight, and they needed to be ready for whatever came next.

Shay placed a hand on her shoulder, his eyes felt for her longing. "We did well, Emily. We'll get her."

Emily smiled, appreciating his support. "Yeah, we will. But for now, let's focus on getting this information out there. We need to make sure everyone knows what Arabella has been up to."

As they continued their work, the enormity of their task weighed heavily on them. They had struck a blow against Arabella, but the battle was just beginning. Emily knew that the road ahead would be fraught with challenges, but she was ready to face them head-on. With Shay by her side and the support of their team, they would see this through to the end.

Chapter 43
The Price of Victory

Emily and Shay surrounded the evidence board, plotting out the new information they found. The room smelt stale of coffee, the morning light creeping through the blinds. Neither could sleep, not while they were so close. The double hit on Arabella's operation meant she was weak.

The data they had recovered included the location where Jamie was being held. It was another hidden site, more remote and heavily guarded than the last. Arabella had gone to great lengths to ensure Jamie's containment, Arabella's empire covered London; the tech queen's control was bigger than they could ever have imagined.

"We have to move quickly," Shay said, his tone urgent. "Arabella will be tightening security even further now that she knows we're onto her."

Emily nodded, her eyes scanning the map spread out before them. "The facility is isolated, but that works to our advantage. We can approach from multiple directions and catch them off guard. I will fetch Caldwell."

Shay leaned over the map, his finger tracing a path through the forested area surrounding the facility. "We'll need to disable the perimeter security first. Once we're inside, we split into two teams. One will handle the guards, and the other will get Jamie."

"Emily," called out one of the analysts, drawing her attention. "We've found something. It looks like a list of high-profile targets Arabella planned to use the neural chip on."

Emily moved quickly to the analyst's side, her heart pounding. She scanned the list of names—politicians, corporate executives, military personnel. This was the smoking gun they needed.

"Great work," she said, her voice steady despite the adrenaline coursing through her veins. "This is exactly what we need to prove the scope of her operation."

Shay joined them, his expression grim. "We need to move on this fast. If Arabella realises we have this information, she'll try to destroy the evidence or worse, accelerate her plans."

Emily nodded. "Agreed. We need to secure these individuals and inform them of the threat. We can't afford to let Arabella get to them first."

As they strategised their next moves, Chief Inspector Caldwell entered the room, his presence commanding immediate attention. "I've spoken with the district attorney. With the evidence we've gathered, we have enough to issue arrest warrants for Arabella and her top associates. But we need to act now."

Emily felt a surge of determination. "What's the plan?"

Caldwell laid out a detailed strategy. "We'll execute simultaneous raids on all known locations tied to Arabella. We need to hit them hard and fast, leaving no room for them to escape or destroy evidence. We'll coordinate with federal agencies to ensure we have the manpower and resources necessary."

Shay interjected; his voice filled with urgency. "And we need to make sure the media is ready to broadcast the arrests and the evidence. Arabella has powerful allies, and we need to control the narrative from the start."

Caldwell nodded in agreement. "Already in motion. We have reporters on standby, and we'll hold a press conference as soon as the raids are underway."

The team sprang into action, making final preparations for the coordinated raids. Emily and Shay double-checked the information, ensuring every detail was accounted for. There was no room for error.

***

As night fell, the operation began. Teams of officers, supported by federal agents, moved to Arabella's known locations. The tension was palpable, the silence before the storm. Emily and Shay led one of the main assault teams, their target a luxurious penthouse where Arabella was believed to be hiding.

The team approached the building with practised stealth. Emily's heart pounded in her chest, each step bringing them closer to the confrontation. They reached the entrance, and Emily signalled for the team to breach.

The door burst open, and the team swept inside, weapons drawn. The penthouse was opulently furnished, a stark contrast to the cold precision of Arabella's operations. They moved methodically, clearing each room with precision.

"Clear," called out one of the officers as they reached the final room.

Emily and Shay entered the room, their eyes scanning for any sign of Arabella. The room was empty, but a laptop sat open on a desk, its screen displaying a series of encrypted files.

"She was here," Shay said, frustration evident in his voice. "But she must have slipped out before we arrived."

Emily approached the laptop, her fingers flying over the keyboard as she accessed the files. "We can still use this. There might be something here that can tell us where she's gone."

As she worked, a commotion erupted outside the room. Emily and Shay rushed to the source of the noise, finding officers restraining one of Arabella's top associates, a man named Leo Vargas.

"We found him trying to escape through the service elevator," one of the officers explained.

Emily's eyes narrowed as she approached Leo. "Where's Arabella?"

Leo glared at her, his defiance clear. "You'll never find her. She's always one step ahead."

Shay stepped forward, his voice cold. "We'll see about that. Take him into custody. He might not talk now, but we have ways of making him cooperate."

As Leo was led away, Emily felt a mix of frustration and determination. They had come so close, but Arabella had slipped through their fingers once again. She returned to the laptop, determined to find something, anything, that could give them a lead.

***

Hours later, back at the safe house, the atmosphere was a mix of relief and frustration. They had successfully raided multiple locations, arrested several key figures, and secured a mountain of evidence. But Arabella was still at large.

Emily sat with Shay, reviewing the data from the laptop. They had found encrypted messages, financial transactions, and plans for future operations. It was a goldmine of information, but they needed more.

"We'll crack this," Shay said, his voice filled with quiet determination. "We have to."

Emily nodded, her eyes never leaving the screen. "We will. Arabella can't hide forever."

As the night stretched into dawn, Emily and Shay continued their work, driven by the knowledge that they were closer than ever to bringing Arabella down. The fight was far from over, but they were ready for whatever came next.

Caldwell and Emily walked back into the room, his expression serious. "You'll lead the rescue team Shay, you handle the diversion."

***

As night fell, the team gathered near the forest's edge, their movements synchronised and silent. The facility loomed in the distance, a dark silhouette against the night sky. Emily took a deep breath, steeling herself for what lay ahead.

"Everyone knows their roles," she whispered. "Let's move."

They advanced through the forest, their footsteps muffled by the thick underbrush. Emily's heart pounded in her chest, each step bringing them closer to the facility and Jamie. The tension was almost unbearable, but she forced herself to focus, to push aside the fear and uncertainty.

Shay's team reached the perimeter first, and Emily watched as they expertly disabled the security cameras and motion sensors. With the perimeter compromised, they signalled for the rest of the team to move in.

Emily led her team to the facility's entrance, where they quickly neutralised the guards stationed there. She could feel the adrenaline coursing through her, sharpening her senses and quickening her reflexes. They slipped inside, the interior eerily silent.

"We split up here," Emily whispered to her team. "Two of you come with me. The rest, secure the exits and make sure no one gets in or out."

They moved through the dimly lit corridors, their flashlights casting long shadows on the walls. Emily's mind raced with thoughts of Jamie, of the danger she was in. She knew they had to find her quickly.

They reached a heavily secured door at the end of a long hallway. Emily used the codes from the recovered data to unlock it, and they entered a small, stark room. Jamie was there, restrained and weak, but alive.

"Jamie," Emily whispered, rushing to her side. "We're here to get you out."

Jamie's eyes fluttered open, a mixture of relief and exhaustion on her face. "Emily…you found me."

Emily quickly untied Jamie, supporting her as she stood. "We need to move fast. Can you walk?"

Jamie nodded weakly. "I think so. Let's get out of here."

As they exited the room, the sound of gunfire echoed through the facility. Shay's team had engaged the remaining guards, providing the cover they needed to escape. Emily and her team moved swiftly, navigating the corridors and avoiding the fire fight.

They reached the exit, the cold night air hitting their faces as they emerged into the open. The extraction team was waiting, and they hurried to the vehicles, helping Jamie into one of them.

"Go, now!" Emily shouted, and the vehicles sped away from the facility, leaving the chaos behind.

***

Back at the safe house, the team regrouped. Jamie was immediately taken to a makeshift infirmary where a medic checked her over. Emily and Shay stood nearby, their relief palpable.

"She's safe," Shay said, his voice filled with a mix of exhaustion and satisfaction. "We did it."

Emily nodded, her eyes never leaving Jamie. "Yeah, we did."

As the medic worked, Jamie looked up at Emily, her eyes filled with gratitude. "Thank you, Emily. You saved my life."

Emily knelt beside her, taking her hand. "We couldn't have done it without you. The information you left us was crucial."

Jamie managed a weak smile. "I knew you'd find it. I knew you wouldn't give up on me. They took out my chip, I remember someone talking about weaponising it further, making it wireless."

***

The team were debriefed, sharing the new critical details of the operation and the evidence they had recovered. Jamie provided additional information about her captivity and the experiments Arabella had conducted.

"Arabella's plans are even more dangerous than we thought," Jamie said, her voice weak but determined. "She's not just looking to control high-profile people; she's looking to create an army of mind-controlled soldiers. We have to stop her."

Emily felt a surge of anger and resolve. "We will. With your help, we'll bring her down for good."

As the team continued to piece together the puzzle, the gravity of their mission became even clearer. Arabella's reach was vast; her ambitions terrifying. But with Jamie safe and the evidence they had gathered, they had a fighting chance.

Chapter 44
The Final Countdown

Emily and Shay surrounded the evidence board, plotting out the new information they found. The room smelt stale of coffee, the morning light creeping through the blinds. Neither could sleep, not while they were so close. The double hit on Arabella's operation meant she was weak. They had made significant strides, but the final push to dismantle Arabella's network was upon them.

Caldwell and the rest of the team appeared in the room, they sat murmuring to each other, waiting to be informed of the plan.

"We should strike the heart of Arabella's operation tonight," Emily began, her voice steady. "We have the evidence we need to bring her down, we need to secure her, ensure she can't destroy any more lives. Our target is Blackwood Tech penthouse, where we believe she's holding the neural chip prototypes and her most crucial data."

The room was silent, everyone focused on the gravity of their mission. Shay stood beside Emily, his expression as resolute as ever despite the toll his condition was taking on him.

"We'll split into three teams," Shay continued, taking over from Emily. "Team Alpha will secure the main control room and the servers. Team Bravo will handle the guards and any resistance we encounter. Team Charlie will be the extraction team, ready to get us all out once we have what we need."

Caldwell stepped forward, his presence commanding. "Remember, this is our best shot. Stay focused, watch each other's backs, and follow the plan. Let's bring her down."

With the briefing concluded, the teams moved out, making their way to the facility. The drive was tense, the silence in the vehicles a testament to the seriousness of their mission. As they approached their target, Emily felt a knot of anxiety in her stomach. This was it—the culmination of all their efforts.

Chapter 45
A Dangerous Gambit

The facility loomed in the distance, its stark silhouette a stark reminder of the challenge ahead. The teams disembarked from their vehicles, moving swiftly and silently through the shadows. They reached the perimeter, and Team Alpha began disabling the security systems while Team Bravo took up positions, ready to engage any guards.

Emily led her team towards the main entrance, her senses heightened. Every sound and every movement could mean the difference between success and failure. As they reached the door, she used the codes Jamie had provided to gain entry. The door clicked open, and they slipped inside.

The interior was just as they had expected—sterile, high-tech, and heavily secured. Emily motioned for her team to spread out, securing the area as they moved deeper into the facility. The sound of footsteps echoed through the corridors, growing louder as they approached the main control room.

"Alpha Team, secure the control room and start the data transfer," Emily whispered into her earpiece. "Bravo Team, be ready. We're likely to encounter resistance."

No sooner had she spoken than the facility erupted into chaos. Alarms blared, red lights flashing as guards poured into the corridors. The sound of gunfire filled the air, and Emily ducked behind a console, returning fire as the guards advanced.

"Hold the line!" Shay shouted, his voice steady despite the intensity of the fire fight. "We need to buy Alpha Team time."

Emily's heart pounded as she exchanged fire with the guards, her mind racing. The facility was a maze, and they needed to secure the main control room before they could make their escape. She glanced at Shay, who was focused and composed, directing their team with precision.

"We're almost there," a voice crackled over the earpiece—Alpha Team's leader. "Just need a few more minutes."

Emily gritted her teeth, pushing forward with her team. They moved through the corridors, clearing rooms and securing their path. The fire fight was relentless, but they were gaining ground.

"We have to keep moving," Shay said, reloading his weapon. "We can't let them pin us down."

They reached the main control room, the door fortified and locked. Emily accessed the security panel, using Jamie's codes to unlock it. The door swung open, revealing a room filled with servers, monitors, and control consoles.

"Alpha Team, get to work," Emily ordered, her eyes scanning the room. "Bravo Team, hold the entrance. We need to secure this room."

Alpha Team moved quickly, plugging in devices and initiating data transfers. The sound of typing filled the room, punctuated by the occasional burst of gunfire from the corridor.

Emily took up a position by the door, firing at any guards who approached. The tension was almost unbearable, each second feeling like an eternity. Finally, the leader of the Alpha Team gave the signal.

"Data secured. We're ready for extraction."

Emily nodded, her heart racing. "Bravo Team, fall back. Let's get out of here."

They moved quickly, retreating through the corridors as the fire fight continued. The facility was in chaos, guards scrambling to respond to the intrusion. Emily and her team fought their way to the exit, the sounds of conflict echoing through the halls.

As they burst through the door, the cold night air hit them like a shock. The extraction team was waiting, vehicles ready to whisk them away to safety. Emily helped the last of her team into the vehicles, and then jumped in herself, slamming the door behind her.

"Go, go, go!" she shouted, and the vehicles sped away from the facility.

***

Back at the safe house, the atmosphere was charged with a mix of relief and exhaustion. The data transfer had been successful, and they had managed to escape without any casualties. Emily stood with Shay, watching as the tech team reviewed the data they had recovered.

"This is it," the tech lead said, his eyes wide with excitement. "We have everything we need to take Arabella down."

Emily felt a weight lift off her shoulders, but she knew the battle wasn't over yet. They had struck a significant blow, but Arabella was still out there, and she wouldn't go down without a fight.

"We need to act fast," Caldwell said his tone urgent. "We have the evidence, but we need to make sure Arabella can't retaliate. We need to coordinate with other agencies and secure arrest warrants."

Emily nodded her resolve hardening. "We won't let her escape. We'll bring her to justice."

As the team continued to work, Emily felt a surge of determination. The road ahead was still fraught with danger, but they were closer than ever to bringing down Arabella and her operation. They had the evidence, they had the resolve, and now it was time to see it through to the end.

Shay placed a hand on her shoulder, his expression filled with quiet strength. "We did well, Emily. Now let's finish this."

Emily met his gaze, her eyes reflecting the same determination. "Together."

The night was far from over, but they were ready for whatever came next. The battle against Arabella was nearing its climax, and Emily knew they wouldn't rest until justice was served.

Chapter 46
The Fall

The air in the briefing room was thick with anticipation as the team assembled to finalise the raid on the underground complex. Every piece of evidence; every scrap of information was meticulously reviewed to ensure nothing was overlooked. Emily Harper stood at the head of the table, her eyes scanning the faces of her colleagues. They were all tired, but their determination was unwavering.

Chief Inspector Caldwell began the briefing. "We've confirmed the location of the underground complex near the coast. Our intel suggests it's heavily fortified, and Arabella has a significant number of armed guards protecting the site. This will be a high-risk operation, but it's our best chance to stop her."

Emily nodded, her mind focused on the task ahead. "We'll divide into three teams. Team Alpha will breach the main entrance and secure the control room. Team Bravo will handle the guards and any resistance we encounter. Team Charlie will locate and secure the neural chip prototypes and any additional evidence."

Shay Walsh stood beside her, his presence a reassuring constant. "Timing is critical. We need to move fast and hit them hard. Our objective is to secure the facility and prevent Arabella from launching Project Echelon."

Caldwell added, "We'll have aerial support and backup teams ready to move in if needed. This is a coordinated effort, and everyone needs to be in sync."

The team members nodded, their expressions resolute. They knew the stakes and the dangers, but they were ready. Emily felt a surge of pride in her colleagues. They had come so far, and new they were on the brink of ending Arabella's reign of terror.

***

Night had fallen by the time the teams reached the staging area near the underground complex. The cold, salty air from the ocean mingled with the tension of the impending raid. Emily adjusted her gear, her mind running through the plan one last time.

Shay approached her, his eyes filled with determination. "We've got this, Emily. We're ready."

Emily nodded, taking a deep breath. "Let's do this."

They moved swiftly through the darkness, using the cover of night to approach the facility undetected. The complex was hidden beneath a rocky outcrop, its entrance concealed from view. Team Alpha took the lead, reaching the main gate and disabling the security systems.

"Gate's open," Emily whispered into her comms. "Alpha Team, move in."

They entered the facility, their movements silent and precise. The corridors were dimly lit, casting eerie shadows on the walls. Emily led her team through the maze-like structure, following the intel they had gathered.

"Bravo Team, secure the perimeter," Shay ordered. "Keep the guards busy."

The sound of gunfire echoed through the facility as the Bravo Team engaged the guards. Emily's heart pounded in her chest, but she forced herself to stay focused. They had a job to do.

"Control room is just ahead," Emily said, motioning for her team to advance.

They reached the control room, its door fortified with a heavy lock. Emily accessed the security panel, using the codes Jamie had provided. The door clicked open, and they stormed inside, weapons drawn

The room was filled with monitors and servers, the nerve centre of Arabella's operation. Technicians scrambled to react, but Team Alpha quickly subdued them.

"Secure the room," Emily ordered. "Start the data transfer."

As the tech team began downloading the files, Emily scanned the screens, looking for any signs of Project Echelon. She found a series of encrypted files labelled with the project name and began decrypting them.

"Emily, we've found the prototypes," came a voice over the comms. "They're in a secure lab on the lower level."

"Copy that," Emily replied. "Team Charlie, move in and secure the lab. We need those prototypes."

The operation was running smoothly, but Emily knew they couldn't afford any mistakes. She continued decrypting the files, her eyes widening as the details of Project Echelon emerged. Arabella's plans were more ambitious and dangerous than they had realised.

"We have the prototypes," Team Charlie reported. "They're secure."

"Good work," Emily said. "Prepare for extraction. We need to get out of here before reinforcements arrive."

Suddenly, the facility's alarms blared, and the lights turned red. Arabella's voice echoed through the intercom, filled with cold fury. "You think you can stop me? You have no idea what you're dealing with."

Emily felt a chill run down her spine. "We need to move, now. Bravo Team, fall back to the extraction point."

The teams converged, moving swiftly through the facility. The sound of approaching guards grew louder, and the corridors were filled with the chaos of the fire fight. Emily led her team towards the exit, her mind racing with the implications of what they had discovered.

As they reached the extraction point, the sound of helicopters overhead signalled their escape. They boarded the helicopters, the rotors kicking up dust and debris as they lifted off. Emily looked down at the facility, its lights flashing in the darkness. They had struck a significant blow, but the fight was far from over.

***

Back at the safe house, the atmosphere was a mix of relief and anticipation. The data transfer had been successful, and they had secured the neural chip prototypes. Emily and Shay stood with Caldwell, reviewing the evidence they had gathered.

"This is it," Caldwell said, his voice filled with resolve. "We have everything we need to take Arabella down."

Emily nodded her mind racing with the possibilities. "We need to act fast. She knows we're coming, and she'll try to destroy any remaining evidence."

Shay added, "We'll coordinate with federal agencies and prepare for the final push. This ends now."

As the team worked to compile the evidence and prepare for the next steps, Emily felt a surge of determination. They had uncovered the truth about Project Echelon, and now it was time to bring Arabella to justice. "Let's finish this," Emily said, her voice filled with resolve.

Shay met her gaze, his eyes reflecting the same determination. "Together."

Chapter 47
The Lost Path

The first light of dawn barely peeked through the blinds as Emily entered the police station. The station was a whirlwind of activity, but now it was time to bring their findings to the broader force and solidify their next steps. The corridors buzzed with officers starting their shifts, unaware of the monumental operation that had taken place overnight.

Emily walked briskly to Chief Inspector Caldwell's office, her mind focused on the pressing task at hand. She knocked once and entered, finding Caldwell already poring over the evidence they had gathered. His expression was one of grim satisfaction.

"Morning, Caldwell," Emily greeted him, closing the door behind her.

Caldwell looked up, a hint of a smile playing on his lips. "Morning, Emily. Good work last night. We've hit Arabella where it hurts, but we need to follow through."

Emily nodded, taking a seat. "We need to secure arrest warrants for Arabella and her top associates. The evidence we've gathered is damning, but we have to ensure there are no loose ends."

Caldwell leaned back in his chair, nodding in agreement. "I've already contacted the district attorney. They're on board and preparing the necessary paperwork. But there's another matter we need to address."

Emily's brow furrowed. "What is it?"

Caldwell's expression turned serious. "There's been some chatter within the department. We believe Arabella has a mole on the inside. Someone who's been feeding her information and helping her stay one step ahead."

Emily felt a chill run down her spine. The thought of a traitor within their ranks was unsettling, but it also explained how Arabella had managed to evade them for so long.

"Do we have any leads on who it might be?" Emily asked, her voice steady.

Caldwell nodded. "We have a few suspects. Internal affairs is already conducting a discreet investigation, but we need to be careful. If the mole realises we're onto them, they could do significant damage."

Emily's mind raced with possibilities. "We'll need to monitor communications and track any suspicious activity. We can't let them sabotage our efforts."

Caldwell agreed. "I'll coordinate with internal affairs. In the meantime, I need you and Shay to stay vigilant. We can't afford any mistakes."

***

Later that morning, Emily found Shay in the evidence room, meticulously reviewing the data they had recovered. His face was drawn with fatigue, but his focus was unwavering.

"Shay, we need to talk," Emily said, closing the door behind her.

Shay looked up, concern etched on his features. "What's going on?"

Emily filled him in on the potential mole within the department. Shay's expression darkened as he absorbed the news.

"A mole explains a lot," he said. "But it also complicates things. We need to find out who it is before they can warn Arabella."

Emily nodded. "Caldwell is working with internal affairs, but we need to keep our eyes and ears open. Any slip-up could tip them off."

They spent the next few hours reviewing the data, looking for any signs of internal sabotage. The work was tedious but necessary. As they combed through the evidence, Emily couldn't shake the feeling that they were running out of time.

***

By midday, the station was a hive of activity. Officers moved with purpose, briefing each other on the latest developments. The atmosphere was tense but focused. Emily and Shay met with Caldwell and the lead investigator from internal affairs, a no-nonsense woman named Detective Sarah Vaughn.

"We've narrowed it down to a few suspects," Vaughn said, spreading out a series of files on the table. "These officers had access to sensitive information and have exhibited suspicious behaviour over the past few months."

Emily scanned the files, noting the names and faces. Each suspect had a plausible connection to the leaks, but proving it would be another matter entirely.

"We need concrete evidence," Shay said. "Something that ties them directly to Arabella."

Vaughn nodded. "Agreed. We've set up surveillance on each suspect, monitoring their communications and movements. It's only a matter of time before one of them slips up."

As they discussed their next steps, an officer burst into the room, breathless and urgent. "We've got a lead. One of the suspects, Officer Jenkins, just made a call to an untraceable number. We managed to intercept part of the conversation. He's planning to meet someone at a warehouse on the outskirts of town."

Caldwell's eyes narrowed. "This could be it. Emily, Shay, I want you two to handle this personally. Take a team and get to that warehouse. We need to catch them in the act."

***

The drive to the warehouse was tense, the air thick with anticipation. Emily and Shay briefed their team, outlining the plan to capture Jenkins and his contact. As they approached the location, they parked a few blocks away and proceeded on foot, using the cover of abandoned buildings to stay out of sight.

The warehouse was a dilapidated structure, its windows broken and walls covered in graffiti. Emily signalled for the team to spread out, covering all exits. They moved silently, their senses heightened.

Emily and Shay approached the entrance, listening for any signs of movement inside. Voices drifted through the broken windows, confirming that Jenkins was indeed meeting someone.

"Ready?" Emily whispered.

Shay nodded, his grip tightening on his weapon. "Let's do this."

They burst through the door, weapons drawn. The scene inside was chaotic—Jenkins stood in the centre of the room, his face pale with shock. Across from him was a man Emily recognised as one of Arabella's top lieutenants.

"Hands up! Don't move!" Emily shouted, her voice echoing off the walls.

Jenkins hesitated, but the lieutenant reached for his weapon. Shay reacted instantly, firing a warning shot that sent the man sprawling to the ground.

"Drop it, now!" Shay ordered.

The lieutenant complied, raising his hands in surrender. Jenkins, realising the game was up, dropped his weapon as well, his expression one of defeat.

"Cuff them," Emily instructed her voice steady. "We need to get them back to the station."

As the team secured the suspects, Emily felt a surge of relief. They had caught the mole and one of Arabella's key operatives. It was a significant breakthrough, but the fight was far from over.

***

Back at the station, Jenkins and the lieutenant were separated and taken to interrogation rooms. Emily and Shay watched through the one-way mirror as Jenkins was questioned by Vaughn.

"He's scared," Shay observed. "He'll talk."

Emily nodded. "He knows he's got no way out. Let's see what he has to say."

Jenkins broke quickly, the weight of his betrayal evident in his tear-streaked face. He confessed to passing information to Arabella in exchange for money, revealing details of their communications and meetings.

"He's given us enough to secure a warrant for Arabella," Vaughn said, turning to Emily and Shay. "This is the break we needed."

As the team prepared for the final push, Emily felt a mix of emotions—relief, anticipation, and a steely resolve. They were closing in on Arabella, and nothing would stop them now.

"We're almost there," Shay said, his voice filled with quiet determination.

Emily nodded, her eyes fixed on the horizon. "Let's finish this."

Chapter 48
A Glimmer of Hope

The press conference room at the police station was filled with a palpable tension. Reporters from various news outlets jostled for position, their cameras and microphones ready to capture every word. Emily Harper stood off to the side, her eyes scanning the crowd. This was the moment they had been working towards—the moment when they would expose Arabella Blackwood's criminal empire to the world.

Chief Inspector Caldwell stepped up to the podium, his presence commanding immediate attention. He waited for the room to quiet down before speaking, his voice steady and authoritative.

"Ladies and gentlemen of the press, thank you for coming on such short notice. We have significant developments in our on-going investigation into the activities of Arabella Blackwood and her associates. This operation has uncovered a web of criminal activity that includes illegal experimentation, conspiracy, and attempts to compromise the security of our nation."

A murmur ran through the crowd, the weight of Caldwell's words sinking in. Emily glanced at Shay, who stood beside her, his expression resolute. They had worked tirelessly to reach this point, and now it was time to reveal the truth.

"Over the past several months," Caldwell continued, "we have gathered substantial evidence linking Arabella Blackwood to a clandestine project known as Project Echelon. This project involves the development and intended deployment of neural chips designed to control the minds of individuals, including high-profile targets within our government and military."

The room erupted in gasps and exclamations as reporters scribbled furiously in their notebooks. Emily watched the reactions closely, knowing that public opinion would be a crucial factor in bringing Arabella to justice.

"As part of our operation," Caldwell said, "we conducted coordinated raids on multiple facilities linked to Blackwood's organisation. We have secured numerous documents, digital files, and physical evidence that detail the scope of her plans. Additionally, we have arrested several key members of her network who are now in custody and cooperating with our investigation."

Emily stepped forward as Caldwell gestured to her. She took a deep breath and approached the podium, her heart pounding. This was her moment to speak directly to the public.

"My name is Detective Emily Harper," she began, her voice clear and firm. "I have been leading this investigation alongside my colleagues. The evidence we have gathered is irrefutable. Arabella Blackwood and her associates have been engaged in illegal activities that threaten the safety and security of our society. Their goal was to use advanced neural technology to exert control over individuals, stripping them of their free will."

She paused, letting the gravity of her words sink in. "We will not allow this to happen. We are committed to bringing Arabella Blackwood to justice and dismantling her network. This is not just a fight for legal justice; it's a fight for the fundamental freedoms we all hold dear."

The room fell silent, the weight of the revelations hanging in the air. Reporters began to raise their hands, eager to ask questions, but Caldwell stepped forward to take control of the situation.

"We will take a few questions," Caldwell said, pointing to a reporter in the front row.

"Chief Inspector, how soon can we expect arrests to be made?" The reporter asked.

Caldwell's expression was resolute. "Arrest warrants have already been issued for Arabella Blackwood and her top associates. We are coordinating with federal agencies to ensure they are apprehended as swiftly as possible."

Another reporter spoke up. "Detective Harper, can you provide more details about Project Echelon and its intended targets?"

Emily nodded. "Project Echelon was designed to use neural chips to control high-profile individuals, including politicians, corporate leaders, and military personnel. The goal was to influence decision-making at the highest levels, essentially creating a puppet regime under Arabella's control. The evidence we have secured includes detailed plans and prototypes of the neural chips."

As the questions continued, Emily felt a sense of relief mingled with determination. They were finally bringing the truth to light, exposing Arabella's nefarious plans to the public. The fight was far from over, but they had taken a crucial step forward.

***

Later that day, Emily and Shay returned to the safe house, where the team was already hard at work preparing for the next phase of the operation. The press conference had been a success, but they knew that Arabella would not go down without a fight.

Caldwell gathered everyone in the main room, his expression serious but hopeful. "The public is on our side now, thanks to the press conference. Arabella will be feeling the pressure, and she may attempt to flee or destroy any remaining evidence. We need to stay one step ahead."

Emily nodded, her mind focused on the task at hand. "What's our next move?"

"We need to secure the remaining facilities and ensure that Arabella has no place to hide," Caldwell replied. "We've identified a few more locations that may be linked to her operations. We'll conduct simultaneous raids to prevent her from slipping through our fingers."

Shay stepped forward, his determination evident. "We also need to protect the individuals listed as targets in Project Echelon. If Arabella still has the means to activate those chips, we need to make sure they're safe."

Caldwell agreed. "We'll coordinate with federal agencies to provide protection for those individuals. This is a multi-front operation, and we need to be thorough."

As the team prepared for the upcoming raids, Emily couldn't help but feel a mix of anticipation and anxiety. They had come so far, but the final confrontation with Arabella was looming. They had to be ready for anything.

***

The following night, the team mobilised for the simultaneous raids. The atmosphere was tense as they approached their targets, the weight of their mission heavy on their shoulders. Emily and Shay led one of the assault teams, their target a secluded mansion rumoured to be one of Arabella's safe houses.

They moved swiftly and silently, their movements coordinated and precise. As they reached the mansion, Emily signalled for the team to breach the entrance. The door burst open, and they swept inside, weapons drawn.

The interior was lavishly decorated, a stark contrast to the cold, calculated nature of Arabella's operations. They moved through the rooms methodically, securing each one and neutralising any resistance they encountered.

"Clear," Shay called out as they reached the final room.

Emily stepped inside, her eyes scanning the space. It appeared to be a study, with bookshelves lining the walls and a large desk in the centre. She approached the desk, her gaze falling on a laptop and a stack of documents.

"Start the data transfer," she instructed, plugging a flash drive into the laptop. "We need to see if there's anything here that can lead us to Arabella."

As the data was transferred, Emily rifled through the documents, her heart racing with each new discovery. There were financial records, communications logs, and detailed plans for Project Echelon. But there was one document that caught her attention—a map marked with several locations.

"Shay, look at this," she said, holding up the map. "These locations...they could be safe houses or other facilities linked to Arabella."

Shay studied the map, his expression serious. "This could be the breakthrough we need. If we can hit all these locations, we might finally corner her."

The data transfer was completed, and Emily pocketed the flash drive. "Let's get this back to Caldwell. We need to analyse it and plan our next move."

As they exited the mansion, the sound of helicopters overhead signalled the success of the other raids. They had struck a significant blow, but the fight was far from over.

***

Back at the police station, the team reviewed the data and documents they had recovered. The map provided crucial insights into Arabella's network, revealing several previously unknown locations.

"We have her on the run," Caldwell said, his voice filled with determination. "But we can't let up. We need to hit these locations hard and fast."

Emily felt a surge of determination. They were closing in on Arabella, and she knew they couldn't afford to falter now. "Let's finish this," she said her voice resolute.

Shay nodded, his eyes reflecting the same resolve. 'Together.'

As the team prepared for the final push, Emily felt a renewed sense of purpose. They had exposed the truth, rallied public support, and dealt significant blows to Arabella's operation. Now, it was time to bring her to justice once and for all.

Chapter 49
The Choice

Arabella Blackwood sat in her opulent office, the walls lined with bookshelves filled with volumes on science, technology, and philosophy. The room was tastefully decorated, a testament to her impeccable taste and the vast resources at her disposal. Her desk, a massive antique, was covered with meticulously organised papers and a sleek laptop. She had always prided herself on maintaining control, on staying a step ahead of her enemies. But today, as she watched the news broadcast on the large flat-screen TV mounted on the wall, that control slipped away.

The screen showed Chief Inspector Caldwell and Detective Emily Harper addressing the media, detailing the extensive evidence they had gathered against her. The camera panned to show the faces of reporters, their expressions a mix of shock and determination. Caldwell's voice echoed through the room, outlining the criminal activities linked to her name—illegal experimentation, conspiracy, and attempts to compromise national security.

Arabella's hands gripped the arms of her chair, her knuckles turning white. She felt a surge of anger, a burning rage that threatened to consume her. She had been careful; meticulous in her plans, yet here they were, exposing her to the world.

The camera zoomed in on Emily Harper as she stepped forward, her voice clear and firm. "Arabella Blackwood and her associates have been engaged in illegal activities that threaten the safety and security of our society. Their goal was to use advanced neural technology to exert control over individuals, stripping them of their free will."

Arabella's vision blurred with fury. She slammed her fist on the desk, sending papers flying. The carefully constructed façade of calm and control was crumbling, and she felt powerless to stop it.

"We will not allow this to happen," Emily continued. "We are committed to bringing Arabella Blackwood to justice and dismantling her network. This is not just a fight for legal justice, it's a fight for the fundamental freedoms we all hold dear."

Arabella let out a scream of rage, the sound primal and raw. She stood up, her chair toppling over behind her. The screen now showed the arrest warrants being issued, the coordinated raids, and the detailed plans for Project Echelon. Every word felt like a dagger, each revelation a blow to her carefully constructed empire.

With a sweep of her arm, Arabella sent everything on her desk crashing to the floor. The laptop skidded across the room, smashing against the wall. Papers fluttered to the ground like fallen leaves, and a glass of water shattered, the liquid spreading across the polished wood.

"You think you can stop me?" She shouted at the screen, her voice hoarse with rage. "You have no idea what you're dealing with!"

She stormed across the room, grabbing books from the shelves and hurling them to the floor. Her breath came in ragged gasps, her heart pounding in her chest. The news continued to play, the reporters now discussing the public reaction and the swift actions being taken by law enforcement.

Arabella's mind raced, the realisation of her precarious situation sinking in. She had always been one step ahead, but now she was cornered, her plans unravelling before her eyes. She felt a cold, hard knot of fear in her stomach—something she hadn't felt in years.

In frenzy, she tore down the paintings from the walls, their frames splintering as they hit the ground. The meticulous order she had maintained was gone, replaced by chaos and destruction. Her sanctuary had become a battleground, her anger the only weapon she had left.

As the broadcast ended, Arabella stood in the midst of the wreckage, her chest heaving. She looked around at the destruction, her eyes wild. She had to think, to regroup. This wasn't over. It couldn't be.

She grabbed her phone and dialled a number with shaking hands. "Get me my security team," she barked into the receiver. 'Now.'

There was a pause on the other end and then a hesitant voice replied, "Yes, ma'am. Right away."

Arabella ended the call, her mind racing. She needed to find a way out, to salvage what she could of her plans. They had taken her by surprise, but she would not go down without a fight. She was Arabella Blackwood, and she would not be defeated so easily.

She moved to the window, staring out at the city below. The sun was setting, casting long shadows across the skyline. Her reflection in the glass showed a woman on the brink of desperation, but also one filled with a fierce, unyielding resolve.

"I will not be broken," she whispered to herself, her voice trembling with anger. "They will pay for this. Every single one of them."

As night fell, Arabella began to plot her next move. She would regroup, reassess, and retaliate with a vengeance. The game was far from over, and she was determined to reclaim her place at the top, no matter the cost.

Chapter 50
The Last Battle

The morning after the public exposure of Arabella Blackwood's criminal activities, the police station was a hive of activity. The press conference had sparked a media frenzy, and the pressure was mounting to apprehend all those involved in the conspiracy. Emily Harper and Shay Walsh were at the centre of it all, coordinating the arrest operations and planning the interrogations.

Arrests began at dawn. Teams of officers, supported by federal agents, moved swiftly and efficiently, rounding up several of Arabella's top associates. The suspects were brought to the station one by one, each under heavy guard. The atmosphere was tense, every officer acutely aware of the stakes.

Emily stood in the main operations room, monitoring the progress of the arrests on a series of screens. She felt a mix of satisfaction and urgency—satisfaction that they were finally bringing these people to justice, and urgency because Arabella herself was still out there.

Shay joined her, his expression serious. Despite the physical and mental toll of his condition, his insights remained invaluable. He had been instrumental in identifying the key players and devising strategies for their capture.

"Seven of her top associates are in custody," Shay reported, his voice steady. "We need to start the interrogations immediately. Every minute we delay gives Arabella more time to cover her tracks."

Emily nodded. "Agreed. Let's get started."

They moved to the interrogation rooms, where the suspects were being held. The first was Leo Vargas, a key lieutenant in Arabella's organisation. He was known for his ruthlessness and loyalty to Arabella, but under the intense pressure of his capture, he appeared shaken.

Emily and Shay entered the room, the door closing with a resounding click behind them. Leo sat at the table, his hands cuffed, his eyes darting nervously between them.

"Mr Vargas," Emily began her voice calm but firm. "You're facing serious charges. Cooperation could make a significant difference in your situation."

Leo sneered, attempting to mask his fear with bravado. "You think I'll betray Arabella? You don't know her. She'll find me, and she'll find you."

Shay leaned forward, his gaze piercing. "Arabella's days are numbered. We have enough evidence to bring her down, but your cooperation could help us ensure she faces justice sooner rather than later. Help us, and we can help you."

For a moment, Leo's defiance wavered. He looked between Emily and Shay, weighing his options. The silence stretched; tension thick in the air.

"Alright," he finally said his voice barely above a whisper. "I'll talk. But you have to guarantee my safety."

Emily nodded. "We can arrange that. Now, tell us everything you know about Arabella's current operations and her plans."

Leo began to speak, each word drawing them closer to understanding Arabella's network. He provided details about safe houses, contacts, and the logistics of Project Echelon. It was clear that Arabella had been preparing for every eventuality, but her confidence had led her to make mistakes.

***

The interrogations continued throughout the day. Each suspect provided pieces of the puzzle, slowly tightening the net around Arabella. Shay's insights were crucial, his ability to read people and connect disparate pieces of information proving invaluable.

However, Shay's condition also began to complicate the operations. During one of the interrogations, he suddenly paused, a look of confusion crossing his face. Emily noticed immediately, her concern evident.

"Shay?" She prompted gently.

Shay blinked, regaining his focus. "Sorry, just a moment." He took a deep breath, his hands trembling slightly. "I'm fine."

Emily nodded, but her worry grew. They couldn't afford any lapses, not now. She made a mental note to speak with Caldwell about the situation later.

***

By evening, they had gathered a significant amount of information. The arrests and interrogations had been fruitful, and the pieces of Arabella's plan were falling into place. Emily and Shay returned to the operations room, where Caldwell was waiting.

"We've made good progress," Emily reported. "Leo Vargas and several others have provided valuable intel. We know where Arabella might be hiding and more about her plans for Project Echelon."

Caldwell nodded, his expression serious. "Excellent work. But we need to move quickly. The longer Arabella remains at large, the more dangerous she becomes."

Shay spoke up, his voice steady but weary. "We need to prepare for a coordinated strike. Use the intel we've gathered to hit her remaining strongholds simultaneously. It's the only way to ensure we catch her."

Caldwell agreed. "I'll coordinate with the federal agencies. We'll need all the resources we can muster."

As the team began to plan the final operations, Emily pulled Shay aside. "Are you alright? You seemed...distracted earlier."

Shay gave her a reassuring smile, though it didn't quite reach his eyes. "I'm fine, Emily. Just tired. We're close to the end, and I don't want to let anyone down."

Emily placed a hand on his arm, her concern evident. "You're not letting anyone down. We need you at your best. Promise me you'll let me know if it gets too much."

Shay nodded. "I promise."

As they returned to the planning session, Emily felt a renewed sense of urgency. They were close, so close to bringing Arabella to justice. But the final push would be the most dangerous yet. She glanced at Shay, hoping that his strength would hold out.

They couldn't afford any more mistakes. The net was tightening around Arabella, and they had to ensure it closed without leaving any gaps. The next few days would be critical, and they needed to be ready for whatever came next.

Chapter 51
The Endgame

The tension in the air was palpable as the team assembled in the briefing room. Maps, blueprints, and photographs covered the walls and tables, each one a crucial piece of the puzzle they had been working to solve. The final raid on Arabella Blackwood's main headquarters was imminent, and every detail had to be perfect.

Emily Harper stood at the front of the room, her eyes scanning the faces of her colleagues. Each one reflected the same mix of determination and apprehension that she felt. This was their last chance to bring Arabella down, and they all knew it.

Chief Inspector Caldwell stepped forward, his presence commanding immediate attention. "We have confirmed the location of Arabella Blackwood's main headquarters," he began. "This is it. The final push. We'll be hitting her with everything we've got, and we need to be prepared for anything."

He pointed to a large map pinned to the wall, detailing the layout of Arabella's headquarters. "The building is heavily fortified, with multiple layers of security. Our plan is to divide into three teams: Team Alpha will breach the main entrance and secure the ground floor. Team Bravo will handle the upper floors and any resistance we encounter. Team Charlie will focus on securing the control room and gathering any remaining evidence. Emily and Shay would be leading Team Alpha, their experience and knowledge are critical to the success of the mission." As the briefing continued, Emily felt a sense of resolve solidify within her. They had come too far to fail now.

***

Later, as the team finalised their preparations, Emily found a moment to speak with Shay privately. They stepped outside, the cool night air a welcome relief from the intensity of the briefing room. The city lights twinkled in the distance, a stark contrast to the darkness of their mission.

"Shay, we need to talk." Emily said, her voice soft but insistent.

Shay turned to her, his expression weary but resolute. "What's on your mind, Emily?"

Emily took a deep breath, choosing her words carefully. "I've noticed how hard you've been pushing yourself. This mission is critical, but so is your health. I need to know you're okay."

Shay's eyes softened and he looked away for a moment before speaking. "Emily, I've been trying to ignore it, but the truth is, I'm scared. Scared that my condition would make me a liability. That I'll put you and the team at risk."

Emily placed a hand on his arm, her touch both comforting and grounding. "Shay, you're one of the strongest people I know. We wouldn't have gotten this far without you. But if you feel like it's too much, you need to tell me. We'll figure it out together."

Shay met her gaze, his eyes reflecting a deep well of emotions. "I just don't want to let anyone down. Especially not you."

Emily's heart ached for him, but she held his gaze with unwavering determination. "You could never let me down, Shay. We're in this together, no matter what. And we'll face whatever comes next, side by side."

The two stood in silence for a moment, the weight of their words hanging in the air. The bond between them had grown stronger through the trials they had faced, and now, as they stood on the precipice of their final challenge, that bond felt unbreakable.

***

Back inside, Emily checked in on Jamie. She found her in a quiet room, sitting by a window with a faraway look in her eyes. The physical wounds had healed, but the emotional scars were still fresh.

"Jamie," Emily said gently, pulling up a chair beside her. "How are you holding up?"

Jamie's eyes flickered with a mix of pain and determination. "It's been hard, Emily. What Arabella made me do…the things I saw. I keep replaying them in my mind, and it's like I can't escape."

Emily reached out, taking Jamie's hand in hers. "You've been through so much, Jamie. But you're here now, and you're safe. We're going to stop Arabella, once and for all. And we'll make sure she pays for what she did to you and so many others."

Jamie nodded, tears welling in her eyes. "I know. It's just…it's hard to move past it. I feel like a part of me is still trapped there."

Emily squeezed her hand gently. "It's going to take time, but you're strong. And you're not alone. We'll get through this together."

Jamie managed a small smile, the first Emily had seen in days. "Thank you, Emily. I don't know what I'd do without you."

Emily felt a surge of emotion, and before she could overthink it, she leaned in and kissed Jamie softly on the lips. Jamie's eyes widened in surprise, but she didn't pull away. Instead, she leaned into the kiss, a tear slipping down her cheek.

When they finally broke apart, Emily whispered, "I'm here for you, Jamie. In every way. We'll get through this together, I promise."

Jamie nodded, her eyes shining with gratitude and something more. "I feel the same, Emily. We'll face whatever comes next, together."

***

The final preparations continued late into the night. Equipment was checked and rechecked, plans were reviewed, and every possible contingency was considered. The team moved with a sense of urgency, knowing that any mistake could be their last.

As dawn approached, Emily and Shay gathered the team for one final briefing. The room was filled with a quiet intensity, each member focused and ready.

"This is it," Emily said, her voice strong. "We've worked for this moment, and now it's time to finish it. Stick to the plan, watch each other's backs and we'll bring Arabella down. Let's do this."

Shay added, "Remember, we're not just doing this for ourselves. We're doing it for all the people Arabella has hurt, and for those she would hurt if we don't stop her. Stay strong, stay focused, and we'll come out of this victorious."

With a collective nod, the team moved out, ready to face the final challenge. The sun was rising, casting a new light on the path ahead. They were ready for whatever came next, knowing that together, they could overcome anything.

Chapter 52
The Sacrifice

The morning sun cast long shadows as the team assembled near Arabella Blackwood's main headquarters. The building was an imposing structure, fortified and bristling with security. Emily Harper, Shay Walsh, and the rest of the team stood ready, their faces set with determination. This was it—the final showdown.

Chief Inspector Caldwell addressed the team one last time, "Remember your training. Stick to the plan. And watch each other's backs. Let's bring her down."

Emily and Shay exchanged a glance, a silent acknowledgement of the stakes. Emily's heart pounded, but her resolve was unwavering. They had prepared for this moment, and now it was time to execute their plan.

"Team Alpha, move out," Emily commanded.

Emily and Shay led Team Alpha towards the main entrance, their movements synchronised and precise. The team reached the heavy steel doors, and Emily signalled for the breaching charge to be set. The explosion was deafening, and the doors flew open, revealing a corridor lined with armed guards.

"Go, go, go!" Emily shouted, leading the charge.

Gunfire erupted as the team pushed forward, each member moving with practised efficiency. The resistance was fierce, but Team Alpha was relentless. Emily's focus was razor-sharp, her training kicking in as she returned fire and advanced through the chaos.

"Shay, cover the left flank!" she yelled, her voice barely audible over the cacophony.

Shay nodded, taking the position and providing cover fire. Despite the intensity of the battle, Emily noticed him falter for a moment, his expression pained. Her concern for him flared, but she pushed it aside. They had a job to do.

***

Meanwhile, Team Bravo, led by Detective Thompson, breached the upper floors. The corridors were a maze of security checkpoints and armed guards, but they pressed on. Thompson's voice crackled over the comms.

"Team Alpha, we've secured the second floor. Moving to the third."

Emily acknowledged her mind racing. They needed to reach the control room and secure the critical evidence.

"Team Charlie, what's your status?" She called over the comms.

"We've breached the control room," came the response. "Beginning data transfer now."

"Copy that. Hold your position," Emily replied, her heart pounding.

As they advanced deeper into the building, the resistance intensified. The guards were well-trained and heavily armed, but the team's strategy and determination kept them moving forward. Emily's thoughts flickered to Jamie, who was monitoring the operation from a safe location, providing real-time intel.

"Emily, there's a heavy contingent of guards converging on your position," Jamie's voice warned through the earpiece. "You need to move, now!"

"Roger that," Emily replied, signalling for the team to pick up the pace.

They pushed through another wave of guards, the fire fight becoming increasingly intense. Shay was by her side, his movements steady but she could see the strain in his eyes.

"Shay, are you alright?" She asked, her concern evident.

"I'm fine," he grunted, but Emily could see the toll it was taking on him.

As they rounded a corner, they were met with a barrage of gunfire. Shay took point, his determination unwavering, but then it happened. He stumbled, clutching his head, his vision blurring.

"Shay!" Emily screamed, catching him before he fell.

The team formed a protective perimeter around them, fending off the guards. Emily's heart raced as she tried to get Shay back on his feet.

"Come on, Shay. Stay with me," she urged, her voice filled with desperation.

Shay blinked, trying to focus. "I…I'm okay. Just.. give me a second."

"Take your time. We've got you," Emily said, her grip on his arm tightening.

With a monumental effort, Shay regained his composure. He took a deep breath, nodding to Emily. "Let's keep moving."

They continued their advance, the final objective within reach. The control room was just ahead, but the last line of defence was formidable. The guards were entrenched, their firepower overwhelming.

"Flashbangs, now!" Emily ordered.

The team deployed flash-bang grenades, the explosions disorienting the guards long enough for them to breach the final barrier. Emily and Shay led the charge, their combined determination cutting through the resistance.

They burst into the control room, the guards inside caught off guard by the sudden assault. Emily and Shay moved with precision, subduing the remaining guards and securing the room.

"Team Charlie, what's the status of the data transfer?" Emily called out.

"Transfer complete. We have everything we need," came the response.

"Good. Let's secure the building and prepare for extraction," Emily commanded.

As the team worked to secure the facility, Emily turned to Shay, her eyes filled with concern. "Are you sure you're, okay?"

Shay managed a weak smile. "I'm good, Emily. Just a little…worn out."

Emily nodded her relief palpable. "We did it, Shay. We're almost there."

As they prepared for the final sweep of the building, Emily couldn't shake the feeling of pride and determination. They had faced incredible odds, but they had come through. The raid had been a success, but the real victory was in sight—bringing Arabella Blackwood to justice.

The team regrouped, their expressions a mix of exhaustion and triumph. They had fought hard and won the day, but the mission wasn't over yet. Arabella was still out there, and they needed to finish what they had started.

"Let's get this place locked down and make sure Arabella has nowhere left to hide," Emily said, her voice resolute.

Shay nodded, his eyes reflecting the same determination. "Together, Emily. We'll see this through to the end."

As the sun set on the battlefield, the team prepared for the final phase of their mission. They had come this far, and they would not rest until justice was served.

Chapter 53
The Aftermath

The atmosphere in Arabella Blackwood's main headquarters was tense, the air charged with the anticipation of the final confrontation. Emily Harper and Shay Walsh moved through the building with purpose, their team securing every corridor and room. They were getting closer to Arabella, and the stakes couldn't be higher.

"Emily, we've cleared the west wing. No sign of Arabella yet," came the report over the comms.

"Copy that. Continue the sweep," Emily replied, her focus razor-sharp. She turned to Shay, who was by her side, his expression resolute despite the toll of his condition.

"Are you ready?" She asked, her voice steady but filled with concern.

Shay nodded, his determination unwavering. "Let's finish this."

They moved towards the central command room, where they believed Arabella was hiding. The corridor was eerily quiet; the only sound was the faint hum of the building's systems. As they approached the heavy steel door, Emily felt her pulse quicken.

"Jamie, we're at the command room. Any movement inside?" Emily asked, her hand hovering over the door control.

Jamie's voice crackled over the earpiece. "I've got eyes on you. There's activity, but I can't get a clear view. Be careful."

Emily nodded, signalling for Shay and the team to take positions. "On my mark. Three, two, one."

The door slid open, and they burst into the room, weapons drawn. Arabella stood at the far end, her demeanour calm and composed, a stark contrast to the chaos outside. Her piercing eyes locked onto Emily and Shay, a twisted smile playing on her lips.

"Well, well, well. Detective Harper and Mr Walsh. I've been expecting you," Arabella said, her voice dripping with contempt.

"Arabella, it's over," Emily declared, her weapon trained on the woman. "Surrender now and this can end without more bloodshed."

Arabella laughed a cold, mirthless sound. "Do you really think it's that simple? You've only scratched the surface of what I'm capable of."

Before Emily could respond, Arabella reached for a small device on her desk. "This is where it ends for you."

Emily's eyes widened as she recognised the neural chip controller. "No!"

But it was too late. Arabella activated the device, and a wave of energy pulsed through the room. Emily felt a sharp pain in her head, her vision blurring. Shay stumbled, clutching his head, his condition exacerbating the effects.

Arabella's laughter echoed through the room, cold and triumphant. "You cannot resist. The neural chip technology is far beyond anything you can comprehend."

Emily struggled to stay on her feet, her mind fighting against the invasive control. She could see Shay beside her, his face contorted with pain, but still standing. "Shay, fight it!" she screamed, her voice strained.

Shay's eyes met hers, filled with determination. "I'm trying, Emily," he grunted, his hands trembling as he gripped his weapon.

Arabella stepped closer, her smile widening. "You're too late. My plan is already in motion. Soon, I'll have control over the most powerful minds in the world."

Emily's vision blurred further, but she refused to give in. "Jamie, we need you!" she called out, hoping that her voice would reach their ally.

Jamie's voice came over the comms, filled with urgency. "Emily, distract her! I'm working on overriding the system from here."

Emily gritted her teeth, forcing herself to focus on Arabella. "You're a monster, Arabella. You'll never win. We'll stop you."

Arabella sneered, her eyes cold. "You're delusional. This world needs my control. You're just too blind to see it."

As the neural chip's influence intensified, Emily felt herself weakening. But then, the lights flickered, and the hum of the systems grew louder. Jamie was doing something, creating a feedback loop to disrupt the controller.

Arabella's expression shifted to one of confusion and anger. "What are you—"

Suddenly, the lights flickered, and the hum of the systems intensified. Jamie had managed to create a feedback loop, causing the neural chip controller to malfunction. Arabella screamed in frustration, her grip on the device faltering.

"Now, Shay!" Emily yelled, seizing the moment.

With a final surge of strength, Shay lunged at Arabella, knocking the device from her hand. They grappled, their struggle fierce and desperate. Shay's condition made every move a monumental effort, but his determination fuelled him.

Emily, her vision clearing slightly, joined the fray. Together, they managed to subdue Arabella, pinning her to the ground. Shay's breath came in laboured gasps, but his grip was firm.

"Stay down!" Shay growled, securing her wrists with a pair of cuffs.

Emily looked around the room, her heart pounding. "Jamie, what's the status of the override?"

Jamie's voice was breathless but triumphant. "I've disabled the neural chip controller. You should be free from its effects now."

Relief flooded through Emily as the pain in her head subsided. She turned to Shay, her gratitude and admiration for him overwhelming. "We did it, Shay. We stopped her."

Shay managed a tired smile. "We did it together, Emily."

Arabella glared up at them, her eyes burning with hatred. "You think this is the end? You're fools. My work will continue, with or without me."

Emily shook her head, her resolve unshaken. "No, Arabella. It ends here. We have all the evidence we need to dismantle your entire operation. You've lost"

As they secured Arabella and prepared for extraction, Emily felt a wave of emotions wash over her. Relief, exhaustion, but most of all, a fierce determination to see justice served. They had faced incredible odds and come out on top, but the fight wasn't over yet. There were still loose ends to tie up and a world to protect from the remnants of Arabella's network.

Shay, despite his condition, stood tall beside her, his courage and quick thinking having played a pivotal role in their victory. Emily placed a hand on his shoulder, her gratitude and respect for him deepening.

"Thank you, Shay," she said softly. "We couldn't have done this without you."

Shay gave her a tired but genuine smile. "We did it together, Emily. Now, let's finish what we started."

As they led Arabella out of the building, Emily knew that they had taken a significant step towards justice. The road ahead would be challenging, but with Shay, Jamie, and their team by her side, she felt ready to face whatever came next.

The sun was setting, casting a golden glow over the city. It was a new dawn, a fresh start, and Emily Harper was determined to make the most of it.

Chapter 54
A New Dawn

As Emily, Shay, and the team escorted Arabella out of the command room, the atmosphere was tense. Arabella's threats still echoed in Emily's mind, and she knew they couldn't afford any mistakes.

Suddenly, a loud alarm blared through the building, and Arabella's twisted smile returned. "You think you've won? You're more naïve than I thought."

Emily's heart sank as she realised Arabella had one last trick up her sleeve. She glanced at Shay, who looked equally concerned. "Jamie, what's going on?" She asked over the comms.

Jamie's voice was frantic. "She's activated a secondary device. It's a failsafe to ensure the neural chips are activated remotely. We have to stop it, or all these people will be under her control."

Emily felt a surge of panic. "Where's the device?"

"It's in a hidden chamber beneath the command room," Jamie replied. "I'm sending the coordinates to your devices now. You need to get there fast."

"Team, split up!" Emily ordered. "Half of you stay here with Arabella. The rest, follow me and Shay."

They raced through the corridors, the alarm blaring incessantly. Emily's mind raced with the implications of Arabella's plan. If they didn't stop the activation, countless lives would be controlled by her twisted technology.

They reached a concealed door at the end of a corridor. Emily used the coordinates Jamie had sent to unlock it, revealing a staircase leading down into darkness.

"Move quickly," Emily urged, descending the stairs two at a time.

The chamber below was filled with servers and control panels, the nerve centre of Arabella's operation. In the centre stood a tall, cylindrical device, its lights flashing ominously.

"There it is," Shay said, his voice strained. "We need to shut it down."

Emily rushed to the control panel, her fingers flying over the keys. "Jamie, I need you to guide me through this. How do we deactivate it?"

"I'm on it," Jamie replied, her voice a steadying presence in the chaos. "First, you need to override the primary control system."

As Emily worked, Shay stood guard, his eyes scanning the room for any threats. His condition was worsening, but his determination kept him focused.

"Emily, you need to hurry," Shay said, his voice tight with pain.

"I'm doing my best," she replied, frustration lacing her words. "Jamie, what's next?"

"Now, disable the failsafe mechanisms. There should be a series of switches on the right side of the panel."

Emily located the switches and flipped them one by one. The device's lights began to dim, and the hum of its machinery slowed.

"We're almost there," Jamie said. "Now, initiate the final shutdown sequence. It's a code: Alpha-Delta-9-3-7."

Emily entered the code, her heart pounding. The device's lights flickered, then went dark. The room fell silent, the only sound was their ragged breathing.

"We did it," Emily whispered, relief flooding through her.

Shay staggered, and Emily rushed to his side, supporting him. "Shay, are you okay?"

"I'm fine," he said, his voice weak. "Just…need a moment."

Emily nodded, her concern for him mingling with the relief of their victory. They had stopped Arabella's final plan, but the toll it had taken on Shay was evident.

"Let's get out of here," Emily said, helping Shay to his feet.

As they ascended the stairs, Emily felt a renewed sense of purpose. They had faced incredible odds and come out on top. Arabella's plans had been thwarted, and justice would be served.

They re-joined the team above, where Arabella was being secured. Her expression was one of cold fury, but Emily felt no sympathy for her. The lives she had tried to control, the chaos she had caused—it was all over.

As they led Arabella out of the building, Emily knew that they had taken a significant step towards justice. The road ahead would be challenging, but with Shay, Jamie, and their team by her side, she felt ready to face whatever came next.

The sun was setting, casting a golden glow over the city. It was a new dawn, a fresh start, and Emily Harper was determined to make the most of it.

Chapter 55
The Phoenix Rises

The dawn light filtered through the clouds as Arabella Blackwood was led in handcuffs from her once-impenetrable headquarters. The triumphant yet exhausted team surrounded her, ensuring she had no opportunity to escape. The battle had been long and arduous, but justice was finally within reach.

The media had gathered outside the building, capturing every moment of Arabella's arrest. Reporters shouted questions, cameras flashed, and the world watched as one of the most dangerous criminal masterminds was brought to justice. Emily Harper and Shay Walsh stood by, watching as Arabella was placed into a police van, her face a mask of cold fury.

Chief Inspector Caldwell approached Emily and Shay, his expression a mix of pride and exhaustion. "You did it. Arabella Blackwood is finally in custody. The evidence you gathered will ensure she faces the full extent of the law."

Emily nodded, the weight of the moment sinking in. "We couldn't have done it without the team. Everyone played their part."

Shay, though visibly tired, managed a smile. "We've taken down a monster. Now we need to make sure she can never hurt anyone again."

***

Back at the police station, the atmosphere was electric. Officers and agents buzzed with activity, cataloguing the mountains of evidence collected from Arabella's headquarters. Every document, hard drive, and neural chip was meticulously logged and secured.

Emily and Shay entered the main operations room, where Jamie was already at work, her fingers flying over a keyboard. She looked up as they approached, a relieved smile spreading across her face.

"You did it," Jamie said, her voice filled with admiration. "Arabella is finally going to pay for everything she's done."

"We all did it," Emily corrected, placing a hand on Jamie's shoulder. "Your efforts were crucial. We couldn't have stopped her without you."

Shay leaned against the table, his exhaustion evident. "We need to ensure every piece of evidence is airtight. Arabella will try to fight this every step of the way."

Jamie nodded, her expression determined. "I'm already on it. We have enough to bury her."

As they reviewed the evidence, Caldwell joined them, holding a file. "There's something else we need to address," he said, his tone serious. "Sarah Bennett."

Emily's heart sank. Sarah had been a trusted ally, but the revelation of her true role had been devastating. "What about her?"

Caldwell handed the file to Emily. "We've confirmed that Sarah Bennett was responsible for Robert's murder. She was working with Arabella, likely under duress or manipulation, but it doesn't change the fact."

Emily felt a surge of anger and sadness. Robert's death had been a personal blow, and knowing Sarah's involvement made it even harder to bear. "We need to bring her in. She has to answer for what she's done."

Caldwell nodded. "Agreed. We'll issue an arrest warrant and bring her to justice as well."

***

Later that day, a press conference was held to update the public on the outcome of the raid and the arrest of Arabella Blackwood. The room was packed with reporters, their cameras trained on the podium.

Caldwell stepped forward first, his presence commanding the room. "Today, we have taken a significant step in dismantling a criminal network that posed a grave threat to our society. Arabella Blackwood has been apprehended, and we have secured substantial evidence to ensure she faces justice."

He gestured for Emily and Shay to join him. "Detective Emily Harper and Shay Walsh have been instrumental in this operation. Their dedication and bravery have been extraordinary."

Emily stepped up to the podium, taking a deep breath. "This has been a long and difficult journey. We've faced many challenges, but the teamwork and perseverance of everyone involved have led us to this moment. Arabella Blackwood will answer for her crimes, and we will continue to pursue justice for all those affected by her actions."

Shay stood beside her, his presence a reminder of the toll this mission had taken. "I want to acknowledge the incredible efforts of our team," he said, his voice steady despite his fatigue. "We couldn't have done this alone. And while my condition has been a challenge, it's also a reminder of the importance of standing together and supporting each other."

The press conference continued, with questions about the specifics of the evidence and the next steps in the legal process. Emily and Shay answered as best they could, ensuring that the public understood the gravity of Arabella's crimes and the thoroughness of their investigation.

***

As the day drew to a close, Emily and Shay found a moment of quiet in the station's courtyard. The adrenaline of the past hours had begun to fade, replaced by a profound sense of relief and exhaustion.

"We did it," Emily said softly, looking up at the darkening sky. "It's finally over."

Shay nodded, his eyes reflecting the same mix of emotions. "We stopped her. But it's hard to believe it's really done."

Emily turned to him, her expression serious. "Shay, your bravery today was incredible. But we need to talk about your condition. You've pushed yourself so hard, and it's taken a toll."

Shay sighed, running a hand through his hair. "I know. I can't ignore it anymore. But I didn't want to let anyone down. Especially not you."

"You haven't let anyone down," Emily said firmly. "You've been a hero. But you need to take care of yourself now. We'll get through this together like we always have."

Shay managed a tired smile. "Thank you, Emily. For everything."

They stood in silence for a moment, the weight of their journey settling in. The fight against Arabella Blackwood had been long and gruelling, but they had emerged victorious. Justice would be served, and the world would be a little safer.

As they headed back inside, ready to face whatever came next, Emily felt a renewed sense of purpose. They had won a significant battle, but the war against crime and corruption was far from over. With Shay, Jamie, and their team by her side, she knew they could face any challenge.

Together, they would continue to fight for justice, honour the memory of those they had lost, and ensure that Arabella's reign of terror was nothing but a dark chapter in history.

Chapter 56
A New Era

The days following Arabella Blackwood's arrest were a whirlwind of activity and reflection. The police station was a hive of paperwork, interviews, and the painstaking process of ensuring that every piece of evidence was accounted for and ready for the forthcoming trial. The team that had taken down one of the most dangerous criminal masterminds was finally able to take a breath and reflect on the journey that had brought them here.

Emily Harper stood in the main operations room, watching as officers and agents moved with purpose. The relief in the air was palpable, but so was the exhaustion. She saw Jamie in a corner, diligently working through stacks of files and digital records, ensuring everything was in order.

Emily walked over to her, placing a comforting hand on her shoulder. "How are you holding up, Jamie?"

Jamie looked up, her eyes tired but determined. "It's been a lot, but we're getting there. I just want to make sure we have everything nailed down. Arabella can't have any loopholes to escape through."

Emily nodded, understanding her urgency. "You've done an incredible job. We couldn't have done this without you."

Jamie managed a small smile. "Thanks, Emily. It feels good to finally see some justice."

As they talked, Shay Walsh entered the room. His steps were slower, and his expression was a mix of relief and contemplation. Emily excused herself from Jamie and walked over to him.

"Shay, you look like you need some rest," Emily said, her concern evident.

Shay chuckled softly. "Rest sounds good, but I've been thinking a lot. There's something I need to discuss with you and Jamie."

Emily's heart sank slightly, sensing the gravity in his tone. "Alright. Let's find a quiet place to talk."

***

They found an empty conference room, and Jamie joined them. The three of them sat around the table, the weight of their shared experiences hanging in the air. Shay took a deep breath, gathering his thoughts.

"I've been doing a lot of thinking," Shay began, his voice steady but tinged with emotion. "This operation took a lot out of me, more than I expected. My condition has been a significant challenge, and I don't want to be a liability to the team."

Emily and Jamie exchanged concerned glances but remained silent, letting Shay continue.

"I've decided it's time for me to retire from active duty," Shay said, his voice firm. "I need to focus on my health and make sure I'm around for the people who matter most to me."

Emily felt a lump in her throat. "Shay, you've been a cornerstone of this team. We couldn't have done any of this without you."

Shay smiled, his eyes filled with gratitude. "Thank you, Emily. That means a lot. But I've been pushing myself too hard, and it's time to face my limitations. I don't want to put anyone at risk because of my condition."

Jamie reached out and took Shay's hand. "We understand, Shay. And we'll support you in whatever you decide. You've earned this."

Shay nodded, his expression one of relief and acceptance. "I'll still be around to help with the transition and to offer any advice you need. But it's time for me to step back and let you all take the lead."

Emily felt tears prick at her eyes but smiled through them. "You're making the right decision, Shay. Your health comes first. And we'll always be grateful for everything you've done."

They sat in silence for a moment, reflecting on their journey. The victories, the losses, the challenges they had faced together. It had been a long and difficult road, but they had emerged stronger for it.

***

The following days were filled with a mix of emotions. The team celebrated their victory, but there was also a sombre acknowledgement of the toll it had taken. Arabella Blackwood was in custody, and justice would be served, but the scars left by the battle would take time to heal.

A small ceremony was held at the police station to honour Shay's contributions. Chief Inspector Caldwell spoke, highlighting Shay's bravery and dedication. The team watched with a mix of pride and sadness as Shay accepted a commendation for his service.

As the ceremony ended, Emily found Shay outside, looking out at the city. She joined him, standing silently for a moment before speaking.

"You've made a huge difference, Shay. Not just in this case, but in all the lives you've touched."

Shay smiled, his eyes reflecting the gratitude and memories of his career. "It's been an incredible journey. And I'm glad I got to share it with you and the team."

Emily placed a hand on his arm. "We'll carry on the fight, Shay. And we'll make sure your legacy continues."

Shay nodded, his expression peaceful. "I know you will. And I'll be cheering you on every step of the way."

***

As the sun set over the city, Emily, Shay, and Jamie gathered one last time in the operations room. They talked about their plans for the future, the challenges ahead, and the bonds they had forged.

Emily looked at her friends, feeling a deep sense of gratitude and resolve. They had come through the fire together, and while the road ahead would have its challenges, she knew they were ready to face it.

"Here's to new beginnings," Emily said, raising a glass of water in a toast.

"To new beginnings," Shay and Jamie echoed, their voices filled with hope.

As they clinked their glasses, Emily felt a sense of peace. They had achieved justice, but more importantly, they had forged a bond that would endure whatever the future held.

Together, they would continue to fight for justice, honour the memory of those they had lost, and ensure that Arabella's reign of terror was nothing but a dark chapter in history. And with Shay's decision to focus on his health, they knew that their journey would be guided by the strength and wisdom he had imparted to them.

Chapter 57
Redemption

The sun dipped below the horizon, casting a warm glow over the city as Emily Harper prepared for her date with Jamie. The past few weeks had been a whirlwind of activity, and amidst the chaos, she had found herself growing closer to Jamie. Tonight, she wanted to take a step further, to show Jamie that there could be life beyond the shadows of their mission.

Emily chose a simple yet elegant outfit and glanced at herself in the mirror, feeling a mix of excitement and nervousness. She had decided to take Jamie to her favourite café, a place she usually visited with Shay. It held a lot of memories and felt like the right place to start this new chapter.

When she arrived at Jamie's apartment to pick her up, Jamie greeted her with a warm smile that made Emily's heart skip a beat. "You look beautiful," Jamie said, her eyes reflecting the same nervous excitement Emily felt.

"So do you," Emily replied, taking Jamie's hand. "Ready for our date?"

Jamie nodded, and together they walked to the café. The evening air was cool and refreshing, filled with the sounds of the city winding down for the night. They reached the café, its cosy interior glowing with soft, inviting light.

Emily led Jamie to a table by the window, where they could watch the world go by. "This place is special to me," Emily said as they sat down. "Shay and I used to come here a lot. It feels like the right place to start something new."

Jamie smiled, squeezing Emily's hand. "Thank you for bringing me here. It's perfect."

They ordered their meals and talked about everything and nothing, enjoying each other's company in a way they hadn't had the chance to before. As the evening progressed, the conversation grew more personal, the connection between them deepening.

After dinner, they decided to take a walk, the night air cool against their skin. Emily felt a sense of peace she hadn't experienced in a long time, and as they walked, she found herself opening up to Jamie in ways she hadn't expected.

When they finally reached Emily's apartment, she invited Jamie inside. "Would you like to come in for a while?"

Jamie hesitated for a moment, then nodded. "I'd like that."

Inside, they sat on the couch, talking quietly as the night wore on. The atmosphere was charged with a mix of anticipation and tenderness. Emily leaned in, her heart pounding, and kissed Jamie softly. Jamie responded, her touch gentle and reassuring.

They moved to the bedroom, their kisses growing more passionate. Emily's hands trembled slightly as she undressed Jamie, her desire mixed with a deep sense of connection. Jamie's touch was both electrifying and comforting, grounding Emily in the moment.

They made love slowly, exploring each other with a tenderness that spoke of healing and new beginnings. It was a moment of vulnerability and intimacy, a breaking down of walls that had been built up over time. As they moved together, Emily felt a sense of completeness, a feeling that this was where she was meant to be.

Afterwards, they lay tangled in each other's arms, the room filled with the quiet sounds of their breathing. Emily stroked Jamie's hair, feeling a deep contentment as she drifted off to sleep.

***

Jamie woke in the middle of the night, her heart racing and her body covered in sweat. She sat up abruptly, her mind filled with flashes of her time under Arabella's control. The feeling of helplessness, the loss of control—it all came rushing back in a wave of terror.

Emily stirred beside her, instantly alert. "Jamie? What's wrong?"

Jamie tried to catch her breath, her hands shaking. "I...I had a nightmare. It felt so real."

Emily sat up, wrapping her arms around Jamie. "You're safe now. It's over. Arabella can't hurt you anymore."

Jamie leaned into Emily's embrace, trying to steady her breathing. "I know, but sometimes it feels like she's still there, in my mind."

Emily held her tighter, her heart aching for Jamie. "You're not alone. We'll get through this together. Whatever you need, I'm here for you."

Jamie nodded, taking comfort in Emily's presence. "Thank you. I don't know what I'd do without you."

Emily kissed Jamie's forehead, whispering soothing words until Jamie's breathing slowed and she began to relax. "Let's try to get some rest," Emily said softly. "We'll face everything together, one step at a time."

Jamie lay back down, still nestled in Emily's arms. The fear lingered, but so did the sense of safety and love. As they fell asleep, Emily's steady heartbeat against her back, Jamie knew that no matter what came next, they would face it together.

The dawn light began to filter through the curtains, promising a new day. And with it, the hope of healing and new beginnings.

Chapter 58
A Future Forged

The early-morning sun filtered through the curtains, casting a warm glow across Emily's bedroom. She woke to the gentle sound of Jamie's breathing beside her, feeling a deep sense of contentment. The events of the past few weeks had been intense, but now there was a sense of peace and hope for the future.

Emily turned to Jamie, brushing a strand of hair from her face. Jamie stirred and opened her eyes, smiling softly. "Good morning,' she whispered.

"Good morning," Emily replied, leaning in to kiss her gently. "How did you sleep?"

"Better, thanks to you," Jamie said, her eyes reflecting gratitude and love.

They lay there for a few more moments, savouring the quiet intimacy of the morning. Eventually, Emily glanced at the clock and sighed. "We should get ready. It's a big day."

Jamie nodded, stretching and sitting up. "Yeah, back to the station for me, and you've got the agency to run."

They got out of bed and started their morning routine, moving around each other with a comfortable ease. As they dressed, Emily felt a sense of anticipation. This was the beginning of a new chapter, not just for her, but for all of them.

Once they were ready, they stood by the door, sharing one last kiss before heading out. "I'll see you tonight," Emily said, smiling.

Jamie smiled back. "I'll be thinking of you all day."

They left the apartment hand in hand, the city bustling with morning activity. At the corner, they shared a quick hug before parting ways—Jamie heading to the police station, and Emily making her way to the detective agency.

***

Emily arrived at the agency, feeling a mix of nerves and excitement. The familiar building seemed to hold new promise now that she was stepping into a leadership role. She walked through the door, greeted by the familiar faces of her colleagues. They smiled and nodded, their respect for her evident.

She entered her office and found Shay already there, looking through some files. He looked up as she walked in, a warm smile spreading across his face. "Morning, Emily."

"Morning, Shay," Emily replied, closing the door behind her. "How are you feeling?"

"Better," Shay said, his voice steady. "Retirement is suiting me well, but I wanted to be here to help you settle in."

Emily sat down across from him, her heart full of gratitude. "I appreciate that, Shay. I couldn't have asked for a better mentor."

Shay's expression softened, and he reached across the desk to take her hand. "You're more than a colleague, Emily. You're family. In fact, I've been thinking...I'd like to start calling you my niece if that's alright with you."

Emily's eyes filled with tears, her emotions overwhelming her. "Shay, I'd be honoured," she whispered, her voice breaking. "Thank you."

Shay squeezed her hand, his own eyes glistening with unshed tears. "You've earned it. I have no doubt you'll continue the legacy we've built here. You're going to do amazing things."

Emily wiped her tears and smiled. "I'll do my best, Uncle Shay."

They spent the rest of the morning going over cases and discussing the future of the agency. Emily felt a renewed sense of purpose, her determination fuelled by Shay's faith in her. She knew she had big shoes to fill, but she was ready for the challenge.

***

Later that day, Emily visited the police station to touch base with Jamie. As she walked through the familiar halls, she felt a sense of pride in how far they had all come. She found Jamie in the forensics lab, engrossed in her work.

"Hey, stranger," Emily said, leaning against the doorframe.

Jamie looked up and smiled. "Hey! How's your first day as the head of the agency?"

"It's going well. Just wanted to check in and see how you're doing," Emily replied, walking over to her.

Jamie set down her tools and took Emily's hand. "I'm doing good. It feels like we're finally moving forward, doesn't it?"

Emily nodded, feeling the weight of their journey lift slightly. "It does. And I'm glad we're doing it together."

They shared a tender kiss, a promise of the future they were building together. "I should get back to work," Jamie said reluctantly. "But I'll see you tonight?"

"Definitely," Emily replied. "I'll make dinner."

Jamie smiled, her eyes twinkling. "I'm looking forward to it."

***

As the weeks passed, the team began to heal and look towards the future. The agency thrived under Emily's leadership, her renewed sense of purpose driving her to uphold Shay's legacy. Shay, now officially retired, found peace in knowing the business was in capable hands. He spent his days enjoying a slower pace of life.

Emily and Jamie's relationship blossomed, their bond growing stronger with each passing day. They faced challenges together, supporting each other through the ups and downs. The trauma of their past experiences lingered, but they found strength in each other and the promise of a brighter future.

One evening, Emily and Jamie sat on the couch in Emily's apartment, a sense of contentment settling over them. "You know, I never imagined we'd end up here," Jamie said softly, leaning against Emily.

"Me neither," Emily replied, wrapping an arm around her. "But I'm glad we did."

Jamie smiled, looking up at her. "So am I."

As they sat together, the city lights twinkling outside, Emily felt a deep sense of gratitude. They had faced incredible odds and endured unimaginable challenges, but they had emerged stronger and more determined than ever.

Together, they would continue to fight for justice, honour the memory of those they had lost, and build a future filled with hope and love. It was a new beginning, and Emily was ready to embrace it with all her heart.